URBAN ANGEL

BOOK 1 OF THE MASTERS SERIES

A. J. CHAMBERLAIN

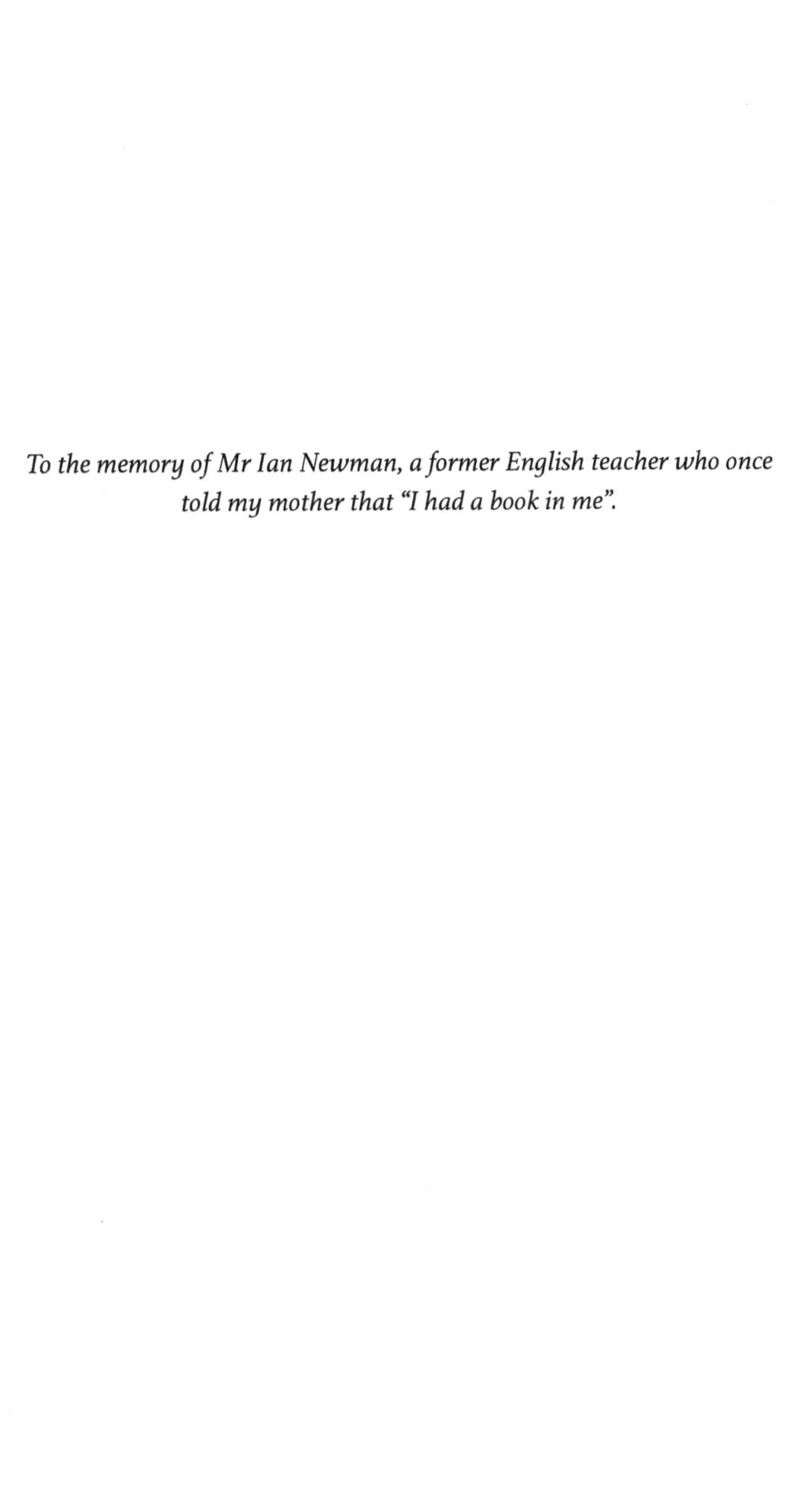

To the memory of Mr Ian Newman, a former English teacher who once told my mother that "I had a book in me".

The Light shines in the darkness, and the darkness has not overcome it.

— JOHN 1 v 5 (NIV)

URBAN ANGEL

1

———

Above all else, Alex Masters wanted to be in control of her life. In a world of inexplicable danger and uncertainty, she wanted to create a blanket of order around herself. She practised this control with diligence, especially in her own home. She had less control over her work environment, but she knew she could come home and withdraw into the safety of the anonymous suburban flat where she lived, unobserved by human eyes.

Most of the time she achieved her desire for safety and security; and yet there were days when uncertainty and disorder would shatter the pattern of her life with casual ease.

Today was one of those days. She was desperately glad to retreat into her own ordered world and regain the control she had lost. Nestling in the big armchair in her lounge, she pondered the afternoon's events, replaying them in her mind. Uncertainty and danger had penetrated her world, and her inability to act in a crisis could have left a child injured, or dead.

The incident had happened on the way home from work. She had been one of a little group of pedestrians who were waiting to cross the busy road. As the traffic rumbled in front of them, a hot and restless child pulled on his mother's hand, looking for attention. For just a moment, the boy distracted his mother and she let slip the handle of the pushchair, which then tipped over the incline of the kerb and moved with titanic grace into the path of the oncoming traffic. The first impact would have come from an articulated lorry, barely thirty yards away; she remembered the hiss of the air brakes, the jarring scorch of tyres on the road.

The mother screamed, and Alex's mind assessed the situation immediately. The pushchair was just about within reach; she could lean forward, grab it, and pull it back to the pavement. It was a metre, two at most, away from her; one step and a body stretched, and the baby would be safe. The thought was translating into action within her when something restrained her, an indecision that didn't seem to come from within.

While something indescribable held her, the young man standing next to her moved. He slipped past her, out onto the road, and hauled back the pram, just as the lorry squealed past them, shuddering to a halt. The mother was in tears with relief, the young man was a reluctant hero, the driver was in shock, and the traffic, stacked up behind the lorry as the scene played out, was soon on the move again. Nobody noticed Alex slipping quietly across the road and away from the scene.

Hours later, in the fading light of that spring evening, she was still picking at the details. She showered, as if she could wash the confusion from her body. But even there, the questions would not go away. How had she missed the chance, the need, to help? Had something restrained her at that moment? It had felt like it, as if someone had literally placed their hands on her shoulders. But how could that possibly be true?

Hot water poured down onto her head as she pictured herself again standing at the crossing. Something had held her back: a gentle but strong force, like the guiding hand of a parent with a small child. The mystery of it shook her, and she tasted something at her throat, the human chemistry of fear reminding her of her vulnerability.

Abruptly she turned the shower off. The thought of something unknown influencing her brought back the old horror: that something outside of her control could impact her life, could take something from her, and she would be powerless to resist it. She could not live with that, and so she chose to believe that her own thoughts had restrained her, maybe she had been dreaming again, absorbed within herself.

Afterwards, from the safety of the armchair, she gained some perspective on what had happened. She thanked God for saving a life, possibly her own, and browsed through the TV channels. This was her home, her own space.

She had bought the flat five years ago and had made her mark on it. This was where she had created the environment that she craved, the place where she could listen, as best she could, to her God.

Alex was a Christian, and she also went to church. There was no cultural reason for this. She lived in an age when there was little to gain from social attendance, and there were plenty of other things for a bright girl in her twenties to do on a Sunday morning. She went to church because she believed Jesus had risen from the dead and was her personal Saviour, and she wanted to be with others who thought the same as her.

She loved her church friends but saw their weaknesses. Many of them loved their faith to have a bit of extra fizz. They wanted drama and emotion in the practice of their faith, but she also knew that beneath the frenzy, God was at work in them all. Their discussions were full of animation, with nervous talk of End Times, descriptions that sounded like a big-budget movie from the Golden Age of Hollywood. They prayed, longing for the desired result, hoping the Deity would deliver the goods, coaxing Him from the dressing room to the stage, like a precocious actor. It was a fraught and uneasy relationship.

The supernatural had its place in the wider scheme of things, but for Alex the quest for safety was the goal. She joined in with some of the exuberance, and all the sincerity, and with the help of her friends she found her place amongst the faithful. But Alex was also separate from them. There was a gravity to her life and a deeper sense of purpose. Jesus was in her house with all the attendant effervescence, but Alex preferred to find Him in the tears of her personal history. Her Saviour understood the human condition because He had tasted it for Himself, and from this unique perspective He had the right to demand everything of her. Bringing her legacy of unresolved emotion, she had given Him everything she had. It had been the only personal concession she had ever made.

Alex knew her faults well, but they differed from those exhibited by her friends. She was prone to introspection, and this could sometimes be so absolute that the demands of the present yielded to it, leaving her stranded and separated from others. Conversations washed over her, and even the hopes and interests of those whom she loved became background noise. Her friends noticed this distraction, of course. Some mistook it for indifference, while those who knew more of her history forgave her.

Alex lived on the outskirts of a great city, which was never at ease with itself, always pulsing with busyness and urgency, full of impatient people living fast, rootless lives. In her own flat, she tried to regulate the pace of time. All the clocks ticked slowly, and she valued the familiar rhythms of her life.

What she didn't realize was that she had shared her home, and her entire life.

Even now, from the corner of the room, he watched her, sensing her thoughts and emotions, sensing the will of the master. He was a servant of God, one who some might call a guardian angel. She was not the first one he had watched over, and she would not be the last, but the fact he was even here meant she must be unusual.

He was aware of her unease: as well he might be since he had caused it. It was not for her to risk her life trying to save someone else. The other life was precious but there was an order to these things, and it had been someone else's destiny to act in this case, so he had restrained her for a moment. He had interacted with the physical world as commanded, standing in the space in front of her and pressing gently on her shoulders. It had taken less than a second to achieve the desired outcome.

He recalled the moment when she had come into existence, conceived in her mother's womb. At that moment he had joined her, and he would be with her for the rest of her life. He had no pride to be offended, but his position was such that the Lord must surely have grand plans for this woman.

As he watched her, relaxing in front of her TV, he reflected on the fact that she was very fond of uttering the words "Thy will be done" at the end of her prayers. It should not surprise her to see those prayers answered.

2

In the weeks preceding her twenty-fifth birthday, Alex resisted the temptation to call Mr Wicks, her solicitor, knowing he would phone or write. He had never forgotten her birthday, and surely, he would not forget the one that was coming up.

Her mornings became dominated by the post. Noises, imagined and real, came to sound like the drop of envelopes into the postbox. After a week of this, she became tired of her own frustrated anticipation and started going into work early to avoid the temptation of spending the morning looking from her window.

A couple of days before her birthday, a handwritten note arrived. With his typical fondness for understatement, Mr Wicks invited her to the office for "a chat". Of course, this was more than a casual conversation; this was about the last wishes of her dead parents, and the last details of the estate they had set up for her. She telephoned immediately and made an appointment for the day before her twenty-fifth birthday.

On the day of her appointment, Alex arrived twenty minutes early. In the reception area, she spent the time fidgeting and pretending to read a newspaper.

Mr Wicks' secretary offered her some tea and smiled at her.

"It's lovely to see you again, Miss Masters!" Miss Goldsworth paused for a moment and then said, "We are expecting your cousin today as well – have you seen her recently?"

Alex stared back at Miss Goldsworth. What would Daisy be doing here? Could she be a beneficiary as well? Alex felt a slight twinge of jealousy. Why should Daisy get anything from her parents?

"I haven't seen her for a while," she said. "What time is her appointment?"

Miss Goldsworth returned to her desk and perched some reading glasses on the end of her nose. "Well, it says here..." She ran her finger down the page of a very large diary on her desk. "Alexandra and Daisy Masters, ten o'clock. I remember now, Mr Wicks was eager to see you both at the same time."

"I see. I imagine..." Alex stopped mid-sentence, unable to guess what could be delaying Daisy. "I imagine she'll be here soon."

Ten o'clock came and went, and so Daisy was officially late. Alex was aware that someone like Miss Goldsworth would not cope very well with people who were late. It would offend her view of how the world should be. A large carriage clock sat ticking on the mantelpiece, defining the embarrassment of Daisy's absence.

The office had once been a townhouse, but someone had boarded up the grate and turned the bedrooms into offices. Every time Alex visited, Miss Goldsworth would be sitting in the little square office that must have once been a lounge or reception room. Alex imagined the secretary was studying the diary, believing that by an act of will, she could make Daisy turn up.

Just before a quarter past ten a thin girl with large blue eyes and naturally blonde hair peered around the panel door and looked in, as if she were about to enter alien territory. Her face was pale but defiant, suggesting a lack of sleep or an unforgiven hurt, and possibly both. Alex could see that Daisy had lost weight, again. She wore a pair of jeans that should have been tight on her and a bright pink tee shirt, and she clutched an old canvas bag as if it was a source of comfort. Her eyes scanned the room, ignoring Alex, and focusing on Miss Goldsworth.

"I'm here to see Mr Wicks."

"Of course, you must be Daisy Masters," said Miss Goldsworth.

"Yeah, I have an appointment," said Daisy with an unnecessary defiance. She hesitated, then finally perched herself on a hard chair near the door.

"Would you like some tea?" For people like Miss Goldsworth, Alex knew tea was the way to reconcile all humanity, even the young and confused.

"No," said Daisy. There was no courtesy in her reply. She did not acknowledge Alex, although Alex was sure she must have recognized her.

"Hi, Daisy, how are you?" said Alex.

Daisy looked at her cousin and uttered one word: "Fine."

The clocked ticked, and Alex glanced at her cousin.

Daisy seemed like an animal trapped in a cage, nursing an injury that would not heal. She could guess very well why her cousin was like this, since Daisy's parents had sown the seeds of all this pain long ago.

Uncle Simon, Daisy's father and Alex's uncle, had always been the rebel in the family. Here was a man whose moral framework stretched and buckled to accommodate any available business opportunity. He was always talking about his next venture, bragging about trips to Hong Kong and Australia where he was about to clinch some enormous deal. Uncle Simon gave money to people in order to avoid giving himself. It was as if he had looked at the arguments for loving other people and decided it wasn't worth the cost.

His wife, Alex's Auntie Lu, short for Louise, was a woman who, like Alex, had developed her own defences. She had quickly recognized her husband for what he was and had resolved to stay with him. Where he was used to taking risks and pushing the limits, she made their home her domain. The decoration was conservative, as if she longed to compensate for his lifestyle with the trappings of respectability. They did not love each other, but they had an understanding.

It had worked for Simon and Louise, but it had not worked for their only daughter. Daisy was a casualty of the arrangement. She had needed love like any other child but had found herself excluded by people who did not want to love her or were incapable of doing so. Now she was in her first year at college, after a chequered career at school. Alex knew it had taken Daisy two extra years to collect the grades for a place at college, and through family tittle-tattle she'd heard how Daisy had sought the love she craved in the only way she could, via several brief relationships with boys who would probably have only remembered her as a performer of sexual acts.

Alex turned away from her cousin and looked around the waiting room. It was a familiar place with sad and desperate memories. Her first visit to this office had been as a frightened, lonely child, newly orphaned by the traffic accident that had taken her parents. Back then, the room had seemed huge, and every item of furniture had been imposing.

She thought of Mr Wicks, the man who had arranged all the details with her guardians when her parents had died. Together with Auntie Helen and Uncle Max, good friends of her parents from their time in India, he had formed a team that had worked to secure her future. It was only as an adult she had realized how much he had done during those first terrible weeks after the accident.

She suddenly recalled an event that had occurred many years ago. It had been two years since she had lost her parents, but the pain of that loss was acute during that period. She would have been about twelve, and she remembered sitting in the lounge at the table, learning the capitals of the world. She had been stuck on Peru.

Mr Wicks, who was a family friend and their solicitor, was sitting opposite her, putting his papers in his bag. He had been visiting her auntie and uncle as usual to talk business. Alex assumed it was about her, but she had never been party to all the conversations, and she resented the fact that people were deciding her future without asking her what she thought about it. She looked at this strange distant man; his floppy moustache made her think of a walrus in a suit.

On a whim, she had turned to Mr Wicks and asked, "What's the capital of Peru?"

He had looked at her over his glasses.

"Alexandra," (it was so typical of him to use her full name) "important questions need considered answers. I will leave you a note; it will tell you what you need to know." With that, he had bid her goodnight and ambled into the other room to say farewell to her aunt and uncle.

His reaction had upset her. She had asked a simple question, and he had responded by saying he would write her a note! If he knew the answer, why didn't he just tell her? It was typical of adults to be tricky and mysterious, as if this was terribly clever. Alex completed the rest of her homework and then went to bed.

The next morning, at breakfast, she discovered a sealed note on the dining room table addressed to "Miss Alexandra Masters".

"Auntie, what's this?"

"It's a note for you from Mr Wicks."

"What does it say?"

"I don't know, Alex, it's your note. Why not open it and read it?"

She had taken the note and opened it later in her room.

. . .

My Dear Alexandra,

I shall tell you two facts, both of which are true. One, the capital of Peru is Lima. Two, your parents loved you very much, and you were precious to them. I trust you are in no doubt which of these facts is the more important to you.

With much affection,

Mr Wicks

She had stared at the letter and read it perhaps three times before copying the word "Lima" into her geography homework book. As she was doing this, the import of the other things he had written suddenly hit her.

Her parents had loved her very much; she had been precious to them.

It was as if a truth she had not fully comprehended suddenly became crystal clear. Tears came to her eyes as she felt a sense of a love that had been eluding her since becoming an orphan. The note had bridged the gap to a precious realization that she treasured in her heart.

Back in the present, a door opened, and there he was, standing in front of her, peering at her over his spectacles. She remembered the moustache, a little peppered now with age, but his demeanour was the same as ever; here was the Walrus, the fool, the gracious man that she had learnt to respect and love. He glanced first at Alex, and then at Daisy, and smiled.

"Good morning, ladies, do come in."

They followed him into the room. Alex had not seen Mr Wicks' office for some years, but it was exactly as she remembered it, although scaled down from the perceptions of her childhood. The floor still creaked underfoot, and the smell of wood polish pervaded the air. A vast bookcase occupied one side of the room, its shelves heavy with the weight of legal opinion from the last hundred and fifty years. The laptop on the mahogany desk was the only concession to modern technology.

Mr Wicks invited them to sit on a large leather sofa spread with knitted blankets, which was a rather incongruous sight amongst the more formal surroundings of the office.

He lowered himself into a seat opposite them and sighed, and said, "Well now, how are you both?"

"All right," said Daisy, shifting in her seat.

"Very well, thank you." Alex nodded and smiled.

"Let's get down to business then." Mr Wicks sensed the mood and judged that a prompt despatch of his duties was the best course.

"I have called you both here in connection with Paul Masters' will. The will included a clause which stated that when you, Alex, reach the age of twenty-five, and you, Daisy, reach twenty, you should both receive a sum from the estate."

He took a file from the table and placed two envelopes in front of them. "These envelopes contain the amounts made out to each of you. I will be happy to arrange for someone to advise you on the how to invest these sums." He made a point of glancing at Alex over the half-moon glasses.

He passed the envelopes to each of them.

"Thanks." Daisy took her envelope and put it into the inside pocket of her jacket.

"Is that it?" She stood up. "Can I go now?" Her wide eyes stared at him, almost begging for release.

He had no desire to hold her here for any longer than was necessary. "Yes, Daisy, you can go now."

"Right, thanks." She stumbled over to the door and made her escape.

He could hear her running down the steps and out the front door. She must have ignored Miss Goldsworth on the way out.

Mr Wicks let out a long sigh.

"Alexandra, my only consolation is that you have received the much larger sum and will probably use it rather more wisely than your cousin. I see you are fingering the envelope. I will tell you now that the sum is eight hundred and fifty thousand pounds. I have not written you a cheque, although I can if you want me to; I intended to transfer the money to an account of your choice this afternoon."

Alex looked at him and frowned.

"How much did you say?"

Mr Wicks was looking at Alex as if he was wondering whether she had become temporarily, but profoundly, deaf.

"Eight hundred and fifty thousand pounds, my dear."

"I see," she said.

He smiled at her. "Shall I get Miss Goldsworth to bring in some more tea?"

"No, no thank you," said Alex, "I'm fine, it's just I didn't realize how much money they had."

"Well, the sale of the house and the other investments realized a decent sum of money. But tell me, Alex, do you have any dealings with your cousin these days?"

The question took her rather by surprise.

"No, not really, she keeps herself to herself now."

"Hmm," he scratched his head as if trying to figure out some intricate problem, "seeing Daisy today in the state she's in, it makes me concerned for her. It is because I have a duty in law to discharge that I have given her any money at all. Is there anything you think we can do to help her?"

Alex realized he was doing exactly what he had done so often in the past: challenging her and encouraging her. It wouldn't have been his style to just give her the money and send her on her way.

"You see," he continued, "I never had that level of understanding with Daisy that I had with you. I could never fathom the pain inside her. My fear is that she will use this money to do herself harm."

Alex placed the envelope in her bag and was silent. Was he inviting her to take responsibility for her cousin? It wasn't a commitment she would welcome at the moment. Or would she? She really didn't know what she felt. There were too many uncertainties but helping Daisy would take time and emotional effort. Her cousin was a liability. If she'd ever doubted that, this morning's performance confirmed it. She thought again about Daisy, running back to college, clutching her cheque.

Then there was her money, eight hundred and fifty thousand pounds.

"I had no idea it would be that much," she said, and laughed, suddenly embarrassed.

"Alex." Wicks leant forward slightly as if to emphasize what he was about to say. "Be bigger than the money. Master it; don't let it master you, if you will excuse the pun."

He chuckled and sat back again in his chair.

"I will arrange for a transfer to your account, just leave your bank details with Miss Goldsworth. In the meantime, say a prayer for your poor cousin when you get the chance."

He was about to say something else when the phone on his desk rang. He let out an audible sigh, and he reached for the phone.

"Hello, yes," he said, "yes, I should be with you in about twenty minutes, see you then."

Replacing the phone, he made his way to the door and opened it for her.

"Well, goodbye, my dear, you know where I am if you need me."

"Yes, of course," she said. "And thank you."

Even as she said the words, she felt she was thanking him not just for looking after this money but for all the years of caring, thinking of her, praying for her.

She stood and walked to the door and suddenly realized he had used the shortened form of her first name. He had never done this before, and she didn't even know what his first name was. On an impulse she turned and came back to him.

"Mr Wicks, what is your first name?"

"Caleb, Caleb Wicks," he said, smiling.

They looked at each other, and then she offered her hand to him.

"Thank you, Caleb. I appreciate all that you've done for me."

He smiled slightly, and took her hand, and she felt the relationship between them shift.

Alex left the office, closing the door behind her, and gave her account details to Miss Goldsworth. Then she walked out into the sunshine with a figure bouncing around inside her head: eight hundred and fifty thousand pounds!

Back in his office, Caleb placed his files into his leather bag and smiled to himself, realizing that the frightened little girl he had first encountered had grown into a woman, and he should therefore treat her as an adult from now on. Then his thoughts turned to Daisy, and he eased himself down on to his knees and prayed for long enough to make himself rather late for his next appointment.

DAISY MASTERS CURLED into a seat on the train. None of the other passengers had a view of her, so she took the envelope out of her pocket and looked at the cheque inside. Ten thousand pounds, ten thousand pounds!

In this private space, she allowed herself a smile. Daisy rarely smiled, and it was a desperate, alien gesture that made the muscles around her jaw ache. She was not used to being given good things – Daisy was a sufferer; that was familiar territory. That was what she knew best.

When she got back to the city, she took her cheque and walked in and out of branches of the two banks she used to juggle her finances. In a rare moment of prudence, she paid it into the account with the larger overdraft. The cashier must have recognized her and could not disguise her surprise. Daisy liked that. She wanted her to inspect the cheque, to appreciate what it meant.

Then she asked for two hundred pounds in cash.

The cashier was frowning at her, "I'm sorry, Ms Masters, but that amount would take you over your limit."

"But I've just paid in ten thousand!" Daisy was leaning against the counter, gripping the little black pen she had used to fill out a credit form. Her knuckles had turned white.

"Yes, but the cheque will need to clear before you can draw funds on it."

Daisy could feel the anger rising, the fear that she was being laughed at again, that they would all look at her and judge her. She could feel her head ache and her mouth go dry. It was so unfair. The one time when she should have been on top, in control, and it was all being taken away from her. Even now she was the loser, the fool.

"You can draw out money against it in three days' time." The cashier's voice grated in her ears, but the woman seemed like a distant figure. There were dark creatures in her mind, climbing into her throat.

"But I want MY MONEY." The words echoed around the banking hall, an aberration in the normally staid atmosphere of the place. The other customers pretended to be busy with their transactions, but Daisy felt judged and found wanting.

Mr Hawkes, one of the personal banking managers, glided into view. Daisy recognized him immediately; she'd been in front of him several times before to explain her finances. There was something exquisitely Dickensian about him, like an officious clerk in a TV period drama. She loathed him. Or at least she loathed the power he had over her financial affairs.

"Are you unwell, Ms Masters?" he said.

"I want my money!" she hissed.

Mr Hawkes looked at Daisy.

"I was explaining to Ms Masters," said the cashier slowly, "that the cheque she has paid in will need to clear before we advance any further money to her."

Mr Hawkes leant forward and reached for the cheque.

"A solicitor's cheque, drawn on a client's account," he said, raising an eyebrow.

He held the cheque as if it were a rare specimen, a beautiful example of its kind.

"I am sure it will be honoured, but you have reached the limit of your facilities with us." He paused and looked at her. "I will let you have one hundred pounds, Ms Masters, but there will be an arrangement fee."

He smiled at her and returned to his office.

DAISY TOOK her money and ran from the branch. As she fled, she could feel the eyes of the staff and customers following her. She could imagine the other customers rolling their eyes and shaking their heads, and the cashiers laughing at her during their coffee break.

"Damn them, damn them to hell!" Her mind ran over the words, again and again, as she made her way to the public toilets and locked herself in one of the cubicles. Then she burst into tears.

Curled in a ball on the lavatory floor, she wept for about ten minutes. Above her, on the wall, someone had drawn a large letter E and then turned it into the word "Escape". God, didn't she want to do just that. Escape from her life, from the people who despised her or ignored her. In these moments, she saw herself with a clarity that eluded her for the rest of the time.

She leant against the door and thought about the wreckage of her life. The little girl pampered and accommodated by a mother who hadn't wanted her, and a father who treated her like an inconvenience. Inadequate parents who had told her that her conception was an accident and had implied that her arrival was an enormous inconvenience in their lives.

Her mother probably loved her, but also resented her. Her father did not love her, and when his wife or his conscience got the better of him, he simply bought a gift to stand in for his affections.

She was fifteen when she finally admitted to herself that the presents were a substitute and that she was essentially unloved. She had locked herself in the bathroom and shaved the hair off her head, screaming as she did it. Her parents had heard her scream, and they thought she had slashed her wrists. Her father had broken down the bathroom door and stared at her. Half of her hair lay in the bath. When he didn't see any blood, he let out an audible sigh of relief and then walked away. She knew his concern was only for how her behaviour would affect him, how her actions would intrude on his world. Whatever was left of her relationship with him died that day. Her mother had hugged her, but that had seemed like commiseration in defeat rather than an offer of support.

She sought affection in a succession of aimless relationships, but these only reminded her of the fact that no one really loved her. It had taken her some years to realize, and then admit, that the only people who had shown any genuine compassion for her were from the "Holy Joe" branch of the family, Alex's family, and half of them were dead now. She had drifted into depression and despair. Nothing could ever reach her, and she thought she was completely, irredeemably alone.

But she was wrong: she was not alone. And if she had known who her constant companions were, she would have preferred loneliness to their company.

Even now, three figures stood in the cubicle with her. They surrounded her, observing and enjoying her pain, speaking words of defeat, rejection and self-pity. They whispered directly into her soul.

"Hate them, despise them, and despise yourself." The whispers continued at a level just beyond her consciousness. *"They hate you, your parents, the bankers, all of them. You are an inconvenience. Nobody wanted you, nobody..."*

She thought these things as if they were a conclusion she had come to herself.

"All these years, and you were just in the way. Mum and dad? You have no mum and dad. They never cared; nobody cares. You are merely..."

Suddenly it stopped.

Just when they were really getting into their routine, they found her suddenly shielded from them. The figures bounced off her, and it was their turn to feel the frustration. A most offensive thing had occurred: someone had prayed for the girl.

They circled her for a few moments and then withdrew, nursing their anguish, knowing there would be other opportunities. But who had prayed for her? Until this moment they had believed their own propaganda, that nobody really cared about the human, but that was wrong, someone cared. In one sense it was no comfort to Daisy, there was more suffering to come for her, but the spirits knew that this was a very unwelcome development.

Daisy came out of the daydream and hunched against the side panel of the cubicle. In the respite from the torment, she realized a truth about herself that she had never quite touched on before. As she mouthed the words, the tears started again, hitting the floor and giving her pain some substance: "I just want to be loved."

She whispered it, conscious that others might be in earshot of her. An image of Mr Wicks flickered into her mind. She saw him looking at her with something like concern in his eyes.

But why? she thought. *Why him?*

In her mind she heard him utter some words; she saw his mouth moving: *"I love you."*

She was at once attracted and repelled. Wicks, of all people? Disgusting! But it wasn't like that, and she knew it; it was as if the Mr Wicks in her vision was speaking on behalf of someone else. In response, she whispered her own words one more time: "I just want to be loved."

She told herself that the image in her mind just showed how desperate she was for real, simple love. It was a little piece of clarity amongst the confusion.

Then it was over. The image faded, and she was herself again. Out of the corner of her eye, she could see the toilet roll, a crumpled end touching the floor. Her shoulder was aching where she had leant against the toilet bowl. Daisy dragged herself up off the floor, pulled at the toilet roll and then wiped her eyes and nose. When there was no noise from the other side of the door, she slid the lock back. She stumbled over to the basin and washed some of the despair from her face. She could feel the banknotes in her pocket, and she wanted a drink.

She headed further into the city, towards the college where she was studying for a degree in Fashion and Design. She went into the Union, and headed for the bar, and when she got there, she felt like she had just reached sanctuary. The noise crowded out her pain. There was always music, voices, and the chatter of the pinball and fruit machines. This was a place to sit and relax, a place where nobody made demands. She bought herself a lager and sat in the corner.

The alcohol warmed her, and she relaxed a little. She bought another bottle, and after a while, the bar filled up. She kept the change from twenty pounds on the table, but she tucked the rest of the money away in her pocket.

"All right, Daisy."

A young man appeared in front of her. This was Will, a friend from the course. He sat down next to her and took a swig from her bottle. Like her, Will was slim to the point of skinny, with an unkempt shock of blonde hair and pale blue eyes. His selection of tee shirts from the most unlikely bands was a kind of uniform. Today he wore something advertising the Bacon Sandwich Tour 2014 from a band whose name had long since faded from the shirt.

"Where've you been this morning? I'd saved you a seat."

"Nowhere," she answered. "So what did I miss?"

"Can't remember, I'd lend you my notes, but you wouldn't be able to read my writing; do you want another beer?"

"Please." Daisy always said yes to another drink.

She was pleased to see Will. He was friendly, but they'd never gone beyond that, although she hoped they would one day. He was a good mate, but she had no difficulty imagining him with her in bed. The memories of the incident in the bank and her tears in the cubicle were becoming fuzzy now, unreal in the sea of warmth and noise around her. The wall she placed between herself and the world was once again secure.

Yet, there was something – she felt it now as she watched Will getting the drinks. She remembered the image of Mr Wicks, and her own response, the sense of the love he represented. It would be easy to dismiss it here in the bar, but somehow, she could not. A new hunger had awakened in her. A deeper, more fundamental need. She had tasted just a little of what genuine love could be like, and now she not only wanted it, but she also felt in danger of believing she could have it. Deep in her mind sat the notion that she could be valuable, even precious to someone. Just thinking about it made her eyes prickle with tears.

She had known nothing like this before, and while she pondered on the novelty of love and sipped her bottle of lager, the spirits that had camped on her soul for all this time gibbered and howled and waited for their next opportunity.

3

<hr>

ALEX HAD no intention of playing the lottery winner and ditching her job, and so the day after her appointment with Mr Wicks she went to the office very early as usual. It was just before seven and the morning air was crisp, but she could feel the promise of the heat that would come later in the day.

The main doors of their smart office block were already open, and she smiled at the familiar face of the early shift concierge. He could see she was juggling a large platter of breakfast croissants and called the lift for her. The croissants were for a working breakfast, a management gathering where Alex took the minutes.

She already knew that this meeting would not go well.

She wanted everything to be ready when her boss, Lewis Ashbury, turned up. Lewis was the Managing Director of Sound Light and Music, or SLaM as they called it, an entertainment conglomerate with interests in music, publishing, social media and fashion. Lewis had started his career in the music business, and he still kept the energy and restlessness of his early days. SLaM was his baby; he owned the company and had built it up by hiring the right people at the right time. He issued short contracts but paid the best rates. He only really had one long-term employee, and that was Alex. He called her his "little saviour", partly to tease her about her faith, but also because she was a reliable fixed point in his life. As his secretary and PA, Alex knew there was no one else in the company he trusted as much as her.

They'd got off to a rocky start when his initial flirtations had almost made her leave the company. However, instead of quitting she'd confronted him and told him how their professional relationship would work, and he had apologized, and the matter was closed.

Now after five years, he trusted her with more and more of his business affairs. Trust was key for him; it was a precious commodity in a company full of jostling egos and selfish interests.

He had asked Alex to call together his senior team that morning to talk about a fresh assault on the "youth" market, as he called it. To any outsider it would look like a business meeting, but Lewis preferred to think of it as an arena. He referred to his team as the gladiators and he, of course, was the Emperor, ready to give the last judgement. That was how he liked to do business: let them fight it out and may the strongest win.

The proposal on the table had come from Martin Massey, Head of Music and Promotions. Also present would be Dave Somerville, the Head of Media, and Bridget Larson, who looked after the small fashion team, designing clothing-based merchandise to complement SLaM's other products.

They were all in before eight, and by nine o'clock Martin had presented his ideas with a series of colourful slides, but his arrogant, grating voice, combined with the stuffiness of the room, had given Alex a thumping headache.

"It doesn't matter what kind of music it is," said Martin, "they can play skiffle for all I care. We set them up the social media presence, bring them under the brand, and then the other activities flow from that."

"Other activities?" said Dave, raising an eyebrow.

"You know what I mean. We just have to understand what is happening out there. Different substances can come onto the market and then disappear just as quickly. If we are clever, we can ride all that and cream off the benefits."

There was silence in the room. Martin had presented his project as bigger and potentially more lucrative than anything else they had ever done. There would be significant financial returns, but it required an initial investment, and the decision to make that investment was the subject of the meeting.

Nobody spoke. The smell of coffee and pastries lingered in the air. The air con had stopped, and Alex was thinking about opening a window, when Dave Somerville spoke. She knew he would oppose the plan on principle because he despised Martin and didn't hide the fact that he thought of him as an arrogant upstart. At the head of the table, Lewis sat back and watched as the games played out before him.

"It won't work, Martin," said Dave, "it's too risky, and it's too illegal, even for us. We'll look like we are pushing the stuff ourselves. You know the line we have to tread; the lawyers will have a fit."

Alex knew a reference to the lawyers was a mistake. Lewis made no secret of his opinion of the legal profession.

"Well, fortunately, the lawyers don't run this company," retorted Martin, unable to suppress a smile that Alex saw forming at the corner of his mouth.

"We'll need one if we go ahead with this plan," retorted Dave. He leant forward, sniffed at the croissants and then grabbed one from the tray.

"How about some bacon sandwiches next time," he said to Alex, "not all this pastry stuff."

Martin, who was standing, looked down at him with contempt.

Lewis had once told Alex that he had taken on both Martin and Dave with the express intention of seeing them clash with each other. He thought the conflict would produce the right creative mix. It seemed to Alex that most of the time it only produced argument and bad feeling.

She glanced across at the other person in the room, Bridget Larson. Lewis had also told Alex, privately, that he would go with Bridget's advice. The gladiators probably didn't realize that this performance was being played out primarily for her benefit. Bridget sat silently, watching the contest, moisture showing on her forehead.

Bridget Larson was the only person in the room who frightened Alex. Nobody knew very much about her other than she was in her forties and lived by a regime that was both precise and clinical. Every morning, she worked out at the gym, and by seven thirty she was at her desk, the blonde hair and red lipstick immaculate. She would then keep going without a break until seven in the evening, when she would get up and leave.

Alex let the exchange between Dave and Martin drift away from her consciousness as she focused on Lewis, who was now looking at Bridget as if expecting some silent message from her. Alex could never fathom the relationship between Lewis and Bridget. Were they lovers? Adversaries? A bit of both?

Bridget chose this moment to speak:

"Tell us more about where you expect the revenue to come from, Martin. Where's the detail?"

"It will come from all the usual places," he answered. "The magazines, the merchandise, the advertising and the downloads. If we're smart with the social media, we can set the trend. Isn't this what we've always wanted to do? Make the culture, change it and mould it for our purposes? If we can get it right then SEEKA will be worth...well, who knows?" He moved his hands in a wide arc, implying a vague but very large number, "it will be the crown jewels for SLaM, it will make us a fortune."

Lewis pushed Martin a little harder to see what he'd say. He frowned slightly and leant forward.

"No, Martin," he said, "it's a bad idea. We can't look like we're encouraging the consumption of drugs. I'm not having our merchandise with tabs all over it. I am not taking that risk."

Alex watched as Dave smirked behind his coffee cup. Everyone in the business knew about this rivalry. Dave would want Martin's idea to sink without a trace. He thought Martin was an arrogant fool who took too many risks, and he'd told Alex this on a number of occasions. He'd even predicted that Martin would have them all doing a ghastly publicity stunt in Oxford Street, snorting something off the pavement.

Martin shut his eyes and breathed the stale air. His scheme was in the balance. He had hoped for more support from Bridget, but yet again she had played the role of Lewis' inquisitor. He realized that in a public forum she would never show him favour, despite what they had. In the back of his mind, he made a decision, and the result of this meeting would not change it. He thought he had conquered Bridget, but now he knew he was still a long way off. It was hot in this room, and he couldn't think straight. With some effort, he tried to relax and spoke again.

"Look, we aren't saying, 'here, kids, take the stuff', we're not selling it, are we? It's just our merchandise, just the usual products at the usual margin."

There was silence in the room again. The air con started up at last but seemed unable to shift the heavy atmosphere.

Dave leant back in his chair and feigned indifference: "I don't think we need to risk the business with this deal," he said, "we can sell all the current lines without looking like we're feeding off the dealers and the pimps. You don't want to drag us through the gutter, do you Martin?"

Alex glanced at Martin, who looked like he was about to explode.

"A proper little saint you turned out to be," he spat. "Well don't worry, I won't mess up your precious media operation, for what it's worth. Sometimes I think you've forgotten what SLaM is about."

Dave leant forward, and the atmosphere in the room changed.

"Excuse me?" said Dave.

Only the air con disturbed the silence, lumbering away with its breathy moan. When Dave spoke, there was an edge to his voice.

"No Martin, I haven't forgotten what SLaM is all about. I want to make money, I'm just not as reckless as you are, and don't start lecturing me about what we're trying to do here. You're the one who has forgotten our roots; you'd sell your own mother if you thought the money was right."

And much to Alex's relief, that was the moment when Lewis brought the games to a halt. He glanced over at Bridget and she looked up at him and Alex thought she could just detect a slight nod of Bridget's head.

"Okay. I think we need to see a few of these ideas fleshed out," said Lewis. "You may be on to something, Martin, I mean the branding, the clothing; the whole thing is really powerful. There is money in it, but we have to get it right. I think we will give it a go. I want you all to go away and work out how we could launch this thing, and we will reconvene next week. Alex will confirm a time with all of you. Thank you."

Alex could almost see the arrogance boiling out of Martin. He had come into the arena and he had won, and everybody in the room knew it.

THEY LEFT Alex to sort out the mess. There was food left untouched and wasted on the table. As she cleared up the mess, she wondered just why she worked for this firm. They were all playing games, and they all despised each other, and she knew that was exactly how Lewis liked things to be.

Gradually her thoughts turned into a prayer, and as she brought it all to God, her mind filled with a picture, in some ways very clear, in others quite hazy. She was looking into a crowded room, and the people there were mostly teenagers. It might have been a canteen or a café. The room was bright, and there was a dusky light coming in through the windows. She sensed this was a summer evening. She was there calling for their attention and introducing someone, and then she turned towards a small, elevated stage where her brother, Conner, was playing his guitar. The picture faded, and she returned to the debris in front of her.

That afternoon she pushed the conduct of her colleagues out of her mind and finished transcribing the notes of the meeting. Then she left work early and went home.

THAT SAME EVENING, Martin was working late, feeling focused and energized by his triumph. It was a victory he felt he had won over all of them, not just Dave. He was so engrossed in his work that when the phone rang, he almost jumped in his seat. He nearly didn't answer it, he didn't want to talk to anyone at the moment. Then he realized who the caller might be and picked up the receiver.

For a moment, there was nothing except a faint modulation of static, and then a human voice reached his ear. "Martin! Martin, is that you?" The small voice sounded as if it was coming from the other end of a long tube.

"Yes, this is Martin, who is this?" He tried not to sound too impatient.

"Martin, it's George, I'm on my mobile. I'm calling from Greece."

"Hello, George," said Martin, "there's no need to shout."

Greece? Martin wished he had left the phone to ring. The last time he had spoken to his younger brother was about six months ago, when George had been trying his luck as an itinerant salesman, and as usual, that had ended in failure. The last thing Martin wanted now was a dependant calling on him.

"Martin," the voice was full of excitement, "I've been trying to reach you. I'm working on a farm here...I've gone into partnership–" The phone cut out and Martin was about to slam it down when he heard his brother's voice again. "Now I know you, Martin, you're going to be cynical about this, but really it's a great opportunity. I mean it this time. Believe me, it beats trying to sell stuff; I'm going to see a complete return on my investment within two years."

"Good for you, George." Martin wondered where his brother had got the money from to invest in a business, since he was usually penniless. The phone hissed in his ear again.

"Anyway, we've got this enormous villa on the property, so if you ever want to come over for a break, just let me know. Hey, if you hit on hard times, you can even come and work for me!" George was laughing at the other end of the line.

Martin considered the chances of him working for his brother to be practically zero. He knew very well what would happen: the entire enterprise would either prove to be a con or fail dismally, and George would creep back, invade Martin's spare room for a while, and then find some other scheme to try.

But George wasn't finished. "Seriously, Martin, if you ever want to come over here; we have the sun, the women...I don't know why I didn't do it years ago. Anyway, look, let me give you my address and phone number."

At the third attempt, Martin got the spelling of the address right and scribbled down the phone number on a scrap of paper. He could imagine George trying to impress the local girls with his legendary charm and wit. Well, George was a fool, and if the women didn't see through him, they deserved everything they got.

"Great, George, I'll be in touch, yeah, bye." He didn't want to hear any more, and he put the phone down before George could reply. Folding the scrap of paper, he then slipped it into the back of his wallet.

He was about to turn his attention back to the SEEKA project when the phone rang again. He snatched at the receiver: "Yes, who is it?"

"Hey, take it easy, Martin." Bridget's cool voice was in stark contrast to the distant excitement of his brother.

"Oh, Bridget, I'm sorry."

"Forget it. Do you want a break from all this hard work?"

Martin sighed and struggled to switch emotional gears.

"Sure, yes. That would be good. I'll see you up there in a few minutes."

BRIDGET REPLACED the receiver and looked out to the cluster of desks where her team sat. No one was there to see her open a drawer and remove a tin of furniture polish and a soft cloth.

It was about half-past seven when she went up to the meeting room again. Martin was already there, the lights half on, filling the room with shadows. Well, that was one thing at least – she had made him wait for her. She smiled across at him, but she could see his mind was on something else. It wasn't like Martin to be this distracted. He should have been looking forward to engaging with her, and Bridget did not appreciate having to compete for her lover's attention. Of course, she knew what the problem was. This SEEKA thing had absolutely consumed him for the past couple of months.

"Martin, it'll be okay," she said smoothly. "You've won, you know that. All you need to do now is make it work." She tried to smile, but he wasn't even looking at her. She continued anyway. "And don't worry about Lewis; he wants this project to happen."

She dropped into a chair. Martin seemed to look past her, at something on the wall. He walked over to the window and looked down onto the streets below.

"There's still a lot to do. And then there's Dave."

She laughed and shook her head. "Dave? Dave is irrelevant; he has nothing more to say." She leant forward, her eyes at last catching his. "Martin, you are in control of this. Now stop worrying, okay?"

Martin fingered the rim of the table, tapping an irregular beat onto the wood.

Bridget frowned again, genuinely disturbed by his attitude; they both knew the rules here, no one was going to pledge eternal love, but this was almost cruel. It was as if he was merely going through the motions, almost judging her and then rejecting her like a piece of meat at the market. She felt her own resolve harden. She had come here for a purpose and she would see it through. He was going to make love with her on this table, she would make sure of it. Then she would choose what happened after that. Placing her bag on one of the empty chairs, she stood up and walked over to him. She was now so close to him she could sense his intensity, feel the heat coming from him. It reminded her why she wanted this to happen.

"It will all come to you in time, Martin – it will all come to us." She placed a hand on the front of his shirt so she could feel the body heat coming from him. With her eyes closed, she could concentrate enough to detect an increase in his heartbeat.

Bridget did not think of herself as particularly manipulative, no more than any ambitious woman might be from time to time. Some of her acquaintances were of course married, and they manipulated their husbands, allowing them some licence while achieving their own objectives. Bridget felt no desire to criticize any of them, she just chose a different path to the same end. Without the encumbrances of a partner and children, she could focus on her desire to get the luxuries in life that she wanted.

Until now she had thought of Martin as an amusement rather than a challenge. He was exciting to be with, there was an energy about him she found strangely alluring. She felt it again now, as they stood in the twilight, in this meeting room alone together, and she allowed herself another chance to look him over. He was one of the most intense men she had ever met, with his thin face, sharp features and dark eyes, adding to the tension that surrounded him.

Bridget wanted him now. She felt the need to move on to the engagement, and further delay would be foolish. She moved over to the control panel used for corporate presentations and dimmed the lights so she could only make out shapes and contours in the room, then she strode over to where he was and rested her head on his shoulder. His breathing was becoming deeper and more rapid. She was winning him back, as she knew she would. It was only to be expected. She was very, very good at this sort of thing.

He eased away from her slightly.

"Martin? What is it?" She frowned. He was usually in the mood by now. It had been the slightest movement, but she had noticed.

"I wanted to look at you."

She studied his shadow, the glint in his eyes heightening her expectation.

"How hungry are you tonight, Martin?" she said, speaking in a whisper.

With all the lights out, he was like a silhouette, a ghost, except she could still make out the moisture across his forehead. Before he could answer, she slipped out of the minimal clothing she wore in the office and stood before him naked. Taking his right hand, she made him feel the contours and intimacies of her body. She knew well that the fire had started within him, even if his fingers were icy cold. She eased herself onto the table and stood, feet slightly apart, looking down at him.

"I said: how hungry are you?" Her question was more of a command, an irresistible demand for attention.

"Ravenous." For the first time that day his voice was quiet, almost hoarse. He moved to engage with her, but within five minutes he was finished, and gone.

Bridget listened to the breath of the air con, still going through its routine, trying to snuff out the last traces of coffee and human bodies in the room. She was still on her back, and she was alone. The sting of brutality persisted inside her. At the best of times, he was energetic, but tonight the engagement had been almost brutal. He had had no regard at all for her; she had been an object to him, and she knew it. It occurred to her he might have been trying to release some of his own tension. She suspected he had failed.

She got up, dressing quickly, removed the polish and cloth from her bag and started work. She rubbed at the table, polishing and dusting at it as she replayed the activities of the past few minutes in her mind. A dull ache in her arm reminded her she was polishing a spot on the table that was already clean, and so she forced herself to stop. Placing the items back in her bag, she walked out, closing the door behind her.

Tonight, she knew she would be lonely as she got into her bed. Her encounters with Martin had always been part pleasure and part contest. Their bodies worked together, but their minds, their personalities, were at war. It was an issue of personal pride between the two of them. But tonight, there was none of the mutual understanding of combatants, none of the respect. Instead, he had worked over her with an almost vicious energy. She felt just a little frightened of him. It was an emotion she thought she had exorcized many years ago, but it came back to her now as all the old emotions settled in her again. She reached for the little packet of tissues in her bag and blinked at the unfamiliar tears.

She took a deep breath and refocused her mind on who she was.

"No," she whispered to herself, "no, no, no."

4

____

THE WARM SPRING evening was heavy with the promise of a long hot summer ahead. Alex stood at the open window looking out onto the High Street and then closed her eyes and listened. There were the immediate noises: cars and voices from the High Street just fifty yards from her flat. The air was full of that familiar urban smell: vehicle exhaust fumes mixed with a pungent aroma of foods from around the world, all side by side, and beneath the bustle and the colour and the smell, that constant, subliminal roar of the city. She kept her eyes shut and listened to the crowded chatter of the urban jungle.

Something rose above the noise, a clatter of sounds. She sensed it first before her ears heard an emerging click-click on the paving stones, an arrhythmic tapping that grew to a crescendo beneath her. Opening her eyes, she looked down on two figures, a couple of girls, high heels tapping, hurrying to some venue in the centre of town. They looked to be about fifteen or sixteen. The taller one was almost shouting in conversation with the other, although they were only a metre apart. To Alex's ears, they sounded loud and confident in their urgency, ready for whatever the evening would bring.

Alex studied them closely: the tight black skirts, skimpy blouses, generous make-up; the facade of self-assurance betraying their youth. She pitied them, but she also felt the bite of envy. They seemed to share a secret community that excluded her. She felt isolated, like a fading princess locked in her ivory tower.

Loneliness had been a familiar feature of her life for a long time now. She had been alone since childhood when she had lost the two people who had meant the most to her. She looked across to the mantelpiece, to where three carved wooden elephants stood in procession alongside the old black-and-white photograph of her parents. She treasured this picture of them; it seemed to capture the love they must have shared. Every time she looked at the photo, it yielded another secret to her; the way her mother held on to her father's arm, the aspects of his character caught in the line of his lips: determination and compassion. The image also reflected the consuming purpose of their lives. The darkened angle in the background must have been the roof of the medical mission where they worked in Kerala in South West India. She could not look at this picture now without feeling a breach in her defences, the hot moisture in her eyes betraying her vulnerability.

Alex had been ten when they had died, and she had felt the need to be very brave about it all. She had sealed herself away emotionally, and nobody could reach her. A succession of experts had tried to bring her out of herself, and she had decided she would need to be on her best behaviour with all of them. No one had broken through to the little girl inside.

In fact, it was one of her classmates who managed to break through to her. One particular day Alex had found her friend Lucy crying, and so Alex emerged from her shell and talked to her friend. Maybe she felt a sense of community with the tears in her friend's eyes. Lucy had eventually confessed the cause of her anguish: "Our dog Billie died yesterday."

This confession had given Alex the permission she needed to

grieve. Her reply had been almost inaudible in the playground: "My mummy and daddy died three months ago."

That was the day Alex had discovered the relief that could be found in tears.

Standing in the living room of her flat, Alex considered the two opposites of life: loneliness and belonging. Her sense of exclusion from the girls who had walked so confidently beneath her window contrasted with the flavour of community she had felt with Lucy that day. Lucy's shared grief had been enough for her then, but now her needs were more complex.

Auntie Helen and Uncle Max had not been blood relatives, although she'd always called them Auntie and Uncle. They had been the close friends of her parents, the four of them bound by the joys and tragedies of their work at the mission.

When Alex had become an orphan, Max and Helen had adopted her and she had become a daughter to them, and a sister to their son, Conner; and she loved them all. She was thankful to God that she hadn't ended up with her father's brother and his wife, Daisy's parents. God forbid! But even with her adopted family, she had still felt the detachment. Somewhere deep inside her, there was an ache, an unresolved longing.

It wasn't until she became an adult, she realized that while some of that longing inevitably sprang from her experience as an orphan, the rest, buried even deeper, came out of a desire to explore and understand her identity, especially from her mother's side of the family. Her mother's parents had come to England soon after the Second World War, and their daughter Shefali, Alex's mother, had been one of the first women of colour to graduate from medical school.

Her adoptive parents had given Alex all the love and support she could ever want from her adoptive parents, but her identity as a person of both Indian and British heritage was something she would have to work out for herself. And in those moments when she could be really honest with herself, she admitted the other longing that dwelt deep inside her – a desire she did not name, did not speak of to anyone – that one day she would love and be loved with such a depth and commitment that the emptiness in her heart would be filled and the loneliness overcome.

And yet, wasn't this a longing that God should fill? Didn't she want Him above all else? These were the questions Alex struggled with. Did she want a man, a husband, more than she wanted God? What if it was her destiny to remain single? What if that was what God wanted for her? Could He fill that need?

And she knew that, for her, the comparison made no sense. She wanted God, wanted to love and serve her Lord with all her heart. But she also wanted a partner, someone to share her life with, someone to touch and to be with.

The wind blew the scents of the city into her flat again. She would have shut the window, but at that moment she saw a car draw up to the kerb on the road outside her apartment. She watched the driver emerge and there was a curious pressure within her, a taste of expectation. Here was a visitor whom she would welcome into her home.

Angel had been watching her all this time, and sensing her mood, he moved to the window. Her visitor was a man who had visited before, but never when Alex was alone.

Alex tidied some newspapers away and paused in front of the hall mirror to check her appearance, unaware of what she was doing. Angel stood next to her, his instructions quite clear: *"Wait, watch – do not influence this exchange."*

There were footsteps approaching. Alex opened the front door before the visitor could ring the bell, and in her enthusiasm, she startled him.

"Oh, hi, Alex."

"Sorry, Joel, I made you jump, please, come in." Now she felt embarrassed. He hovered in the doorway, regaining his balance.

He looked as though wasn't sure he should be there at all. This was Joel Stamford, thirty-one, blue eyes, a kind face, and married for three years to Alex's friend Laura.

Like Alex, Laura had a passion to see serve young people, and the pair of them worked well together at the church youth club, where Laura's easy-going personality proved to be a good complement to Alex's more structured approach to life.

Angel could read the thoughts and motivations of a person, and these things said as much as anything seen in the visual world. Here was a man who had done something that was not entirely wise. It had been a spur-of-the-moment thing for him to come here, and when he eventually got home, he might not tell his wife he had been here at all.

When Laura first started seeing Joel, she had been anxious that he make a good impression on her friend. She need not have worried; Joel and Alex had hit it off from the start, and from Laura's point of view they had exhibited just the right amount of friendliness. It was all very relaxed. Joel had been courteous but had kept his distance. He had made sure that whatever he said to Alex, he said to his wife. He patrolled his boundary with care.

Angel thought of the range of human relationships he had come across throughout the ages of his service: the frustrated couples who talked but never listened; the lifelong friendships that were true love even if they weren't acknowledged as that; the short-lived, destructive liaisons, which bristled with the enemy's work – secrecy, lies and sex, mixed in the most damaging way.

So what was happening here, now? When the door opened, Angel could see that these two people were fond of each other. It was not the love of a husband and wife, but it was also not quite the love between brother and sister. This was something else that sat on the boundary between different emotions. It had always seemed to Angel that human relationships were another example of why the human project – God's human project – was a very high-risk strategy. But he was not God and did not expect to understand everything that happened. He knew his place. He was simply Angel, an angelic being, occasionally a divine emissary, and always a servant of God.

Alex and Joel embraced by the door, and Angel sensed their emotions. There was pleasure in their meeting, genuine affection, and the undercurrent of excitement engendered a quickening pulse and a release of adrenaline. He concluded that some temptation would manifest itself. It was going to come soon.

"I was just passing," said Joel, "and thought I'd bring the home-group notes round." He hovered inside the doorway, clutching some papers. "I don't want to disturb you."

Alex shook her head. "I wasn't doing anything." She beckoned him in, but he continued to hesitate, like a rabbit caught in the headlights.

Alex feigned impatience. "Come in so I can shut the door!"

"Sorry, yes." He took a couple of strides and then followed her into the lounge.

"I was about to make some coffee," she said.

JOEL HESITATED. How long could he spend here? Was there time for a coffee? When was he expected home? He heard himself accept the offer of a drink even as he asked himself these questions, and then he sat down in one of Alex's armchairs.

He hadn't just been passing; he had gone out of his way to be here. He could have given the notes to her on the following Sunday if he had wanted to. He was out on a limb here, but Alex was making him feel welcome, and he liked it. And why not? He was her friend's husband.

They made conversation for a few minutes. The kettle boiled. Joel made a point of studying the items on the mantelpiece while

Alex busied herself in the kitchen. He glanced through to her in the kitchen, and she looked up and smiled at him. He smiled back and imagined her for a moment confiding in him, confessing her sins to him as if he were the parish priest. He would have taken pleasure in granting her absolution.

"So," he said, "what's happening with the youth group?"

"There are just so many of them," she called back, "and they need somewhere to go, somewhere that's not a pub, and not out on the street. I think if we delivered the Gospel out there with the same passion and determination as the pushers and dealers showed..." She left her statement unfinished.

Somewhere out on the High Street, another car glided past.

"They need somewhere to go after school," she continued, "and at the weekend. If I could find somewhere for them, I would run it myself."

And he knew she would. He was familiar with her conviction, and he admired her strength of will; and there was something else there too, something else within the curious mix of feelings he had for her. He did not want to say what it was.

Alex came in with the coffee on a tray, and from the corner of the room, Angel continued to watch them. He wanted to understand the situation here, but it would require more observation. He was thinking about some aspect of Alex's destiny, the purpose God had for her when his senses screamed at him. Something was coming. Something was rising, slowly, forcefully; even now, something spiritually toxic was approaching them, moving up from beneath the floor. He did not know this one, but he felt the familiar revulsion and outrage.

It emerged through the carpet, and the stench of it filled Angel's senses. It must have sensed Angel's presence long before it entered the room, and now the two spiritual forces faced each other, sizing each other up. The demon stopped and sniffed the air, its eyes darting back and forth.

"You have no rights here," it ventured.

Angel was well used to the enemy appealing to authority. This was a typical preliminary skirmish.

"I will go where the Lord bids me," he said, *"and you have no authority over me."*

The thing flinched, but then it steadied itself and crept slowly towards Angel, its eyes flicking back and forth between the two humans and its angelic foe.

It appeared in human form, in a dark clerical cassock, with jet-black hair and a thin moustache. The eyes betrayed the boiling lust within it. The demon surveyed the room. It looked at Alex and a leering smile stretched across its face.

"If I could have her," it whispered, taunting Angel, curling its bony fingers into a fist. The eyes widened slightly, and it moistened its lips. Angel returned the stare.

"The living God has authority over you and your master," said Angel, *"and I have charge of this one."* He pointed to Alex. *"You will not touch her."*

The demon sneered: *"Have the female, but you will look on helplessly as I soil them both yet."*

ALEX ALLOWED herself a closer look at Joel as she handed the drink to him. She had always found his personality attractive, and she had told Laura that she approved of her taste in men, but the depth of her feelings seemed to be more apparent this evening. She placed the tray on the table and then passed him a mug, but she'd filled the mug to the brim and so as she passed the mug to him, some coffee slopped onto the table.

"Oh sorry," she whispered, and she got up to find a cloth.

As she disappeared back into the kitchen, Joel had an overwhelming sense that he was dealing with someone who was vulnerable, fragile. He wanted to whisper reassurances to her and hold her in his arms. When she returned, he noticed for the first time she had recently had her hair cut short so that the nape of her neck was now visible. The act of her movement captivated him, and he continued to stare as she mopped up the spilt coffee. Without realizing what he was doing, his eyes searched out the form of her under her shirt. He could just see some firmness beneath the material, the contour of her body.

Angel watched as the demon scuttled over to Joel and then bent down to whisper something in the man's ear. Angel could see the demon's lips moving, but he could not hear what it said.

"There," said Alex, putting the cloth on the tray, "all sorted now."

Joel smiled up at her and he was suddenly aware of the hum of the city from the open window, the heat in the air, and a sense of dislocation, which seemed to marginalize his senses. He felt like he was looking into her soul. It was too much, and he glanced down at the Bible notes on the chair beside him. His eyes caught a fragment of the scripture at the top of the paper: "But amongst you, there must not be even a hint of sexual immorality..."

There was an abrupt sensation as all of his spiritual intellect snapped back into place. He thought about his wife Laura for a moment and remembered who he was. "Jesus." He whispered the name under his breath, not as blasphemy but as a prayer.

He picked up his coffee and sipped it, eager not to spill any on either himself or the carpet.

Alex turned around with the cloth and walked back to the kitchen. He lowered his eyes and felt as if something dangerous had just passed them, and he remembered how he was supposed to treat the friend of his wife.

...not even a hint of sexual immorality.

When she came back, they chatted about Alex's work with the young people of the church.

Joel finished his coffee and stood up. "I should go."

"Okay, thanks for the notes."

...not even a hint...

At the door they briefly embraced in a way that made neither of them vulnerable, and he left.

Another spirit accompanied Joel as he made his way down the corridor to the lift. This angel had also observed the skirmish but had not tried to intervene. Whatever happened here was Angel's responsibility. They did not share any discussion during the whole incident: there was nothing to say. What they did share, though, was the beautiful moment when Joel had remembered that he was a follower of Jesus, and the Spirit of God had swept into the room, blowing the enemy aside like a leaf in a storm.

5

THE NEXT DAY, summer hit the city. The heat lingered in the air, rippling off the roads and the vehicles. The sun hovered over the metropolis, fierce and insistent. At the offices of Sound Light and Music, ideas became plans, and those plans were turned into products and media.

The company would invest heavily in a new range of music, clothing, accessories, and a new website that would ride the drug culture and promote it. They would introduce the concept immediately with some material they had already produced, and a couple of Lewis' contacts on the club circuit had agreed to carry out a pilot launch before the real thing later in the year.

Alex had been party to all of it, from attending meetings to typing up agendas. She had seen the entire plan unfold, and the spiritual tone of it hardened the lingering queasiness she felt into disgust. SLaM was going to feed off the drugs culture, and profit from it, and if it promoted the drugs scene, then so be it. There would be several new fashion lines and a new logo. They had settled on a single brand for the complete range, from magazines to music to fashion. The logo showed a unisex head with wide staring eyes and the word "SEEKA" in swaying typeface underneath. Below that, the simple catchphrase was completed with the words "after the truth". The underlying philosophy behind the whole initiative being that everyone could explore any experience: music, drugs, sex and fashion, and so find their own truth.

That the phrase had an almost biblical ring to it made Alex feel even more uneasy. It was as if evil was daring to use the very words of scripture to serve its own ends. She had no power to affect this situation directly, but she knew she could pray.

That evening, before she was hosting her home group, she knelt in her room and pleaded with God to stop this somehow, to stop it or give her a way out. She loved her job, but she knew she couldn't stay and be part of what SLaM was doing now. When she thought about leaving, it was regret at not working with Lewis anymore that surfaced in her mind.

———

Joel was on a hot commuter train, heading home. He was an electrician by trade and preferred to work close to home, but a big contract right in the centre of town offered an irresistible day rate and so he took the job and joined the commuters.

The train carriage was humid, the open windows doing nothing to ease the heat or the dilemma in his head. His mind turned constantly back and forth between opposing views. He felt like the caricature of the person with the devil on one shoulder and the angel on the other.

His external life was functioning normally, but it felt like a lie. In his heart, his feelings for Alex gnawed away at him. He had told no one because he had not wanted to risk his reputation in the church. He tried to fill his mind with other thoughts, his baby son, his wife, his work, but always his thoughts came back to her, waiting to catch his attention. His imagination played back the moments they had had together, unable to stop himself analysing these moments to discern his motives, and hers. What did she really think of him? What were her feelings? Half of his mind was focused on the day to day of his life, but the other half was wrestling with emotions he did not want to admit to anyone.

Now he was thinking about her at night, and in the morning, within seconds of waking up, the issue descended on him like a weight. There had even been an occasion recently when Laura and he had switched on the answering machine and gone up to bed early. As they made love, his mind suddenly flickered to Alex. It had been only for a moment, but the intrusion had shocked him – this was their space, just him and Laura, and thinking about Alex made it feel like a violation.

Just supposing I was alone, or if something happened to Laura if I was single.

Then another voice in his mind seemed to counter the first.

I need to get a grip on this. Laura is my wife, and I am committed to her. My feelings for Alex will not defeat me, I will stand firm.

He remembered his last conversation with her as they sat on the sofa in her flat. He remembered the ease with which they had chatted about things, the warmth of the evening. He pictured Alex's front room, the little elephants lined up on her mantelpiece, the black-and-white picture of her parents and the tick of the clock, the aroma of coffee. His mind flashed to the moment he had looked at her, discerning the contours, seeking the shape of her.

"Enough," he whispered under the noise of the train. "I don't want to know about her anymore, I don't want this anymore. I want my wife."

And he meant it. He loved Laura and wanted to be with her, but there were moments when he just wanted to cry out to God and say: "I love her," and in his turmoil, he was never quite sure which of them he meant.

And how circumstances conspired! It was the summer, and the women on the train were dressed in their short skirts and blouses, and he didn't have to look very far to see things that only hindered him in his present state.

The train pushed against the heat, and Joel withdrew from the battle, burying himself in his paper. He was not looking forward to the evening's home group. It was his turn to go, and it was at Alex's flat. The train pulled into his station, and he walked home, still absorbed by the struggle.

Bridget stared at the phone, and then, finally, she picked it up and dialled the number.

"Martin, it's me." She used her cool voice, determined to gather him in on her terms this time.

"What time is it?" he said.

"It's seven thirty." She frowned; he shouldn't be worrying about the time. "Am I going to see you this evening, Martin?"

"I'll see you ten minutes," he said.

Even as they were locked together that night, she realized she had lost him. He did not utter one word to her afterwards, he just stood up, put on his clothes and walked away. He had been rough with her again, and now she felt used and angry. She dressed and seated herself in one of the leather chairs, and now her frustration turned into anger.

He had relied heavily on her support to get his proposal through and now he had what he wanted, he had dumped her. He hadn't said as much, but emotionally she knew he was gone.

She was angry with herself for expecting it to be any different, and after all this, what did she want from him? It wasn't much more than what she'd got. She knew Martin could never give her the things she really wanted, the desires she admitted only to herself. Not the sex, enjoyable though it was in the right circumstances, not even the power. She had tried these things and found them ultimately unsatisfying. What she really desired was respect, consideration, and connection with someone else that didn't come as a contest. There were even moments when she admitted what she really wanted was love.

She sighed and suddenly felt so tired that she couldn't even bring herself to go through the ritual of polishing the table. Everything was a sham. She placed her tin of polish down on the wood.

"My God," she whispered, looking at the tin, "how pointless, how bloody pointless it all is." Her routines, carefully constructed over the years to defend her, were threatening to unravel before her eyes.

Inevitably, her thoughts went back to her father, a man whose memory she pitied now more than feared. He had dreamed of having a son and was disappointed when Bridget turned out to be a girl. That disappointment had hardened to bitterness when he discovered his wife could not have any further children. Bridget didn't know whether he had loved her mother at all, and now she didn't really care.

It had always seemed to be her fault that after her birth her mother could not conceive again. With no love at home, she had looked for attention elsewhere, in the pubs and clubs of her town, on back seats of boyfriends' cars and in bedsits. When her father had discovered she was sleeping around, he had beaten her. That was when she really perfected the art of hate; she had hated him so much, and she was proud to still feel the raw contempt she had experienced when she first left home. He had hit her mother, and her mother had accepted it as a part of life. But Bridget had resolved that she would not submit to it.

And it all came to a head one night. He had waited up, waited in the kitchen to confront her, and when she came in smelling of drink and cigarettes, he shouted at her, calling her every name he could think of. He was especially fond of calling her "dirty". So often he would say that: "You are dirty, Bridget, dirty!" That phrase was etched in her mind now.

Then he had hit her, slapping her across the face, hard. She had told him to stop, tried to push him away, but he kept shouting at her and hitting her. Then her mother had come in and tried to calm him down, but he had slapped her so hard that blood trickled from her lip. Bridget screamed at him:

"No, you bastard! NO."

That had really got him going.

"What did you call me? What did you call me, you bitch?"

She had known he was going to hit her, hard, and in a moment of clarity something in her had broken. As he had come towards her, she had picked up a kitchen knife lying by the sink and slashed his face. She could remember the light, pattering noise of the blood as it had hit the hard kitchen floor. Her mother had screamed, her father had screamed and called her something, but she had been unmoved. He had already called her every name he could think of, and it didn't really matter if he used the same words all over again. Her parents had gone to the local hospital, and she used the time they were away to pack a bag with clothes and whatever money she could find in the house, and leave.

Her only regret was that he would blame her mother and make her suffer for what Bridget had done. She spent the night at the coach station and got the first ticket to Victoria. All she could hear in her mind was her father's voice calling her "dirty" and the spatter of his blood on the floor.

Bridget looked around the conference room. The air con hummed quietly, and a resolution formed in her: she would not lead a life where the threat of abuse hung over her. She would take back control of her life.

First, she had to deal with Martin Massey. He had used her, and he was going to pay for it. There was going to be a moment of reckoning, and she didn't mind if it meant that his whole precious SEEKA project came crashing down around his ears.

She got up from the table, picked up the polish and dropped it in the bin on her way out.

Back in the office, she could see Martin had already gone. She sat at her desk and thought about her plan of attack. There was Martin, yes, but there were also some other matters to attend to. She would draft some very specific instructions to her old friend and legal adviser, Mr Shand. He had proved to be an excellent solicitor and adviser to her – very efficient, very precise and very discreet. He had always been sympathetic to her particular requirements over the years, and in a way, she was fond of him, and now she was going to need his special brand of tolerance and understanding for the particular job she had in mind. There would need to be a session with the photocopier – a long session – followed by a letter to Mr Shand, and then she would deal with Martin.

In the office's darkness, she focused on the faint sheen of light reflecting off the table and allowed herself a smile; she was always at her best when she was under pressure, cornered like an animal. Now was just such a time.

JOEL THOUGHT Alex's home group was progressing well. Tonight's subject was "Relationships in the Church", and although the group members held slightly different views on this subject, they could agree on the main issues, and he knew Alex could keep them all in line. However, for Joel, the division in his mind between the demands of the present and the deeper issues that were affecting him cast a shadow over any interest he might have had in the debate.

He was pleased to see his friend Aiden here tonight. He was

feeling a particular need for some of his male friends at the moment, and the stirrings of the call for help that he wanted to make. Joel wondered whether his friend had guessed at any of his turmoil. Aiden made his living by analysing companies and numbers, but he could also read people like no one else Joel knew, and tonight he was watching Joel like a hawk.

The Bible study finished, and people chattered amongst themselves. Aiden leant forward and whispered:

"You seem a little distracted tonight, Joel."

"Sorry?" said Joel, feigning confusion.

His friend looked at him and smiled. It took a considerable amount of self-will for Joel not to say something about the conflict inside him.

"No, I'm fine," he said. "Did you enjoy this evening? I'm pleased you could come."

Aiden smiled at an elderly lady who was handing him a cup of tea, but then he leant forward again to whisper in Joel's ear:

"Joel Stamford, you're a liar." He smiled again as the bearer of tea offered him a large plate of cakes.

"Thank you, Margaret," he said, and then leant over towards Joel yet again:

"You can fool some of these people, but you don't fool me. Your brain was here, but your heart was elsewhere."

Joel was silent for a long moment, and then before he could reply, Aiden had turned again to Margaret, engaging her in a conversation that Joel could not hear.

THE EVENING DREW TO A CLOSE, and as Alex went to find some coats, the phone rang. She suddenly thought of Daisy, although she didn't know why. In fact, it was Laura, who wanted to borrow a resource book for the youth club work and wondered if Alex could give it to Joel to bring home.

Alex said goodbye to her guests and asked Joel to stay so she could find the book and he could take it home for Laura, even though she knew exactly where it was.

Why don't I just give him the book while everyone else is around? she thought, but she could find no answer.

She felt as if she were part of a game where the end involved her spending another few minutes with Joel, alone.

***

JOEL WATCHED as Aiden headed for the door.

"Just be careful, okay?" said Aiden, as he brushed past.

"Sure," said Joel.

When Alex and Joel were alone, Joel watched as Alex quickly found the book that Laura wanted, and he took it from her.

"Well, I'll see you on Sunday," he said, placing the book in his bag. "I think things went well tonight."

"Yes, they did," said Alex.

"Well, goodnight," said Joel.

She moved towards him and he dropped the bag as they embraced. Catching again the slight scent of her, he shut his eyes, and felt himself falling into this embrace as if it were a pool of water to a thirsty soul. She held him and there was silence in the room. Again, he felt that sense of dislocation, the rush of adrenaline and an inner stirring he did not want to acknowledge.

Across from them, Angel sensed the mood, and concern grew like a shadow in his mind; these two people were having a profound effect on each other. There was a physical and emotional exchange here, enough to alert his enemy to another opportunity. It would happen. He knew it was coming and then, sure enough, just as they seemed to part, Angel sensed the spiritual atmosphere in the room change as if the air itself was rotting, heralding an enemy.

"*Can you not smell their lust, angel of Jesus?*" whispered the demon, as it appeared right at Angel's side.

"*Have you not yet learnt what people are? Their religion is a tawdry pretence! In their hearts, they want nothing more than to rut here and now on this floor!*"

Angel looked away from the creature in front of him. He dared to believe he was the better judge of God's people, and the Saviour who loved them. But what the demon said was, in some sense, true; there was always something there, something in each of them that wanted gratification. In His infinite wisdom, God had placed inside humans an almost irresistible drive, and so many of them had tasted ruin through its misuse.

"*You are wrong,*" he replied. "*It is you who does not understand the true nature of humanity. I shall not be the one to enlighten you.*"

But the demon was confident now, and it fixed its eyes on him. "*Naïve! That is what we shall name you, angel of God. I told you, I will soil them both, and however much you are responsible for the woman, I will render her powerless by the act. Look at them, how desperate they are for it, despite all of their religion.*" He said the last word with a sneer.

In the physical world, Alex and Joel looked at each other. Joel bowed his head, and in the same movement put his face next to Alex's. She kissed his lips lightly, and they parted. He could not even find it in himself to say goodbye as he left.

The demon turned again to Angel and smiled its wicked smile. The air between them fizzed as the demon's lips came up close to Angel's ear.

"*Oh yes, that is enough for now. We are patient when the prize is large. And the prize is large, isn't it? I have seen her potential; I have seen the simpleminded plans that your God has conjured up.*" The demon croaked out a laugh and then gathered itself together, bowed low in mock submission, and bled away into the floor.

As Joel left, Alex walked into the kitchen to wash up. The place seemed silent now, and her mind flashed to when she had kissed him: such a sweet taste, such a piercing inside her. Their embrace had at least told her what she suspected: that Joel felt for her as she felt for him. Glad of something to do as she rinsed the cups and plates, she thought about Laura, her friend Laura, whose husband she had kissed and embraced this evening, and she bowed her head as the consequence of the situation really dawned on her, a disturbing sense of guilt building up in her mind.

There was something else there. It took her a few minutes to identify it before she guessed at the truth. The feel of another body next to hers had been like a catalyst, encouraging something within her that had already started. She felt the need clarifying itself deep within her: irresistible and terrifying and wonderful.

She could no longer continue to be both single and happy.

She eased herself onto her knees, right there in her kitchen, hands soapy and wet, and she prayed, forcing herself to worship God first, before she submitted to the desire to confess, and repent.

At that moment, she also knew she had to leave SLaM. Lewis would try to persuade her to stay, of course, probably offer her more money, but none of it would change her mind. She wondered whether the inheritance was swaying her decision, and maybe it was God's provision for her and a sign that she should go. Whatever the circumstances, she would have to tell Lewis that she needed to leave.

Angel stood in his usual corner and felt compassion for her, and for the coming test she would need to face. The enemy would not be far away, Angel knew it would bide its time, chipping away at Alex and Joel's resolve, and when they were at their weakest moment, it would present them with the temptation. If she succumbed to that temptation, not only would that be a personal tragedy for the people involved, but it might also render her unfit for the plans God had in mind for them both. There was forgiveness, of course, but these things always exacted a price.

As Alex finished her work in the kitchen, Angel remembered something else, a deep sense of God's love for these people, including Laura. They were not pawns in a game, these were real lives bought and paid for. He could sense his Lord's passion for them, a passion that had submitted to the scourge of the Roman whip, to the nails, driven between sinew and bone, pinning a physical body to the cross. Both Angel and the enemy knew how high the stakes were now.

As soon as he got back to his desk, Martin Massey gathered his files together and shoved them into a drawer. He left the office and drove out onto the main road west from the city. Music filled the car, but he kept glancing at the hands-free kit next to the dashboard. He was putting off the call he knew he must make. Even though he had good news, he still didn't want to have this conversation. He never really enjoyed talking to Darius Lench. He was turning the music down when the call came in.

"Yes?"

"Hello, Martin, how are you?" It was the familiar voice, emanating refinement, social privilege and contempt.

"I'm fine. The board approved the ideas, SEEKA has the green light." There was a silence. He cursed himself again. What a poor way to present a brilliant piece of news. Hadn't he wanted to savour this moment? And yet all he had done was mention it as if it were a casual conversation.

"That's excellent news, Martin. We need to proceed now without delay. When will the product be available?"

Martin's brain juggled the conversation with the traffic.

"We'll be ready pretty quickly; the artwork's already done, and we booked a couple of articles today. The other stuff, the merchandise, will take a couple of weeks. The whole thing is really an ad for drugs, just like we discussed. The drugs' theme was what you said you wanted, wasn't it?"

He knew he was jabbering like a fool. Confined by the smart interior of his BMW, his hands were moist on the steering wheel, and his heart was pumping. He needed to relax, and he needed to slow the car down. Lench's voice cut into his thoughts.

"Try not to get overexcited, Martin. What I want is the fulfilment of our master's will. If drugs are a means to that end, then so be it. In so far as they can help us meet our objectives, they have potential. But it is the master's will that is central." There was a slight pause. "Why do I have to keep going back to the basics with you, Martin? It's very disappointing."

Martin could not think of an answer. He took his foot off the accelerator and eased on the brake. The voice continued:

"The magazine, is that Somerville's responsibility?"

"I am sure he will get on with it. He knows what's good for him."

"I am sure he will, and he is not likely to cause you any trouble. But I have to tell you that there is someone else who can cause us some harm."

Martin felt a pressure growing in his skull. Through an enormous exercise of will, he slowed the car right down and pulled into a lay-by. It was impossible to concentrate on a conversation with Lench and drive at the same time.

"I have felt it," Lench continued. "One of them has the power to oppose us. Who is it, Martin, who is our adversary?"

He thought immediately of Bridget. Surely, she wouldn't pose a threat to the SEEKA project, would she? She had supported him, and he would not mention her reticence now. The whole thing was going to be a success, and he was going to make a lot of money out of it. That meant more to him than belonging to the group.

"Martin, are you still there?"

"Yes."

"Think, Martin, who is against us? Please remember you are one of us now. The time for deciding on where your loyalties lie has now passed. Now, who spoke at the meeting, who was for this project, and who was against it?"

Martin knew he was trapped. He'd made his decision, and there was nothing he could do about that now.

Lench spoke again. "I have been very patient with you, Martin, suffering your little ways. Some would say I have indulged you. I will give you some time to think about this, but when I call you again, you will tell me who stands in our way."

The phone line went dead.

Martin sat in the stationary car for a minute, five minutes, ten minutes. There was no doubt about what Lench could do if he wanted to. This wasn't a game anymore; the group did not play games. They could be discreet, but if they needed to, they would act with devastating efficiency.

He thought about Lench, who was easily the most spiritual person Martin knew. The man was totally dedicated to his cause. Calm, decisive, calculating, he would do anything to further his master's will. He wondered what the girl who worked as Lewis' PA would make of someone like Lench, completely opposed to her beliefs. Martin thought further about Miss Masters, the prim PA. He had laughed when he'd found out that Lewis had tried to seduce her, and then he'd laughed again when he heard that she'd rebuffed his advances. But really, she was weak and timid. He imagined Alex cowering in Lench's presence, all her religion falling away.

Bridget was a different person altogether. Strong, determined, a powerful ally and a fearsome enemy. If she really turned against him, she would be much more of a problem than that bumbling halfwit Somerville. Martin didn't seriously think Dave was any kind of problem, particularly now that SEEKA was a done deal, Dave would fall into line. His mind circled back to Bridget. What would she do when he dropped her, now she had finished being of use to him?

"There is no choice." He repeated the words to himself over and over. He was reaching for his phone when a lorry rushed past him as he sat in the lay-by, and the car swayed slightly in its wake. Under his breath he whispered a prayer, though he didn't know why, or who he was praying to.

"I'm sorry, Bridget, God help you."

"Hello?"

Lench's voice startled him. He must have pressed "call" without realizing it.

"The woman," said Martin, "Bridget, it must be her."

There was a pause.

"Why do you think it's her?" said Lench.

"She has had second thoughts, she is suspicious. She will seek to ruin me, and the way she will do it is by ruining the project. I have felt it when I have been with her in the last couple of days. Her body is saying no; I expect her mind is saying no as well."

Lench was silent. Another car whisked past him.

"Bear with me a moment, Martin."

He heard Lench's voice, muffled and distant. He was talking to someone else in the room. Bridget's name was mentioned, and Martin's guts churned; he resisted the temptation to say anything as he waited.

The phone came alive again, and the tone of Lench's voice had mellowed considerably.

"Thank you, Martin. Leave us to deal with this. You have done well. We will meet next week in the usual place at the usual time. I am arranging a reward for you; it will be available on that day. In the meantime, focus on the project. Everything is going to happen as we have planned it. I will see you next week, goodbye."

Martin had not heard that last "goodbye" because when he heard Bridget's name, he finally realized what he had done, what he had condemned her to. The gravity of it all fell on him, and he panicked, and before he could open the car door, his stomach launched its contents onto the smooth leather of the passenger seat beside him.

6

SATURDAY NIGHT WAS PARTY NIGHT, but this evening, Daisy was working on an assignment in her room, and Will was coming over to help her.

They had organized it only that day, and though they were both used to working in larger groups, tonight was different because it was going to be just the two of them, nobody else even knew about it.

Daisy's room was not like Alex's flat, the air tasted of sensuality and disorder, and while Alex defended herself with order and tidiness, Daisy liked to hide behind the chaos.

At around seven, Will turned up with a bag full of folders and books. His rather energetic use of the intercom buzzer brought her running to the door. Once they were upstairs and, in her room, he took three strides into the heart of her living space and slid the folders across an already crowded table.

"All right Daisy, did you get some beers in?"

Out of habit, she looked at the tee shirt he wore to see if she had ever heard of the band it advertised. All Will's tee shirts looked well worn, and this one seemed to be from the Absolution tour by a band called Extreme Unction. Daisy had no idea what either phrase meant.

For the next hour and a half, they sat at the table in her room, and he went through the notes for the last two lectures, talking to her over the frantic background noise of some drum and bass. Will enjoyed giving her an explanation of his notes, but for Daisy, this was just a warm-up for what she really wanted: his opinion on her portfolio of designs.

With the notes completed, she cleared away the folders, a couple of mugs and a plate, and wiped her sleeve over the table surface.

Once she was satisfied, she reached down for her portfolio case, took it out and opened it on the table. Will leafed through the designs, studying each one.

"Yeah, well, there's a bit still to do here," he said, and then he glanced at her, watching the frown appear across her forehead.

"But some of it is just brilliant," he added. "The thing is, Daisy, when you're in the mood you can just knock it out of the park; it's like you think you have permission to create these designs. Some of it looks timid, but other stuff, when you're in the groove, then it's just –boom!" He leant back and smiled at her.

"So you like some of it?"

"Yes, some of it is good."

She had expected more from him. She didn't know what that was, what else she wanted, and she turned away from him.

"Is that it?" she said.

"What?"

"Is that all you can say about these?" She jabbed a finger at her designs.

"Hey! I said some of it is good, okay? I mean it, it really is good. But some of it just, well..." He shrugged, and they both fell silent. Behind them, the radio continued to play its urgent mix.

Will laughed and leant forward in his chair. "I'm sorry, Daisy.

Look, some of it is wonderful, it really is, but I know how good you are, and some of it just doesn't do you justice."

The look on his face suggested genuine care, and she felt her anger starting to melt. She didn't want to be weak in front of Will any more than she wanted to scream at him, so she took a pencil from the table and placed one drawing in front of herself.

"Okay, so I'll get on with this." She added to a rough sketch. She drew a line and then rubbed it out, then she drew another and then another, which she also had to rub out. As she tried to bring the picture together, Will moved around the table and stood behind her. He picked up another pencil and drew one flowing line that seemed to capture her intentions.

She felt the frustration in her heart bubbling to the surface.

"What did you do that for? Can't you just leave me to get on with it?"

Will sat back down and looked at her again.

"Yes, of course, I could just leave you to get on with it, but..."

"But what?" She slammed the pencil down on the table. It bounced and rolled and landed on the floor.

HE LOOKED at her with her anger and her passion and then placed his own pencil down carefully and let out a long sigh.

"Why do you think I came over to help you, Daisy? Why have I come here on a Saturday night when I could have been going out? What do you think my motive is?"

"I don't know," she snapped. "Maybe you just want to sleep with me!"

"Really." He was angry because, in part that was true, he wanted to be with her, but there was more to this than just sex.

"I do like you, I really like you," he said, "but I also want you to do well, I want to see you succeed, and if you weren't so..." he fumbled for the word, "…if you weren't so damaged, you'd be such a good designer."

Daisy looked at him as though she had been walking from the shoreline out into the sea, and suddenly she had just walked out of her depth.

"I mean it." He came round the table and sat down again. "There's such a talent in you."

"Why do you care?" she whispered.

Will wanted to say, "Because I love you," but instead he reached down to the floor, picked up her pencil and handed it to her.

"It's all there inside you," he said, "all the talent, all of that vision, it's just waiting to come out."

"I wish I believed in myself like you do," she whispered.

"I know I am right," he said, "all that potential is right there," he placed his hand just above her heart, "there inside you, it will burst out if you let it."

He wanted to show his respect for her work, and by association his respect for her. He also wanted to sleep with her, but that could wait. For now, he simply wanted to provide her with a little of the dignity she seemed to long for. That was what she needed, not another sexual partner.

He couldn't understand what he felt; it was too complex, too unlike the simple ways that he had enjoyed before. He looked back at the drawing where she'd added a couple more lines.

"Is this what you were trying to say?" he said.

"Yes," she said, "when you told me I could do it, I just did it."

He winked at her.

"I told you it was in you," he said.

In the background, the radio had started to play a familiar club anthem and Daisy began to move slightly in response to it. She added some more lines to the sketch, a little shade of colour, and then she stopped.

"See that," said Will.

"What?"

"You've got a great eye for colour as well, see?"

She smiled and looked up at the clock. He followed her gaze: it was nearly ten.

"I think that's enough," she said, throwing her pencil across the table and leaning back in her chair.

He watched her stretch her body, putting life back into cramped muscles, and then he made a decision.

"Let's go out, Daisy," he said.

"What? Where?"

"Just somewhere. Get your best frock on and let me take you to a party."

She was ten minutes getting changed. In that time, he lit and smoked a cigarette, wished he was in the room with her, then he was glad he wasn't. She emerged in a short blue dress with a light touch of make-up. Will experienced that familiar sensation and blinked twice.

"So where are we going?" she said.

"Ah well, even I don't know that yet," he said, "but we'll need the car."

To go for a ride in Will's car was an experience. That he drove like a maniac was not a problem for Daisy, it was the car that made things interesting. There were two engines under the bonnet, welded together to fit under the hood. Each of the seats had started life in another car, and the sound system took up the entire back seat and part of the boot.

They climbed in, the engine roared, and the car launched out of the parking bay and down the main road. Will switched on the radio, and she expected to hear some of the rave or house music he liked, but all she got was static. She leant forward to tune it.

"Leave it, Daisy, just listen."

The static hiss became absorbed into the bass resonance of the engine. Daisy sat back in her seat and closed her eyes and let the ambient roar take her. It spread to her brain and made her feel as if anything could happen and she wouldn't care. She had been thinking all night, and now she wanted to relax. Closing her eyes, she let the hum fill her brain.

A voice penetrated the hiss of the radio.

"...this is the Shadow Man, telling you how it is, we are at the Shanty Town tonight..." The voice was suddenly lost in the angry crackle of static. "...joined tonight by brother Ethan D and Ellie J. Jax," more hiss "...grime and some old skool, so if you are a SEEKA, seek it here."

The radio reverted again to its tuneless crackle. Will tuned it to the station they had been listening to in her flat. He smiled at Daisy:

"That's all we need to know."

They headed off out of the city on one of the main roads north, then turned off the main road and headed into the countryside. The deep hum of the engine made Daisy feel drowsy, but she wasn't aware she had dozed off until she felt Will's hand tap her knee.

"Hey, we'll be there soon, Daisy. Don't go to sleep on me."

"I'm not asleep," she shouted, grabbing his hand and squeezing it hard. He put his hand back on her knee and left it there.

Daisy slowly closed her eyes again and focused on the pressure of his hand. In her mind, she took the sensation of his hand on her knee and tried to magnify it. Then she imagined the same touch moving up past her knee, the sensation intensifying. She occupied a space between waking and sleeping, and as the sensation moved further up her leg, she recoiled slightly. Then it was upon her and in her mind, she was making love to Will, but it wasn't quite right…it was like she was with the brother she had never had, and they should not be like this. She was irritated now, annoyed that her imagination had tricked her in this way, spoiling the moment for her. She jolted out of her dream as the car turned off the road and bumped down a farm track.

Ahead, she could see a large building, maybe a barn or a warehouse. Light escaped in bright shafts from the wooden structure. Daisy could sense a steady thud through the ground as the car slowed. Will parked in the middle of rows and rows of other vehicles. They got out, and she stretched before taking his arm.

"Stay with me, Daisy, I want to make sure you stay safe. If you get a drink, just keep an eye on it, or someone might put something in it, okay?"

She nodded at him.

"Of course I'll be careful," she said. "I know what I'm doing."

He took her hand, and they jogged up to the building. The music was quite audible now. Four men stood at the door.

"It's fifteen, each," said one of the men as they approached.

As Will dug around for some money, Daisy got out a wad of notes from her jacket pocket and handed a ten and a twenty to one of the security guys, who nodded them in.

They pushed through some heavy plastic slats that were hanging in front of the entrance, and the heat came over them like a wave. Daisy took a step back and squinted into the lights, then like the tide on the seashore, the moist warmth drew them into itself. Will leant in towards her:

"I'll pay you back later," he shouted.

She leant in to say something in reply, but the music swallowed her words. Inside the building, Daisy felt the force of the sound and saw that the place was full of people of about their age.

The noise did not so much hit her ears as invade all of her

senses. The flickering lights disorientated her, red and green in the darkness. She held on to Will's arm, as he mouthed the word "DANCE", and she nodded. She was going to say something back to him, but it was impossible to communicate, so she gave herself up to it all, and let the ocean take her, draw her in and swallow her. Daisy loved how the power of the music and the darkness made her feel safe and anonymous amongst all the people there. She felt free.

Will got a large bottle of water from somewhere and pressed it into her hand, and she drank greedily from it. On a screen to her left, she could just make out a human face with words written around it. Something about seeking after the truth... The words seemed familiar... She remembered the voice on Will's radio talking about seeking, being a seeker... The face appeared to her again...above it she could see the word SEEKA...the spelling was wrong but that didn't seem to matter. They were talking about her. She was seeking the truth – perhaps she would find it here with Will.

She reached out to him and he put something like a little headache pill in her hand and she swallowed it and then moved forward to hold on to him because she wanted to do nothing but dance with him. The face appeared again, and a man's voice...was it the DJ? The music came and went, carrying her along, but her attention was on Will.

Then something unfurled within her. Complete release. Complete acceptance. She belonged here with these people; they were all one together. Moving closer to Will, she put her arms around his waist. Maybe she had taken him rather by surprise, because he nearly stumbled. He passed the bottle to her again, and she drank, breathless by the end of it, and he pulled her to him. She kissed him and tasted him and resolved that she would be ready for more later.

A new DJ came onto the stage and played something she

recognized, and they continued to dance. In the heat, she could feel moisture forming on her face. It trickled down to the neckline of her dress. She thought again about the sensation of kissing Will, the sensation of his hand on her knee. By now she had lost the meaning of time; the minutes and hours moved about randomly, and though she glanced at her watch, the position of the hands meant nothing to her.

Eventually, they sat down somewhere together, and he gave her another bottle to drink. She offered it to him, but he pushed it away. He gave her another one of the little pills and she took it without really registering what she was doing. He mouthed something else to her, but she couldn't hear him, and it meant nothing to her; she just grinned and hugged him.

Then they went back to the music, and she felt herself joining the group again, her and Will and the sound and the light. Complete release. Daisy thought that amongst the drugs and the sweat and the aimless volume of noise, she had found a place to belong, a place where everything came together.

But everything was about to fall apart.

Sometime later, Daisy noticed that the bottle of water had suddenly become empty, and she wasn't sure why, but it didn't seem to matter. Then her foot hit something, and she looked down and saw Will on the floor, and that didn't seem right. That wasn't what was supposed to be happening.

She forced herself to stop dancing and shouted at Will, but he didn't respond. Something about this didn't fit with the feelings inside her. Everyone here belonged together; all of them were all dancing, and it wasn't right for Will to be down on the floor. She wanted him up with her and all the other people here.

Two men emerged from the crowd close to her and came over to where Will was lying. They said something to each other, which she did not hear, and then they hauled him up off the floor. Daisy suddenly felt protective of Will and shouted at the men: "Where are you taking him? What are you doing?"

They dragged him away, ignoring her.

She followed them across the floor, squeezing past other people who now seemed to be strangers to her. The men in front of her worked their way towards a door she had not previously noticed. No one stopped her as she followed them through the door into a dark corridor. The men dragged Will behind them, and Daisy bit her lip as she watched his head slumped between his shoulders, bobbing from side to side between them. And then the old fears kicked in. She was scared and bewildered by what was happening. She shivered as the sweat dried on her.

They passed into a small room surrounded by PA containers, cables and some bottles of water. The music had quietened, and the air was much cooler here. The men turned, noticing her properly for the first time.

"Who are you?" said one, and she didn't answer. Someone shut the door and turned on the light. The other one dropped Will on the floor as if he were a sack of potatoes.

"Are you with him?"

She stared at each of them.

"I said, are you with him? What's he had?"

This wasn't how it should be; she knew that. But the situation was demanding too much of her. It was like a nightmare she had once had where angry people surrounded her, and she didn't recognize them, and they were asking her questions that had no answers. Without quite realizing what she was saying, she whispered one word, just a letter:

"E."

Her voice sounded pathetic to her ears. She was feeling cold now, and she wrapped her arms around herself. The second man looked down at Will and then pulled a phone out of his pocket. He turned around and Daisy couldn't hear what he was saying. She tried to speak to the man who had questioned her.

"We were seekers, the truth, we wanted to…"

"Shut up, you stupid bitch!" His venom shocked her into silence, and then she jumped as the door opened and a third man entered the room. He was tall and lean with sharp blue eyes. He wore a dark suit.

"What's happened?"

"This one's really gone. The girl says he's been on 'E', I don't know how many."

The second man chipped in: "I haven't seen much out there tonight, but you just don't know."

The suited man cursed.

He looked at Will, now prostrate on the floor, and then he checked Will's pulse. He looked over at Daisy. A frown spread across his forehead as he stood up.

"How did you get here?"

"He has a car," she said, "a Peugeot, yellow."

"How many of you are there here?"

"Just us, the two of us." Her voice sounded small and hoarse in this room.

"Right, put them in the van, both of them, and dump them up at the hospital, and tell Spider to get out there and find this car, and make it go away, now."

The men pushed Daisy back through to the dance hall. The sound and light assaulted her again, but now it felt brutal and alien to her. One of them dug into Will's pockets and pulled out his car keys. Daisy wanted to scream, and she wanted to tell them she hated them all, and she wanted to protect Will, but there was nothing in her, except shock and silence. They pushed her towards the entrance and out into the darkness of the night.

Now they were outside, and the music changed to a dull

thump. She shivered again as they approached an old Transit van parked beside another entrance to the barn.

They laid Will on the ground, opened the rear doors and pointed at the hardboard floor within.

"Get in," said one of them.

She clambered into the van, and they heaved Will's unconscious body after her. Then the door shut, and she was in complete darkness. Reaching out, she searched for the fingers of Will's right hand. His skin felt cold and clammy. She leant back against the side of the van and heard the men climbing in the front.

She was scared now, for Will and for herself. She felt exposed and humiliated, and angry, although in her frustration she couldn't decide if she was angry with herself, or Will, or these people who were treating them both like this.

The engine started up and the driver hit the accelerator, the wheels span in the mud as the van lurched forward and bumped over the field.

In the darkness, Daisy shut her eyes and let the tears trickle down her cheeks to her chin. The old familiar despair crowded in on her, ready to feed on her once again.

The van rumbled down the track and out onto a major road. Daisy wiped the tears and snot from her face and looked at Will. Painfully, she moved her legs so she could pull him closer to her and support his head. She put her fingers to his neck to see if she could feel a pulse, and then she leant forward to listen to his breathing. It was difficult to tell if he was dead or alive.

She didn't know how much time had passed, and she was still trying to listen for Will's breath when she heard the men speaking to each other, and the van slowed down. They turned a corner and then stopped sharply. There were footsteps and then the van doors opened. Immediately in front of her were some lights. She recognized the familiar style of hospital signs.

"Get out," one of them said, looking at her.

She stared blankly at him.

"I said, get out, now."

She clambered out and the two men pulled Will from the van and laid his body on the pavement in front of the hospital entrance. They ignored Daisy.

"Come on," she heard one of them say to the other. They climbed back in the van and pulled away, the tyres screeching as they disappeared into the night.

Daisy looked up at the lights of the hospital entrance and forced herself to leave Will and run towards the light. She barged the door open and searched around. Ahead of her was a reception desk with a tired-looking nurse staring at her.

"Help," she said, feeling the tears come again.

AT JUST AFTER three in the morning, one of the shift nurses heard the vehicle outside, and by the time he had come out to the admissions area to investigate, the van had disappeared into the darkness. In the reception area, he noticed the girl immediately. He could see the patches of sweat, and the make-up streaked with tears. She made a pathetic sight in her little blue dress, clutching an empty mineral water bottle as if it were the only thing she had left in the world.

He followed her out to the kerb at the hospital entrance and saw the boy lying on the pavement. He looked at the girl again, shivering and wide-eyed with worry, and the boy pale and motionless on the ground.

"It's okay," he said to her and turned to go back to the door. He'd already made his diagnosis.

7

———————

AT THREE THIRTY in the morning, Daisy was in a visitor's room shivering over a vending machine coffee, and Staff Nurse Michelle Compton was with her, asking questions:

"What has he taken?"

"How many of them?"

"Have you got any of them left?"

Daisy felt weak and exposed and frightened. Someone had found a blanket for her, but it seemed to make no difference to the shivering. Nurse Compton had explained that Will was alive but unconscious and suffering from the consequences of his body overheating.

Anyone in authority made Daisy defensive, and that included people in uniform like Nurse Compton. Daisy felt scared, angry and confused.

She had given no details about herself, and now she was fending off questions about Will, her mind swinging between concern for herself, and worry about Will.

"I don't know what he's taken," she said. "He just said he was taking me to a party, and we drove out to somewhere in the country, I don't know where. Then Will got sick, and they put both of us in a van and brought us here." She pulled the blanket tight around herself.

"Are you absolutely sure you don't know what he might have taken?" The nurse sighed as though she thought Daisy was either naïve or lying, neither of which endeared Daisy to her.

"Your friend has suffered from very severe dehydration, and how we treat him might depend on whether he has taken drugs, and if he has, what they are." She might have added that whether he lived or died depended on that information, too. "And you must tell us if you have taken any drugs or are feeling ill at all."

Daisy looked at the nurse, opened her mouth to speak, and then closed it again.

"Okay, let's start from the beginning. You are…" the nurse glanced at a clipboard in front of her, "…Ms Smith and you don't want to give us your address, but you've said that the patient's name is Will Myers, and you don't know where he lives, is that right?"

"Yes! I've told you all this. Why don't you leave me alone and get on with making him better?"

"That is what we are trying to do, Ms Smith, but we can do that better if we know what's happened to him."

Daisy let out a long sigh. "I've had enough of this; you people are calling me a liar and I'm not having it. I need some air."

"No one is calling you a liar," Nurse Compton said, "but if you really want to be a friend to Will, tell us what happened. I'm not interested in getting the police involved we only want to do the best for Will."

Daisy slid down in the chair and stared at the nurse.

"I think he took something," she said at last. "A pill, and he gave one to me."

"Thank you, Ms Smith. So we think he's taken something, but you can't remember anyone saying anything about what these pills were."

"No," said Daisy. She fidgeted and looked at the door. She needed to get out of here, she needed to have a cigarette, and she needed to get home.

"Ms Smith!" she shouted, and Daisy jumped. "Listen. This is serious. Your friend is alive, still, but that doesn't mean we can just patch him up and send out of here as if nothing's happened. If he has taken a substance like MDMA, or Ecstasy, his body will have become severely dehydrated, and his liver might have been damaged. If the liver damage is severe, he may need a transplant, if he survives at all."

Daisy sat and stared at the nurse.

"Am I spelling it out clearly enough for you? There's a real chance that he could die. That is why we need your help."

The room was silent.

Daisy turned away and stared at the wall. Had she mentioned Ecstasy to the nurse? She thought back...no, it had been a guess, a lucky guess. What was she going to do now? A great swell of self-pity built up inside her, as if the circumstances proved she was constantly the victim of some unfair injustice.

Then a voice shouted from inside her:

"HELP WILL, HELP HIM."

The voice seemed to shout at her from the centre of her head, like some part of her personality had just woken up and wanted to make its presence known. If this had happened even a couple of weeks ago, she might have simply run away from the hospital and left Will on the ground for the medical staff to deal with. But she hadn't run away. Because of what she felt for Will, she was caring about someone other than herself for the first time in her life.

She turned to face the nurse; her eyes moist with tears.

"He gave me a couple of tabs, probably Ecstasy; I'm sure he took some himself."

"Thank you," said Nurse Compton, standing to leave. "I need

to go now, but someone else will come in a few minutes to see if you are okay."

Across the room, unseen by human eyes and just a short distance from Daisy, three demons raged in frustration. Despite Daisy's wretched state, this engagement had not gone as well as they had hoped.

They should have been able to apply the maximum amount of torment. Exhausted and frightened, she should have been easy prey. But again, they had hit a barrier of prayer. Someone somewhere was praying for this girl. It was almost four in the morning, and someone had interceded for her!

Amongst them, the one that encouraged self-pity raged at the impotence of its power. It had seen her show genuine care for someone else, and for that person's own sake, not with some ulterior motive. She'd been brave on behalf of another human being. All the years of careful delusion were unravelling, and now for the moment she was out of their reach. Spewing their anger and rage into the spiritual realm, all of them withdrew, once more, into the darkness.

Across the city, at about the time Will and Daisy were arriving at the hospital, Caleb Wicks woke up and left the warmth of his bed. He did so with some reluctance: no one of his age is at his best in the early hours of the morning. Donning his dressing gown, he padded into his study and lowered himself into his comfortable office chair. There he sat in silence for a few moments before uttering a single word:

"Daisy."

He knew this sleeplessness was not a result of his fondness for an occasional piece of Stilton last thing at night, a weakness that had endured over forty years of marriage. This was about a commitment he'd made to God. He stayed in his study for maybe three-quarters of an hour, praying and interceding for her, getting grumpy, and then praying some more. As the first of the birds were stirring outside, heralding the dawn, he realized he had done all he needed to do. Forcing his aching joints into motion, he smiled and muttered into the darkness.

"Try not to keep such unsociable hours in the future, Daisy." Then he went back to his bed and fell asleep.

Daisy jolted awake and found that she was alone in the waiting room. She looked at the clock, it was just before five in the morning.

She wasn't going to wait for someone else to come and question her. Picking up the blanket they had given her, she abandoned the now useless water bottle and went out to find a bathroom where she could pee and splash some water on her face.

Thankfully, the ladies' room was next to the waiting room. She slipped in quietly and the lights flicked on. She took a good look at herself in the mirror and was horrified by what she saw. A mixture of make-up and tears had turned her into something resembling a circus clown. Her hair looked like someone had tipped glue over it. She tried to push her hair into some order, but it was hopeless; she would have to make her way home looking like this.

No one took any notice of her as she scurried from the washroom to the entry door, and from there out into the early morning air. She could see the first signs of dawn in the eastern sky. She walked to the small park across from the hospital entrance and found a corner of grass, bordered on two sides by some bushes. She didn't want to sleep here, but she was exhausted, and needed to sit down for a moment, away from everyone and everything, to calm herself before she got her bearings and found some way to get home. There was still a twenty-pound note stuffed in her shoe, an old habit from when she first started going out at night. Sitting on the grass, she wrapped the blanked around herself and decided she would rest here for a couple of minutes.

When she opened her eyes again, she was lying on her back with the blanket rumpled up around her. Staring at a morning sky, she felt the cold in her bones, and she shivered violently. Her head ached, her mouth was dry, and her body didn't want to move. She blinked twice and tried to look at her watch: ten minutes before seven in the morning. Then she remembered where she was, and then she remembered Will.

Oh God.

She turned slowly onto her side, then got up on her knees and looked around, fighting through a wave of dizziness.

The park was at the end of a street that included a scattering of cafés, charity shops and takeaways. She recognized where she was, but she was still miles from her flat. Some way off, she could just make out the entrance to an Underground station.

She walked a few steps, her legs tingling and aching, and she thought she might vomit, but the sensation passed, so she kept walking, putting one foot in front of the other. A newsagent at the top of the road had just opened, the proprietor bringing in Sunday papers, tied and stacked for delivery. She bought some water and a bar of chocolate.

There was no one else at the station, but in about twenty minutes a train would arrive that could take her to within a mile of her house. The emotional drain on her was now almost complete. She could think of nothing more as she waited on the platform, sitting on the only available bench. Her eyes scanned the posters dotted along the platform. The one opposite her caught her eye. It was a dark rectangle with white lettering:

"Come to me, all you who are weary and burdened, and I will give you rest.' Matt Ch. 11 v 28."

As if to underline the exhaustion she felt, she read the words three or four times and couldn't understand what they said. She was numb; her brain couldn't serve up an amusing or dismissive response to what she thought was probably some Bible verse. She had no interest in religion. It didn't connect with her life, and it offered no solutions to her pain. But the poster wouldn't go away. She couldn't be bothered with standing, and so she stared at the shapes and the letters, her mind blank.

But then, as the minutes eased by, an idea formed in her head. It was a crazy idea, reckless really, but these were reckless times, and she didn't care about being cautious now.

She was thinking about Will, the one person she'd been closest to loving, the person who had shown some faith in her, had seen that she had value. Maybe she loved him, maybe he loved her, and maybe what they had would grow into love, if they got the chance.

But now she could lose him; she might discover she loved someone and lose them on the same day. The injustice of it all left her stunned, and it also made her think about the one person she knew who had lost loved ones, her cousin Alex. Alex, the orphaned child, Alex who'd had to deal with plenty of this rubbish and survived.

The train pulled in, and she boarded it and sat in the warmth, feeling the drowsiness come upon her again. She opened the bottle and drank half of the water in one go.

She was awake for her stop, and at the station exit she found a taxicab office. Inside, she could see the detritus of free magazines scattered on chairs. She stumbled in.

"I need a cab." She gave her address.

"Be about five minutes, love," said a tired-looking woman in tracksuit trousers and an old leather jacket. From behind the desk, she mumbled into a small microphone in front of her.

Daisy took another long drink of water, unwrapped the chocolate bar, and bit off about a third of it, then drank again, finishing the bottle. She looked at the spindly wooden chairs strewn with magazines and papers, thought better of it, and walked outside. The sun was already beginning to heat the air; it was going to be another warm day.

The taxi home was a warm, faintly scented bubble. Her mind filled with the events of the past few hours, bringing to the fore the events and emotions she felt. She was angry. She was angry with Will: he had given her drugs and not even asked her if she wanted them; he had put her through all the pain of the last few hours by making himself ill. Most of all, he had broken into her life, got past her defences. In her mind, she could see the folly of her own accusations against him.

Offering me drugs is one thing Will, but how dare you break down my defences! How dare you care for me, befriend me, make me care for you, even love you? Then you end up in hospital!

Then she was angry with God, a God she didn't know or care about. An exercise that seemed profoundly futile, but the anger was there all the same.

Where was God in all this mess? Where was Cousin Alex's God? How dare He let it all happen! Wasn't He in charge?

But the effort of thinking like this drained her. She could not imagine what kind of answers the Deity might offer her, and the next thing she knew, a voice was bringing her back from sleep.

"That will be seven pounds, please."

She awoke to find she was outside her home. She paid the driver and looked up at the front door. The steps up to the entrance were steep and demanded an extravagant effort, as if the proximity of her bed made her feel even more tired. When she got upstairs to her room, she fought the urge to collapse. She had five minutes in the shower, ate some toast, drank some tea and fell into bed expecting to drift away immediately.

But sleep did not come. Turning her head on the pillow, she saw something out of the corner of her eye; Will's bag was sitting in the corner of the room. She wrestled with the need to find a contact address for Will to give to the hospital. She wanted to sleep, but something in her would not let her rest.

She didn't want to move, she really didn't, but she had to. Swearing loudly, she forced herself out of bed and rummaged through the bag. Eventually she found his phone. It wasn't locked and she quickly found a contact called "Mum and Dad". She wasn't going to call them, but she would give the hospital his next-of-kin's contact details.

She used Will's phone to call the hospital, and then panicked and cancelled the call, and then she phoned again. When she mentioned Will's name, the receptionist checked the admission records and transferred her.

"Hello, Intensive Care."

My God, thought Daisy, *he's in the ICU.*

"Hi," she hesitated, "I'm phoning about Mr Will Myers, admitted last night."

"Oh yes, and you are?"

"I'm a friend of his – I heard he was in hospital."

"Well, I'm afraid we only discuss a patient's condition with next-of-kin."

Daisy could feel the old frustration rise in her. She looked around to see if anyone was watching her.

"I came in with him," she said, "I brought him in. He's my friend! Now, how is he?" She was surprised at her own boldness. There was a pause at the other end of the line, and then the voice said:

"Who did you say you were?"

"Ms Smith, Carolyn Smith."

"Ah yes, I see your name on the admission sheet. Well, I can confirm that Mr Myers is in Intensive Care and is likely to stay here for at least a couple of days. We are running some tests to establish the seriousness of his condition. We are trying to contact his next-of-kin. Do you have a contact name or address for his family?"

"Oh yes, I can give you a contact number." She gave the number for Will's parents, switched off the phone and crawled back into bed.

And still sleep did not come. Lying motionless, listening to the noises of Sunday morning outside her house, she could hear, very faintly, the sound of church bells somewhere, and imagined huddles of people dressed in their drab greys and browns shuffling into church. She always thought the same thing about religious people: well-meaning but clueless, naïve. What did these people know about life? They lived in a delusional huddle, away from reality. But then she remembered Cousin Alex. If "reality" meant bad things happening to you, then Alex knew what reality was all about. Her faith must have given her structure to her life, some comfort. And that was why Daisy had made Alex part of her reckless plan. She had resolved to pay her righteous cousin a visit. As for the whole religion thing, who knew what the truth was? She couldn't deal with this right now and so she closed her eyes and whispered into thin air:

"Not now, not yet, thanks."

As she drifted off to sleep, the last thing she knew was the sound of church bells ringing, faint and somehow joyful, ringing far off across the city. If she had not been so tired, she would have tried to listen to them, tried to follow the pattern of the notes, but she was exhausted, and by the time the bells had finished, she was fast asleep.

8

———

THAT NIGHT, Alex had a dream. It was an emotional as well as visual experience as all the strongest dreams are.

For months now, Alex had nurtured a vision to open and run a café for the young people in her town. She'd even identified a place to rent, and in her dream, she could see it now, the old shop at the end of the High Street, empty and neglected with its dark grey and green walls.

Alex had seen the state of the place when she had visited it a few weeks ago, but in her dream, her imagination transformed the shop into what it could be: a riot of colour – sunny yellow and warm orange, vibrant red and mellow green, sunny blues and bold purples; a place full of life and chatter and music. She had always known she would need the help of her church friends to renovate the place, and in her dream, she had that help; she saw a man wearing overalls, fixing some wiring to the wall, doing some kind of electrical job she assumed.

It was Joel.

In her dream, she was happy to have him help, and he was happy to be there; there was no feeling of guilt, no discomfort or awkwardness, he was just doing his part to make the vision come to life.

When she awoke, the dream was still there, for a moment stronger in her mind than the reality of waking and starting another day. She tried to get some sense of what the dream meant, but aside from a general sign of encouragement to get on with the café, she could discern no deeper meaning to it, and certainly no meaning attached to Joel's presence.

THAT EVENING, Alex went to church. She preferred the Sunday evening services. They were more informal, and the reflective worship suited her, particularly at the moment when she had so much on her mind. The service was a comfort to her, but still left her with unanswered questions. She'd long ago learnt that coming to God gave the reassurance of His presence rather than answers. This was about relationship, not solutions. It seemed to her that God wanted His people to experience the challenge of the journey, and to work out a lot of what life was about through that experience.

There was so much in Alex's mind as she drove home that she didn't even notice the figure sitting on the steps to her flat until she had stopped and turned off the engine. From where she parked, she could make out an outline of someone, but in the gathering dusk, she wasn't sure who it was.

As she got out of her car, the figure rose and Alex could see that it was a woman, a young woman. As the figure approached her, it resolved into a familiar face: Cousin Daisy.

"Hello, Daisy," she said, "are you all right?"

Daisy didn't answer, but Alex could see the look on her cousin's face, and she knew that something had gone badly wrong. But why would the girl come to Alex? What did she have to offer her?

Alex was about to speak again when her cousin launched herself at Alex and hugged her. There was desperation in that embrace, and Alex felt both flattered and apprehensive. Flattered because she knew Daisy had decided that she, Alex, was worth a request for support, but apprehensive as well because she didn't know what kind of support she would be required to give.

Once they were back in the flat, Alex noticed Daisy's bag and realized that this was going to be a bit more than an evening visit. She put the kettle on, and Daisy sat in the lounge, and cried, and carried on crying while Alex made some tea, brought in a box of tissues, and waited.

After a minute Daisy said:

"I have a friend who is very ill, he's at the hospital now."

"Tell me about him," said Alex.

"His name is Will," Daisy reached for a tissue, "and we are on the Fashion and Design course together. He's been good to me; he didn't run away when I shouted at him, he hasn't tried to take advantage or anything like that, you know?"

Alex nodded; she knew exactly what Daisy meant.

"Why is he in hospital, Daisy? Can you tell me what's wrong with him?"

Daisy started to speak but all she could do was sob into the tissue.

"We went to a party – a rave – last night. He was on some drugs and he got ill. They took him to hospital. I was with him. He's been very kind to me. You know how messed up I am."

She drank half of the tea Alex had given her and reached for another tissue.

"They said he was really ill. They said he might have damaged his liver – he might need a transplant. I don't know what's going to happen to him."

The tears started again.

"Do you want to go to the hospital and visit him?" Alex ventured.

Daisy nodded, and then Alex said something she had not planned to: "Do you love him?"

Immediately, she wished she hadn't said it, but it was too late.

"I don't know," said Daisy. "I think I do." She paused for a moment. "I don't want to lose him."

She pulled at another tissue and buried her face in it. She was silent for a moment and then Alex could see her moving back and forth, silent aching sobs, beyond even tears.

"I'm sorry," said Daisy, "I couldn't think of anyone else to talk to. You know what it's like to lose people you care about. I know this isn't like your parents and all, but if he dies, you know what that's like, to lose someone, to lose people."

Alex was silent. Even after fifteen years, losing her parents was still painful, the memory could still pierce her heart. She couldn't pretend she had figured out that part of her life, not completely. God knew how many hours she had spent thinking about it, turning over the question:

If He is such a good God, why this pain, why this suffering?

She still had no clear answer. All she had were those who had been companions on the journey, and with everything that had happened to her, she wasn't scared of being with someone who was suffering.

"I'll help as much as I can," she whispered, "but it's not like I've got it all worked out."

"Yeah, but you've been there," said Daisy. "Look at yourself, you lost your mum and dad when you were ten, but you got your act together. You got your flat and your job and all your church mates; you've got your life in order. You've survived, you're okay!"

Daisy was almost shouting now. Alex thought briefly about her neighbours, but then she stopped herself, if Daisy needed to shout a bit, then let her shout.

"How do you know I'm okay?" said Alex, wondering herself where those words had come from.

Daisy didn't seem fazed by the question.

"You just are," she said. "Or you've found out how to be at peace with it, you've found some strength somewhere."

"You know where I get my strength from, Daisy, I know I am loved by Jesus. It doesn't stop the hurt, but it gives me a way to deal with it." She looked up at the photo of her parents.

"So how is it," said Daisy, "how is it that you have to deal with all this and you're still so..." she couldn't find the right word, "...so nice? How is it that you're still so nice and well behaved? Is it all this religion? What about the people who have loved you? I haven't had that; how do you get that? How do you do it?"

From the corner of the room, Angel watched them both. He'd been wary of opposition from the enemies within Daisy, but they seemed to be bound at the moment and much weaker now than when he had encountered them in the past, so he focused on these two young women.

Alex looked at her cousin and then reached down for her tea. "I'll tell you how I do it, shall I?"

Daisy nodded and let out a deep breath. "Yes, tell me."

"When my parents died, I withdrew into myself. It took someone my own age expressing grief over losing a pet to break the hold over me and allow me to grieve myself. My stepparents were very good with me; they gave me the room I needed, but they still let me know that they loved me. Even old Mr Wicks, bless him, somehow, I knew he cared about me, even though he bumbled around and seemed very strange to me. I used to think he was like a walrus in a suit, with his shirts and ties, and big moustache." They both smiled.

"So I think I had something you might not have had, I grew up surrounded by love and security, enough love to let me feel accepted, enough love even to allow me to rebel and still come home."

Daisy raised her eyebrows.

"Yes, I know you might find that surprising, but I wasn't always a good girl. I was angry, especially with God, for years I was angry. I took it out on those around me, especially my adoptive parents, and Conner; but then he gave them a bit of trouble as well."

"Conner?" said Daisy, "really? I can't believe either of you were that bad."

"Believe me, he's had his moments," said Alex. "But yes, I was hard work for a while. I remember I was coming up to eighteen and I knew I was leading some kind of double life. I was still going to church and had friends there, but I was also doing some other stuff as well, not exactly what I'd been taught in Sunday school. I was finding it harder to live with that contradiction. I was saying to myself: 'Do you want all this religion, or not? Make your mind up.' I didn't mind going to church, that was all right. But what did I think of a God who let a little child's parents die?"

"At that time, I was seeing this boy, his name was Neil. We had been together for about six months; I think I did love him. He was gentle, and kind."

"Really?" said Daisy, "I don't remember you ever mentioning him."

"We didn't know each other that well though, did we," said Alex.

"I guess not. Anyway, so what happened?"

"Neither of us were big fans of going out, and we didn't have that much money, so we just stayed in my room and listened to music, and we talked and argued, and well, you know... He didn't try to push anything but we both knew things were getting serious; the way he was with me I knew something was going to happen."

The phone rang, and Alex didn't move. The answering machine clicked, and she heard Joel's voice. He left a short message asking Alex to phone him. She half stood when she heard him, but then forced herself to sit back down and carried on:

"So anyway, things came to a head." Alex paused. "I asked him to sleep with me."

"*You* asked *him*?" said Daisy.

"Yes, it was me who wanted it, but he said no. I admired him for it afterwards, but at the time I was annoyed, and embarrassed. And inevitably, the fact that I had asked him to sleep with me finished off our relationship and we split up, but I couldn't get the incident out of my head. What made him say no? He was male, and I think a bit of him wanted it as much as any other man. But he made a choice, and I knew I had to make a choice as well. I felt like I was at a crossroads. It wasn't just about the sex; it was about God."

Daisy sipped her tea and stared at Alex.

"Anyway," said Alex, "it bugged me so much that one evening I took Uncle Max's church keys and let myself into the building. I knew the alarm code; they hadn't changed it in years. There was nobody else there. I can remember that moment, how it felt, the sun was setting, and there was this warmth in the place, a sense of order and peace. I stood at the front of the church and it was strange; I was so used to the place being full of people and here it was just God and me."

Alex paused, and the room fell silent.

"Go on," said Daisy.

"There was a simple cross at one end of the building; I had been aware of it all my life. I stood right in front of it as if that might help me get through to God, and I thought:

Are you a loving God, or are you a sick evil monster? In fact, do you really exist at all?

"I'd never believed there wasn't a God, that wasn't an issue for me, it was just what kind of God? One who was laughing at me, mocking me, or one who was shedding tears with me?"

Daisy opened her mouth to say something, but then closed it again. She looked at Alex and raised an eyebrow.

"So what happened?" said Daisy.

"As I STOOD there I tried to listen. At first, there was nothing, and I was beginning to think I'd wasted my time; then I heard a voice in my head, and I didn't know if it was real or I was imagining it. I still don't completely know now. *'Let me in, Alex,'* it said. And I knew no one else was there, no other human, so I just thought:

God. God is here now.

"It was weird; what had been an empty church building suddenly became full. I mean there was nobody there, but somehow the place was full."

Alex paused. This was the core of her story, the pivotal moment in her life.

"In my mind, I saw a picture, like a vision or something. There was Jesus on the cross. He was hanging there with the nails in his hands and feet, the blood running from them. Then there was Mary, his mother, and one of his disciples, John. Jesus said to Mary: *'Dear Mother, here is your son.'* And he said to John: *'Here is your mother.'*"

"That sounds like something from the Bible," said Daisy.

"It is," said Alex, "I'd heard it several times, but now I was seeing it like a movie clip. I realized I was shivering on a warm summer evening. I didn't know why. Then this voice spoke, and it said something like:

'Just as my son gave Mary and John to look after each other, so I have given you Uncle Max and Auntie Helen to look after you. And they have looked after you well, but you will always be my child. I love you.'

"Nobody had ever said to me that I was their child. How could they? The only people who could have said that were dead. There'd been this massive hole inside me all this time and as soon as I was really aware of it, God filled it up, as if suddenly I was a complete person; I was who I should be. Then I was on my knees and I'd made my decision. I still had a lot to learn, but something changed, something happened at that moment."

She looked up at the photo of her parents on the mantelpiece.

"I still feel the pain of losing them, Daisy, God knows I do, but I am okay. You ask me how I deal with stuff. I deal with it because I am loved, and that's the only reason why I haven't given up. I am loved, and nothing and no one can take that away from me."

Alex stopped and looked again at Daisy. She felt completely exposed. Daisy could take this personal testimony of hers and accept it or ignore it, but it was too late to worry about that now.

"That's how I do it," she added. "That's how I survive."

There was silence in the room. A car passed by at the top of the road. Alex looked away, unwilling to face Daisy and see her verdict on what she had said.

"I wish I could believe it like you do, Alex, and I really respect who you are and how you've dealt with this stuff. I'm glad I came here, and I'm glad you told me about yourself." She paused, like a child asking a favour of an adult. "Can I stay with you please? For a couple of days – please?"

"Of course you can, and we'll go and see Will tomorrow if that's what you want."

"That would be good. I want you to come with me."

And with that, the intensity of it all eased away; Alex made up a bed in the spare room and told Daisy to find something on the TV if she wanted to. There was a comedy show on, and it soon had them both giggling, and by this time Alex had even forgotten about Joel's call.

And from the corner of the room, Angel watched them both and smiled.

9

———

The Lord commands His angels, and they obey His will.

And so it was that the command went out one early summer night, and at that command, a messenger was sent from heaven across the expanse to earth. He didn't know about the larger purpose behind his mission, and he felt no desire to discover it. He would complete the task before him, and that was all.

His journey took him across the great divide of unimaginable space to earth, and more specifically to the kitchen of Bridget Larson's very well-presented flat in an affluent part of the city.

He stood on the cool hardwood flooring and looked around. Everything was clean, functional and expensive, a room full of symmetry and neglect. The serving spoons hung in their place on the wall, the surfaces were precise and angular, even the kitchen stools reflected Bridget's taste: a thin seat atop a set of straight vertical steel rods. Throughout the flat, the art on the walls was directionless and aggressive, reinforcing the amoral environment.

Looking past the décor, he focused on the task at hand. He moved out of the kitchen and into the hallway. He opened one cupboard and saw the slim white boiler, which was humming quietly to itself, giving off a very gentle warmth. He reached out and was permitted a brief interaction with physical reality; as he did so, the flames within the boiler sputtered and died.

He withdrew his fingers and listened. Where there had been a murmur of burning gas, now all was silent. With his purpose fulfilled, he took one step back and vanished silently into the void.

SINCE HER LAST meeting with Martin, Bridget's mood had hardened from anger into cold, focused determination. She'd made preparations and would be spending some time in the office over the weekend.

These were not going to be extra hours for SLaM's benefit. She had given the company enough of her weekends over the years; this time she was looking after her own interests.

The day had started badly, souring her mood even further. The shower produced nothing but a jet of cold water, and investigation had revealed an inexplicable fault with her supposedly high-tech super-efficient boiler. She remembered her parents' old boiler, which was a hopelessly inefficient piece of junk, but at least you could relight it by poking a long piece of curled up paper into it and pressing the stubby ignite button on the front. The one in her apartment certainly wasn't going to respond well to that kind of treatment and so she called the service company. The receptionist promised her that an engineer would be round later in the afternoon. She would have argued for a quicker response time, but Bridget had other, more important things to deal with that day.

Her thoughts turned back to the job at hand. On the Friday, she had mentioned to the security team at SLaM's office that she would be in at the weekend. Nobody was surprised; it was quite usual for a workaholic like Bridget to put in extra hours over the weekend because, as some of her more cynical colleagues pointed out, if you haven't got a life outside the office, you tend to spend more time in it.

On Saturday morning she went to the stationery store near her apartment and bought some paper and a flash drive. She was going to get a copy of everything she could in Martin's office, paper and electronic. That meant accounts, personal correspondence, notes relating to the SEEKA project, and of course anything marked confidential; nothing would be off limits. She would be reasonably careful to cover her tracks, but if he suspected something, so be it, let him fret about someone going through his files, let him challenge her if he dared.

What she most wanted to find was a copy of some market research that Martin had commissioned, looking at young people's attitudes to drugs, music and fashion. For that, she would have to get into his computer, but she was pretty sure she knew the password. When she was finished, she was going to take it all home, open a bottle of Chianti, listen to some opera, and sift through all of the evidence.

The office block was deserted, except for one lone security guard whose job it was to potter around the whole building at the weekend and keep an eye on things. She knew this man and his habits. He was punctilious and liked to do his rounds at hourly intervals making a point of visiting every office. He would think nothing of seeing Bridget in for a weekend stint, but she didn't want him to see her in Martin's office. Her instinct was always to be careful, and she wasn't going to break that habit now.

She placed her bag on her own desk and pulled out the paper and the flash drive. She glanced at the clock and then sat down, pulling a couple of pieces of paper in front of her.

The wall clock ticked up to the hour and, sure enough, the guard came and went, nodding a greeting to her, unsurprised by her presence. She gave him a casual wave and continued with her pretend work. When she was sure he had disappeared, she closed her eyes, let out a deep breath and listened. He would not be back for another hour.

Bridget knew that the security guard had no suspicions about her. She didn't guess it; she knew it because she had a gift for these things.

Years ago, Bridget had discovered she had an innate ability to sense the motives and intent of another person. She had used the gift many times in the past, for business and pleasure. It had required practice in her early years, but there had been plenty of opportunities for that. She had quickly learnt to sense the fear in her mother as well as the anger and violence in her father.

As she grew up and went into her early teenage years, she realized she often knew what another person wanted, before they uttered a word to her.

It was a valuable weapon in life, but it came with a cost. Now, it was impossible for her to trust anyone, she would always be looking for the ulterior motive, the real agenda behind the way people were. She decided to check one more time for anyone with hostile intent, exercising the gift once more, just to be careful, just to be sure.

With her eyes shut, she explored the space around her. In the immediate area, there was nothing, she was alone in the office and free to do what she liked. The security guard was still wandering around, calm and harmless.

She was about to open her eyes and make a start when something stabbed at her mind. At the edge of her perception, she could feel the jab of an enemy. It was subtle but real. The sensation was different to any she had felt before; she could not really be sure whether this was a true feeling or not. If there was something or someone, it wasn't nearby, the office was deserted, she could see that. She sat motionless, like an animal sensing its predator. What was it?

Eventually, her desire to get on with the task won her over.

"Enough of this," she whispered under her breath. She got up and walked into Martin's office. Knowing he was not disciplined about locking cabinets, she pulled open the first drawer, lifted a stack of files from it and took them to his desk.

She sifted through the files and selected a few papers for photocopying; rather helpfully the machine was directly outside his office. She loaded her own paper into the tray and photocopied the sheets she wanted, replacing them where they had been in each file, and returning these files to their proper place once she had finished.

Happy with the process, she repeated it seven or eight times and then returned to her desk with about fifty sheets of paper, which she looked through again. After a few minutes, the security guard passed by and waved. She waved back and smiled.

She repeated this cycle every hour, working through Martin's files before returning to her desk. She was into her third set of papers when she found the gem she was looking for. There were two slim files placed together separately from the other documents. One held the results from the Market Research, the other was Martin's own work. The research dealt with youth culture: exploring the attitudes of young people to fashion, sex, drugs, work and music, trying to link all these things into a cultural framework. The other file contained the sales and marketing plan of the SEEKA project. The first section explained how the SEEKA ethos of trying anything to find "the truth" could be linked to this culture, and how SEEKA merchandise and the drugs trade could work together, with one encouraging the sales of the other. She wondered whether he had connections with the some of the main dealers; he'd never even hinted at that, but she'd believe anything of him now.

Bridget decided she had enough to achieve her purposes; there was no need to spend any more time on this exercise.

After another circuit from the guard, she was ready for the

most difficult part of the morning's work – she wanted to break into the files on Martin's PC.

Getting into Martin's computer was easy. IT security was something that passed Martin by and when she tried what she thought was his password, it worked first time.

Once she was in, she scanned through his emails, and then his own personal directories. Nothing really jumped out as being helpful, but she was about to close the machine down again when she took a guess that there might be something in his temporary files folder.

As she expected, it was full of all kinds of junk, but she made herself look at each file, copies of reports, presentations, maps and documents. It really was boring stuff and eventually her mind turned to the little wine bar by the river where she would go for her lunch; it would be her treat, her incentive for getting this job done. The thought of lunch blunted her attention and because of this, she almost missed it.

Buried in the hundreds of files, she saw a document bearing her own name.

It seemed to be the remains of an email he was going to send her. It was abandoned and unfinished, certainly he'd never sent it to her, but the draft was still on the PC. The pressure inside her head intensified as she read the words:

BRIDGET,

I am not sure I will even give you this note, but if you do get it, treat it seriously, and then destroy it, properly. If knowledge of its existence is discovered, then I will be dead. This is not about our relationship; this is about your life.

I belong to a group who have an interest in seeing the SEEKA project succeed as I do. They will let no one stand in the way of the success of SEEKA, and they have decided that you pose a threat to the project. You must understand that these people are completely ruthless, and their actions will be beyond my control...

IT STOPPED THERE. She stared at the screen for maybe fifteen or twenty seconds.

"What the hell is this?" she hissed. "What are you on about, Martin? What have you done?" Her anger rose with a noise like thunder inside her head.

Her first reaction was to grab her mobile and punch out Martin's home number, to confront him right now, and get an explanation. But then something held her back, she had been cautious so far and she reasoned that it would be wise to continue with that strategy. She didn't want to start screaming down the phone at Martin in the office. She took a couple of deep breaths and closed her eyes for a moment.

When she had regained her composure, she reached into her handbag, took out the flash drive, and inserted it into a USB port on the PC. The file was transferred in an instant, and then she retrieved the tag, switched off the PC and left Martin's office exactly as she had found it.

She'd gone off the idea of a leisurely lunch at the wine bar; she wanted to get things done quickly now. Stuffing the copied papers into her bag, she switched off her own computer and headed for the car park.

Before she reached her car, the sting of apprehension caught her senses again. There was someone out there somewhere who was after her. She had sensed it, and this half-finished warning from Martin only confirmed it. She drove back to the apartment complex where she lived and as she pulled into the car park, she saw the gas company van. Remembering the state of her boiler, she marched up to the driver's window and rapped on it. The engineer jolted from his newspaper and wound the window down.

Bridget stared at the man. "Have you come to mend my boiler?"

The engineer fumbled for his paperwork.

"Ms Larson? Boiler problem, wasn't it?"

"Yes, follow me, now."

Bridget turned and walked briskly to the door. In her haste, she nearly tripped over a bucket of soapy water perched on the steps up to the front of the apartments.

"Can you move that, please!" she shouted at the window cleaner, who hastily removed the bucket. When she got into her flat, the repairman followed her in and then she vented her aggression on the substantial front door, swinging it shut with all her strength, so that it slammed with a deep boom that echoed through the whole building.

"In there!" She pointed to the boiler cupboard.

"Yes, madam." The engineer went about his task.

Bridget left him and stormed into her office. She pulled out the tag and loaded the file on to her own PC, reading the note again. The words still held a deadly potential as she stared at the screen trying to work out what Martin would have written. The more she thought about it, the more sinister the whole thing became. What was this group? What hold did they have on Martin? What were they intending to do to her? She could no longer resist the confrontation and so she pulled out her mobile and called Martin's number. There was no answer, so she left a curt message asking him to call her urgently.

She jumped as a loud clang echoed through the apartment from the boiler. Her anger was now tinged by fear and Bridget hated being afraid; she had been there before, as a child, frightened of her father. She had vowed she would not be afraid, ever again. From the window she could see nothing suspicious, the stationary cars were empty, and nobody was looking at her. She thought about the gas engineer, in her home, right now; she could hear him fiddling with the boiler.

"No," she whispered urgently to herself, "surely not, I called him. He's here to fix my boiler. I just need to calm down, and focus."

She drew in a deep breath and released it, slowly.

"Okay," she said to herself, "let's do this."

She had spent years conquering the different fears that sought to overwhelm her, and she wasn't going to give in to this one. Cursing the unease within herself, she flicked on the hi-fi. Bizet's *Carmen* burst into the flat and she got down to the task of sorting the papers into bundles. She ignored the gas engineer; he would come to her when he was finished.

To each bundle, she attached a note explaining what the papers said. The evidence pointed to a conspiracy within the company. Bitterly she wondered whether they should have renamed the firm Sound Light Music *and Drugs* because somehow the acronym SLaM didn't seem to stand for what they were really all about anymore. Now she regretted supporting Martin's project but at least she could do something to bring it all down around his ears.

"I'm sorry Lewis," she whispered to herself. Perhaps he was partly to blame for this, but she had never wanted to hurt him.

She shut her eyes and took two deep breaths.

"Focus Bridget, come on."

She brought the papers together into several bundles and wrote notes to attach to each one, then she put them all into a large, reinforced envelope. She'd decided not to include the note from Martin. That was personal; and she would deal with it herself.

She placed the bundles in a large envelope and addressed it with clear black capital letters as if such clarity would protect the package from the wrong hands. With her work done, she flicked off the music and strode into the kitchen where the engineer seemed to be finishing up. She could not sense anything sinister about him at all.

"Have you fixed it?"

"Yes, madam, it'll be fine now. Quite odd, really. Looks like the pilot went out on its own. Anyway, it's lit now, so it should stay on. Good afternoon." The man let himself out through the door.

Bridget ignored him and searched around before grabbing her keys and picking up the envelope. She left the apartment, double-locking the door on the way out. She felt calmer, more in control now that she was taking action.

At the front door, she took one last look at the contents of the envelope. Everything was in order: each little bundle was there with its attached note, and the covering letter; her instructions were explicit and of course, she had included a cheque to cover payment for Mr Shand's trouble.

She saw the gas engineer driving away and got into her own car.

She drove into the centre of the city; to a post office she knew would be open on a Saturday. She parked illegally outside the doors of the post office, took her package to the counter and sent it by special delivery to her solicitor. The package passed from her hands and she breathed a sigh of relief as it went into a sack behind the counter.

On the way back home, she took a lengthy detour and visited Martin's house, but as she expected, he was not in. She reasoned that she would catch up with him soon enough, and then there would be a reckoning. She wasn't sure what Lewis would think of this, but he would know all about it as well once she was done.

With her work completed, she tried to relax. She noticed she was driving too fast, and so she slowed down, took a deep breath and then another. This evening she would put on her best dress, go out and dance and drink. Who knew what else might happen? She checked her watch – it was two thirty.

Back at the apartment, she turned the music back on again. Rinat Shaham was the mezzo-soprano, capturing all of Carmen's passion and defiance. Bridget skipped forward to Act 4, the Toreadors, and turned the music up, indulging in this, her favourite recording of her favourite opera. She went into the bathroom and turned on the shower, warm water flowed over her hands, confirming that the boiler, like Shaham, was preforming well. Having stripped off her clothing, she stepped into the roaring shower. She usually spent about three minutes in the shower, but this afternoon she indulged herself a little and stayed in for five.

———

WHILE SHE WAS in the shower, the front door latch clicked, turned, and the door eased open. Bridget heard nothing as the door moved lightly, inch by inch, across the surface of the carpet, all sound drowned out by the finale. She finished her shower and stepped out. It was only then, as she began to dry herself, that once again the instinct that had kept her safe for so long, triggered once more inside her. She froze where she was, looking, listening, sensing hostile intent. Reaching to a shelf in the bathroom, she picked up a pair of nail scissors. Her bare feet made no sound as she crept to the edge of the bathroom and looked out into the hallway. From here she could see the front door, now standing open.

She listened to Carmen rejecting the lover who would also be her killer and she smiled and reached for her bathrobe.

Taking a deep breath, she padded quietly across the corridor and into the kitchen, where she took one of the seldom-used carving knives from the kitchen. She slid one of the expensive, silent drawers open and removed a very sharp, very clean Wusthof six-inch chef's knife.

Bridget had had an intruder in her flat before and her approach had been the same then as it would now: confrontation. She emerged from the kitchen, holding the knife, and padded slowly towards the door, wet feet soft on the carpet.

Her body was not completely dry and the draft from the door made her shiver slightly, but the music urged her on. She was not afraid, not intimidated. She would deal with this situation in the same way she had learnt to deal with so many others in her life, by being strong and sure of herself. She felt calm, freed by the finality of the moment. This was not office politics, this was life or death and she felt exhilarated by it.

To the right of her front door, there was an alcove. It had the potential to conceal someone and might do so now, or it might be that there was no one there. She considered the possibility that she might be walking down the corridor of her apartment to her front door holding a carving knife in order to confront thin air. The prospect made her feel almost disappointed, at least she would then be able to enjoy the evening's entertainment.

She walked very slowly now, bare feet on the carpet. Carmen was approaching the fateful moment, and Bridget had already decided her strategy; she was going to leap at the alcove with the knife in front of her. Either her assailant would take a slash from the knife, or she had deceived herself and she was going to feel foolish for a moment. The package she had just posted came to mind, and she felt a peculiar sense of triumph. After one more step, she was close enough. She told herself that life was full of challenges, which you either confronted or you ran away from.

And Bridget Larson never ran away.

In the last seconds of her life, Bridget knew that her instinct had not let her down; someone was waiting in the alcove by the door. She lunged forward with the knife before her sight could confirm that anyone was there, and she felt the slight resistance as the blade connected with flesh. It was her final act, a suitably dramatic end to a dramatic life.

The window cleaner stood before her. She saw the horror and pain in his eyes as her knife slashed deeply across his face, drawing blood. In that same moment two silenced bullets ripped through her and darkness began to close in. She knew it was over, and in her last moments, she enjoyed the satisfaction of watching the blood well up on her attacker's face.

The parallel with her own father was so compelling that it occupied her last second of consciousness before the mist closed over her and she was gone.

10

THE WEEK BEGAN with glorious sunshine and there was already heat in the air when Alex got into the car ready to take Daisy to the hospital. She'd messaged Lewis and booked a day's leave, and now she sat in the car, waiting for Daisy to join her.

She started to think about her cousin, the unexpected guest. It must have been God's will that Alex was able to give Daisy a place to stay, backing up all the talk about faith with some real, practical help.

Daisy's story had only made Alex feel more committed to her café project, and that was just the start of it. Alex could see that the café was part of a bigger cultural battle, a conflict of ideas and visions over the real purpose to life. It seemed to Alex that creating a cultural space for that vision was more urgent than ever.

Just thinking about these things stirred something deep inside her. She wanted nothing less than to bring Jesus into every part of the cultural landscape: music, film, TV, radio, art, literature, magazines, theatre fashion, all of it and everywhere. This was the heart of her vision – to build a Christ-centred culture, one that would contain elements of such quality that it would command a place in the minds of millions of young people across the world and set them free from the tyranny of filling the deep longing they felt with every damaging thing that called out to them.

What she wanted to do was the antithesis of the SEEKA project, and that was why she had to leave SLaM.

She recalled a prayer meeting she had attended a couple of years ago, where someone had spoken some words over her. She remembered them now:

"God is calling you to be a history maker, Alex, a danger to the enemy and a light to millions. He has so much for you, and you can't even begin to guess at it yet."

A tap on the car window brought her back from her thoughts.

"Alex! Hello? Let me in, the door's locked."

"Oh sorry, Daisy, I was miles away."

"On another planet by the look of it," said Daisy getting into the car. She had her hair tied back and was wearing sunglasses.

"You think that will keep you anonymous?" said Alex, nodding at the glasses.

"I don't know," said Daisy. "I wanted to defend myself a bit, as much as I want to see him."

Alex nodded and started the car.

They were both quiet as they eased out onto the main road, and Alex's mind turned from the high ambition of her vision to a more earthly preoccupation: her friend Joel, and how she felt about him. It seemed crazy that one minute she could be contemplating a calling from God that might have global implications, and the next she was struggling with the sexual feelings that welled up when she thought about her best friend's husband. She wished these feelings would go away, she didn't want them, however sweet they felt to her, and the prospect of falling into sin with Joel filled her with horror.

It wasn't simply that it would be wrong in itself; it would also be a profound betrayal of her friend Laura if anything happened between Joel and her. Not that Alex seriously thought that was likely. She was reminded of something she'd heard in a sermon about how Jesus, even though he was perfect, had known what it was to be tempted. He had spent forty days in the desert before facing the enemy. Then she remembered that Joel had called her, and she had not returned the call. She felt a sudden desire to reach for her mobile and speak with him.

The car approached the hospital and even though Daisy had not been speaking, somehow, they both sat there and became even quieter. They pulled into the car park and as Alex switched off the engine, she turned to her cousin:

"You still want to go through with this?"

"Yes!" said Daisy, "I have to."

"Are you okay?"

"No," said Daisy. "Well maybe, yes."

"Do you want me to say a prayer?"

"No, it's okay." Daisy paused. "You could say one to yourself, in your head, maybe?"

Alex nodded.

They walked into the hospital reception area. Alex glanced at her phone and saw she had a missed call and a message from Lewis. She would deal with that, and the call from Joel, later. She had to be here for Daisy now.

Walking into the hospital again brought the fear and confusion back into Daisy's mind. Those bare walls and that warm, disinfected air made her nearly turn around and walk out again. She realized she hadn't had a cigarette in nearly thirty-six hours. She paused for a moment and Alex stopped as well, looking at her.

"I'm okay," said Daisy. She was glad she looked very different now, in her jeans and sunflower tee shirt, with her shades on and her hair tied back. At reception, Daisy gave her own name and said she was a friend of Will. She had heard he was unwell and had come to visit him. The receptionist disappeared for a moment and then returned with one of the duty doctors.

"Miss Masters?" Both Alex and Daisy looked at her.

"Miss Daisy Masters? I'm Dr Weldon. I understand you're here to see Will."

Daisy nodded, and the doctor looked at Alex.

"And you are?"

"Alex Masters, Daisy's cousin, I'm here with her."

The doctor nodded. "I wonder if you would come with me, please?"

The doctor led the way down a corridor and into a small waiting room. When the door was shut, he turned to Daisy.

"Miss Masters, I am afraid I have some bad news for you. Will died last night. I am so sorry."

There was silence between them all for a moment, and Daisy felt as if she was falling in on herself, falling away from everyone and everything and retreating into herself. She'd had this experience before, and when it was very bad, she would stay locked within herself for hours, dislocated from reality.

"No," she said. "Why?" She could feel the moisture forming in her eyes and blinked to stop herself from crying.

"Well, Will was very ill. I can't tell you any more than that at the moment, I'm afraid, and there will have to be an autopsy, but his liver had been damaged, and although he regained consciousness briefly, he was still very unwell. During the night there were complications, and I'm afraid we lost him. We'll know more after the autopsy."

A little voice in her mind spoke:

"You knew this was going to happen. They all leave you in the end."

"No," whispered Daisy.

"We told you, you were alone."

And now the spirits who attended her saw their chance again, and closed in.

"It's time for you to think about yourself, Daisy, to look after yourself. It's all very well spending time with your Christian cousin, but she doesn't care what you are going through, and neither does God. Look what He did to Will."

The voices were interrupted, this time not by prayer but by the doctor:

"Miss Masters, do you have some identification on you?"

"Yes sure, why?"

"I have something for you." The doctor held out an envelope.

Daisy got her purse out and found her driving licence. It was still a provisional; she'd never actually learnt to drive, but it did show her name and address.

He glanced at the licence, and then handed her an envelope with her name on the front.

"During the time he was conscious, Will dictated a note which he asked us to give to you if he didn't make it. I am sorry, Miss Masters." There was a pause.

Daisy clutched the note and then got up to leave. The doctor touched her arm as she stood.

"There is one more thing, I'm afraid. Will's death has meant that the police are going to be involved now. They may want to interview his friends. It might be wise for you to call the police station before they call you. I have the number here." He gave Daisy a small card.

Daisy said nothing; the temptation to give in to fear and panic almost overwhelmed her. What would she say to the police? Would she need a lawyer? She suddenly thought about Mr Wicks. Perhaps he would be able to help her. Could she tell him what had happened, or would he sit in judgement over her?

She walked out of the room, through the reception area and out into the warm spring air. Alex followed behind her.

"He's dead," she said, and then she started to walk towards the exit, clutching the envelope the doctor had given her.

Alex was silent as they walked slowly back to the car.

Sitting in the passenger seat on the way back to Alex's flat, Daisy picked up the envelope, then she put it down in her lap, then she picked it up again.

"I loved him, Alex. Jesus, I loved him, and now he's gone." She spoke suddenly, staring ahead of herself while Alex carried on driving.

"Why does everything good get taken away?" said Daisy. "Why does your God give good things and then take them away? What kind of love is that?"

Alex kept driving.

"I'm sorry," said Daisy after a moment.

"It's okay," said Alex. "You're right."

"Am I?" said Daisy.

Alex didn't answer.

When they got back home, Daisy sat on Alex's sofa and fingered the envelope. She watched Alex disappear into her kitchen and now she was on her own, the tears welled up in her eyes, the sobs came, and it felt terrible, and it felt good. She felt safe in this place. Alex brought tea for them and they sat in silence while Daisy released the grief she felt.

"I'm going for a walk," said Daisy finally. "I might be a while."

"Here," said Alex, "take a key. You might as well have it while you're here." She passed Daisy her spare front door key.

"Thanks," said Daisy. She took the key and shoved it into her coat pocket with Will's note, and then she left.

WITH DAISY GONE, Alex felt herself relax, glad to have some time alone now. She didn't begrudge Daisy the support, but she had phone messages to deal with.

Her home answering machine had three messages: one from Joel thanking her for the loan of the book and asking about her plans for the café; one from Conner, and a third one from Lewis, her boss.

The one from Lewis made her forget the other two for a moment.

"Alex, it's Lewis, I don't know if you got the message I left on your mobile, look, I know you're off today, but can you give me a call when you get the chance, something's happened and I need to talk to you, sorry, thanks."

She dialled his number as she tried to imagine what would make Lewis call her on her mobile and her home phone number.

"Lewis, it's Alex here, you called me."

"Alex, thanks for phoning. Look, I'm afraid I've got some tragic news. An intruder broke into Bridget's flat at the weekend, and she was shot."

"Oh no, is she..."

"I'm afraid she died there; she's gone."

Alex was stunned. "That's awful!"

"It is too awful," said Lewis, his voice sounding strained. "The police were in here this morning to tell me what had happened and then everyone here had to give an account of their where-abouts on Saturday, we've all had to give blood samples and try to think of people who would have wanted to harm her."

"So they don't think it was just a burglary gone wrong?" said Alex.

"No, they don't, I'm afraid," said Lewis. "They'll want to inter-view you, Alex, as soon as possible. They've given me a number for you to contact them, but I expect they'll track you down them-selves soon enough. I'd contact them if I was you."

He read out a phone number, and Alex scribbled it down.

"Look, I'm sorry about this, Alex. I'm sure if you have a good alibi for Saturday, they won't bother you again."

She hesitated, and then against what felt like her better judge-ment, she said:

"What about you Lewis, are you okay?"

Her concern seemed to be a welcome surprise to him.

"Bless you, Alex, I'm fine. Well, I'm not fine, but I'll be okay, you know? It's terrible, really terrible. I-I mean, I was very fond of Bridget, as you know, and this is just awful in so many ways."

"I'm sorry, Lewis." She wasn't sure what else to say.

"Look, I'm sure you're busy and I don't want to intrude, just tell the police where you were and that will be the end of it, I should think."

"Okay, Lewis, I'll see you tomorrow, goodbye."

She finished the call and looked at the slip of paper with the number on it. Both she and Daisy would have to have dealings with the police now.

For some reason, she was struck by the conviction that Martin Massey had something to do with Bridget's death. She didn't know why she felt this. She certainly had no proof and wouldn't be mentioning her suspicions to anyone, but the thought was there. She wondered if she could deal with this without telling Daisy; she didn't want to put that burden on her as well.

She listened to the message from her Conner again. He was asking if he could come and visit her in the next couple of days. Her immediate response was to say no. Alex's orderly life, so care-fully nurtured over the past few years was in tatters at the moment and she could feel the old sense of unease rising in her again.

Besides which, the place was going to get pretty crowded if Daisy was going to be here at the same time.

"No!" she said to herself. "This is my space, my private space, I can't have it invaded by people." She frowned as she stared around the room, looking at the sunshine, the little carved elephants on the mantelpiece, and then at the picture of her parents. She stared at them, smiling at her.

"Oh okay!" she said finally. "But if the pair of them start arguing, they'll have to go."

She picked up her phone again and dialled her stepbrother's number.

Conner was a musician. He had always loved music, and gadgets. Over the years his room at home had gradually filled with guitars, computers, laptops, sound equipment and speakers. He'd managed to connect all of it up in a way that Alex had no interest in trying to fathom out. He'd been part of a band for over a year now, but Alex couldn't remember what they were called.

As far as she knew, Daisy and Conner had not seen each other for a long time, probably since her own eighteenth birthday party, seven years ago. She would need to tell him what had happened.

"Hi, Conner." She put on the cheerful voice she always used when she talked to him, whatever her mood.

"Hey, sis, how's it hanging?" The familiar cheerful voice shouted back at her over the ubiquitous background music.

"Do you have to use that phrase?" she said. "I mean, in what context is that ever a phrase to use with me?"

"Sorry." Alex was not convinced that he was sorry, but he seemed to be making an effort to sound contrite.

"So you want to come and stay for a couple of days?"

"Yeah," he said. "Is that okay?"

"Sure, but there's just one issue – Daisy's here at the moment."

"You mean Cousin Daisy?" said Conner. "Wow, what brings her to your place?"

Alex explained what had happened, and he offered to postpone his visit, but Alex told him to come anyway. It was possible that Conner's presence, cheerful and gentle as he usually was, would help Daisy during this time. They agreed a time for him to come over and she finished the call.

From his usual corner in the room, Angel watched all this unfold. There were strands to this story that even the police might never uncover. Alex and her colleagues truly were part of a larger plan, a battle much greater than themselves.

But for now, Alex needed to walk the path before her. She had some money from her parents' estate, she would be free of the entanglement of SLaM, and she would be able to focus on the café, and what that might lead to. That was the way forward for her.

There was just one significant complication in Alex's life at the moment, and it was about to manifest itself again in her next call. Angel watched as she phoned Joel's number.

"Hello?" Alex heard Joel's voice, and felt the warm delight inside her.

"Joel, it's Alex, I got your message."

"Oh yes, I just wanted to say, about your café plan, I'd love to come and help you fit the place out when you've got the lease, I can do some of the electrical work for you if you want."

"That would be really useful, thanks," said Alex, and she meant it.

"Great, I'll see you Sunday, bye."

"Bye."

That was the end of the conversation. As she put her phone down, the excitement within her subsided into a feeling of disappointment. She couldn't carry on like this, torn in different directions by reason and passion. She thought of Jesus' temptation in the desert; even after forty days of fasting he refused to turn the stones into bread. But he'd never been alone, had he? He'd always had his Father with him, and the Spirit to guide him. She breathed out a sigh, and picked up the phone again, and the scribbled note with the police phone number.

Someone on the enquiry team for Bridget's murder took the call and booked an interview for her. She had just finished the call when she heard Daisy come back into the flat.

"You okay?" she said to Daisy.

"Do you think Mr Wicks would be able to help me with the police?" said Daisy.

"I'm sure he can," said Alex. "and there's something else I should tell you."

"Oh, what's that?"

"Conner is coming to visit me for a day or so."

"Oh," said Daisy, "so do you want me to go then?"

"Oh no!" said Alex. "No don't worry about that, if he wants to stay, he can kip on the sofa, you can stay in the spare room."

Daisy smiled. "Yes, that's cool." She hesitated for a moment and then she said, "I opened the letter, from Will."

"Oh, okay. What did it say?"

"Here, you can read it." She passed the note over.

DEAR DAISY,

If you're reading this, it means I didn't pull through, or I suppose something else really bad has happened. Daisy, you are such a great artist, and such a great person. Don't be afraid just because I've gone. Be who you are, be everything you were meant to be.

With love, Will

NEITHER OF THEM spoke for a moment.

DAISY LOOKED AT THE MANTELPIECE. There amongst the other pictures was a photo of Conner, with his blue eyes and curly hair. There was something cheeky about his smile – he reminded her of Will. She turned away.

"We'd better call Mr Wicks then I guess," she said.

Alex nodded and once again, picked up her phone.

11

Darius Lench sat at his desk and in his mind, he ran over the details of the kill, again.

He was surprised and annoyed that the Assassin had made such a mess of it. Of course the woman was now dead, so at least in that sense the operation had been a success, but there had been complications. Some of these were obvious and some were subtler.

Sitting back and placing his hands behind his head, Lench noticed how warm the room had become. There was moistness across his forehead and on the palms of his hands. Confirmation – as if he needed it – that this issue was worrying him.

He nudged the air con control in his office and looked out of the smoked glass, onto the city. Below him, clusters of architecture spread out in all directions. The cars and people on the roads below seemed like toys, and he imagined himself reaching down and picking them from the road, placing them wherever he wanted, having power over them.

Power. It was the thing he hungered for most. Other men craved sexual satisfaction, or wealth, and these things had their place of course, but Lench's passion was for power, a lust for control over as many people and things as possible. It was why he got so angry, so agitated when things did not go to plan. Lench did not like loose ends and there were too many of them now.

His thoughts turned back to the murder of Bridget Larson. Not only had the job gone wrong, but he had subsequently learnt that the target had spent the morning in the office doing he knew not what. She'd then returned home, and had gone out again, clutching a large envelope. On top of all this, there was the fact that the Assassin had dripped blood all over the place as he left. That was more than enough evidence to link him to the crime. It was a shambles. He would not have been surprised to hear that there had been some spiritual interference from somewhere in all of this. The issues churned around in his mind as he thought back to the planning stage of the job.

The preparation had been thorough, certainly no problem there. The hair dye and the window cleaner disguise was a reliable strategy and had allowed the Assassin plenty of time to inspect the building and watch the target. Lench had even taken the time to see her for himself; he could see why Martin had coupled with her; she was an impressive-looking woman.

He looked up at the man sitting across from him, and sighed.

In front of him was the personification of their failure. The Assassin, head now shaved, was staring at a space in front of Lench's desk, waiting for judgement to be passed. A fresh scar snaked across his face, stretching over his nose. The two men had been together for the last hour, going over the details of what had happened, trying to assess the implications.

THE ASSASSIN WAS TRYING to sit still and hold his anger in. This was the first time he had failed to deliver a kill exactly as required. The scarring on his face gave him considerable discomfort, reminding him of that failure, but what was worse was the way it would always mark him out now; he knew that the anonymity which was so vital to his trade had been compromised. Lench's voice grabbed his attention.

"I do not wish to see you for a while. You had better go to the safe house for at least a month."

The Assassin nodded.

"Expect few comforts," said Lench.

The Assassin knew better than to respond or defend himself; excuses would only compound his leader's displeasure. Still the old anger burned in him. Being submissive did not suit him, he felt like an animal held on the leash.

So the Assassin stood up, bowed to Lench and left the room, pulling the door shut behind him. He had known this was the most likely outcome. A stay at the safe house would be a frustration, but it was probably for the best; he needed to recover, and centre himself again. He welcomed the basic Spartan lifestyle that lay ahead.

LENCH WAS NOW ALONE. It seemed he was the only one left to judge and punish for the Assassin's incompetence. He stood up and walked over to the glass, stretching from the floor to the ceiling of his office. He could see his outline in the window. His suit and hair were immaculate as usual, but he could see little signs of the tension he felt, tiny pieces of evidence: the corner of his left eye twitched and his hands were still moist.

What really grated at him was the fact that he could still feel the threat to their efforts, even with this woman out of the way. He had chosen not to share this information with the Assassin. If they'd picked the wrong target, then that was his fault, him and the idiot Martin. He thought about Martin Massey for a moment.

"Another weak, arrogant fool," he whispered to himself, "like all the rest of them."

He'd already talked to Martin, made him aware of the problems they'd had, and the fact that the threat still existed.

It was only under further questioning that Martin mentioned his boss's assistant. It turned out she had been party to many of the discussions that had taken place. Martin had even neglected to tell him that she was a Christian, a gross piece of negligence on his part. It only confirmed Lench's suspicions that Martin was another incompetent, and a liability for their organization.

Lench could have tracked this woman down and released the Assassin immediately to deal with this issue, but now they'd have to be patient. Returning to his desk, Lench unlocked a drawer and removed a small Moleskine notebook. Flipping past pages of notes, diagrams and figures, he came to a fresh page, at the top of which were written two words, a name he had only just recently heard for the first time.

"Alex Masters," he said, tapping the surface of the desk. "Who are you, Miss Masters? And are you really standing in my way?"

She was probably an irrelevance, but if she belonged to the enemy, that had implications, and Martin certainly could not be trusted to work out what they were. Lench sensed the desire within himself to see this woman, to examine her himself. He knew it would be like this; he always had to examine the enemy.

He tried to return to his other work, but his mind would not focus on the papers in front of him. As the clock chimed the hour he finally gave in and decided to visit the place where this woman lived. Something within Lench pulled at him, telling him he was being reckless, but the pressure of frustration needed to be released somehow.

He walked briskly down to the car park and settled into his Mercedes. For Lench, the demonstration of controlled power was everything. Sitting in his just acquired ruby black Mercedes S-

Class Coupé was the closest he could get to a physical manifestation of that power. The sensation was visceral, personal. So many of Lench's associates thought he was cold, aloof, distant, but he knew he was none of those things; they simply didn't understand his tastes.

Just being here in the quiet, cool aroma of this new environment was enough to bring things back into focus, to bring his attention back to the important issues. He sat completely still for perhaps two minutes, exercising the meditative discipline he'd learnt over the years. At the end of that time, he felt calmer, more assured.

But the enemy was out there. He wanted to see this woman, needed to see what he was up against. Perhaps a glimpse would give him some insight, some way into the victory he craved.

A single touch started the vehicle, and for a moment he listened to the restrained power, the potential of this beautiful machine. Then he eased out of the cramped car park, onto the busy city road.

ON THE TUESDAY morning of that week, Alex visited the police station and gave a statement to the team investigating Bridget's murder. Fortunately for her, she had been at the local community summer fair for most of Saturday. This had given her the pick of about a hundred witnesses, and the police had accepted her alibi without comment. She gave the requested DNA sample and promised them her full cooperation if they needed her help.

THINGS WERE NOT SO easy for Daisy, given her much closer involvement with Will's death. While Alex was having her interview at a city police station, Daisy was having an honest conversation with Caleb Wicks. She'd called him after visiting the hospital and he had been surprised to hear from her. When she explained what had happened, he'd offered to help immediately, and reassured her he knew a number of barristers who might be able to defend her if it came to it. He'd called the police station for her, booking a time for her to attend for interview that afternoon, and then he'd cleared his diary and sat down with her to go through her story from start to finish, picking apart every single detail until Daisy had felt like screaming.

Twice she had stormed out of his office to calm her nerves with a cigarette. Both times, her return had prompted Miss Goldsworth to make some more tea, which, on the second occasion, Daisy had accepted – black no sugar. Caleb Wicks had maintained an attitude of infinite patience, and they had carried on where they'd left off. After about two hours of this, Daisy had got her story straight in her head.

After the coaching session, Daisy had made her way back to Alex's flat. Alex had agreed to come with her that afternoon for her police interview.

They were making their way out to the car park that served Alex's apartment when Daisy noticed a very smart-looking Mercedes gliding to a stop and parking illegally on the main road outside.

She had an eye for smart motors, and immediately noticed the sleek ruby black vehicle as it came to a smooth stop amongst the family saloons and city run-arounds.

———

LENCH BROUGHT the tinted window down and looked out at the mediocrity surrounding him, the sunlight dazed him, and he blinked. He was just getting out of his car when he noticed two young women leaving the apartment building.

He recognized Alex immediately, and not just by sight. There was a spiritual presence about her. She belonged to the enemy – that much was patently obvious – and he knew in an instant that this woman was the real barrier to their plans, and that his Assassin had indeed killed the wrong person. He cursed Martin again for the incompetent fool that he was.

Lench was suddenly possessed by a desire to get a better look at this woman, his adversary. It was truly a reckless action for someone in his position, but he could not resist, he wanted to see her, to get a sniff of her spiritual state, to observe his prey.

<hr>

"Do you know him?" Daisy said to Alex, pointing at a strange man – some kind of city banker type.

Alex looked up at the approaching figure. As she did so, she felt the blood start to pump around her body, adrenaline kicking in.

"No, come on, Daisy, let's go."

Alex didn't know why she was reacting in this way, she didn't know this guy but there was something about him that made her skin crawl, something that made her think he was a threat.

The man continued to stare at them both as he walked into the car park. Alex turned towards her car, but Daisy kept her eye on him as he approached them.

He stopped just a couple of metres away and squinted at them; he wished he'd brought his sunglasses with him.

"What you looking at then?" shouted Daisy.

The man ignored her and walked a couple of paces towards Alex.

Alex looked at him and her stomach turned.

"Daisy, we need to go," she said, looking away. She turned back to her own car, but it appeared that Daisy wasn't finished yet.

"I said, what you looking at then?" Daisy stepped forward so she was between Alex and him.

LENCH TURNED his attention to the slim blonde thing standing in front of him. He did like women with a bit of attitude, and he could see she certainly would have been a dainty morsel for some of his group.

"Now," he said smirking, "who might you be?"

"None of your business who I am, pal." The girl placed her hands on her hips. "Now get out of here before I get the police to nick you for stalking."

Her defiance amused him, and he took a step closer to her, smelling the scent of her, then he laughed.

"Well, well, you've got some attitude, haven't you, whoever you are." He smiled at her, running his eyes over her body, taking in more of the detail.

"Daisy, come on, we need to go," said Alex, who was now next to her car.

This encounter caused some tension in the physical realm, but in the spiritual realm the ether crackled with adversarial energy.

Angel watched it all with dread fascination. He'd rarely seen an adversary quite like this. Even before Alex had left the flat, he'd sensed some undefined tension coming their way, like the gathering of forces. He'd guessed Alex was about to encounter a host of the enemy, but how this fitted with her life, and why it was happening now he could not be sure.

But when the stench of the legion that accompanied this human resolved itself, he was astonished to see them all collected together. He even knew some of them by name, ancient beings turned from brothers to enemies, aeons ago. But this was a sight to behold; an assembly of some of the most powerful spirits he had ever seen.

At that moment in the physical world, Lench turned aside from Daisy and started to walk towards Alex. Angel watched as this human host brushed past Daisy and strode towards Alex until he was just a couple of metres from her. Angel stared at the spectacle before him, and in a single instance of human time the spirits that attended Lench turned to him.

Angel stepped a little ahead of Alex in his own dimension. From the assembly before him, one spirit moved forward. He knew this one all too well; it was even more powerful than he was. They stood in their own realm, and as was often the case when Angel encountered a direct spiritual confrontation, a kind of peace came over him, a peace that reminded him of the ultimate source of his own power, his own existence. He muttered the calming prayer, and felt the unanswerable, overwhelming assurance of the Divine presence upon him.

Reassured at the most profound level, he looked up at the presence that was now examining him.

"Ah, Angel. Are you really brought so low?" The voice was gentle, but beneath the surface there was contempt, and some anger, which Angel found interesting, all the bravado couldn't hide the fact that something had riled this demon.

It had chosen to represent itself as a boy of about fifteen, fair of skin with blonde hair and blue eyes. The demon looked truly beautiful and there was something in the eyes that reminded Angel of how this demon had looked before it had rebelled. He felt an immense sadness fall over him at the memories of an era so long past it was as if it were before time. The demon stepped closer to Angel so that in their own dimension its lips were just inches away from his ear.

"Angel," the demon whispered, gently, *"did we not once share a kingdom, were we not once powers before God? And look at us now,*

fallen from grace, brought to this, running errands like slaves, chasing after these meat creations. Tell me, what has happened to us?"

Angel looked up at the boy, and the love he had once felt for this former brother pierced his heart.

"I loved you, my brother," said Angel, *"and you loved me."* And for a moment there was silence between them, then the demon closed its eyes, sighed, and nodded.

"But," continued Angel, *"it is you who has fallen from grace, not I. It is you who is now the slave, and you know all too well that your master is an inferior god and may the Lord rebuke you if you harm this woman."* He pointed at Alex.

The demon recoiled, hissing as it did so, pink spittle spraying from its mouth. The pack of demons behind it fidgeted with unease. Then it laughed, although its mirth sounded forced and strained.

"Brave words indeed, Angel, but as you know all too well, the battle-ground is flesh and blood with all its lusts and weaknesses. Now tell me," it pointed at Alex, still frozen in her own time, *"does she really mean so much to you, this beautiful meat child of your God?"*

Angel stared up at the mighty dark spirit before him and stepped a little between it and Alex.

"Ah, yes," it said with a smile, *"she really does mean a lot to you, doesn't she? You really care about this one, don't you?"*

Some of the other demons sniggered.

Angel winced at the sound and then the demon stretched itself up, so it towered over him.

"You are a fool to oppose us, Angel. The woman will be tested, and she will fail. And the other one," it turned to Daisy, *"well, let's just call her a work in progress, shall we?"*

Angel could see three minor spirits clinging to Daisy's back, holding fast to her, but even as they hung on to her, Angel could see their grasp sliding off, as if she were covered in some kind of oil that stopped them getting a real grip on her.

"But, this woman, Alex Masters," the demon continued, *"will not fulfil the plans that have been made for her. Do you know why?"*

Do not react. The order came to Angel from above. *Do not respond.*

Angel said nothing.

"Do you, Angel? Have you admitted the truth to yourself?" It paused for a moment.

"Of course you have. But my brothers here," it spread out a pale hand to the assembled company behind it, *"might not know, so I shall tell them. She will fail because at the point of testing she will prefer a man to God."*

Angel suppressed a reaction and stared resolutely ahead of him. The demon stepped around Angel, so it faced his side, then it leant in, so its lips were next to Angel's ear.

"You know what I am saying is the truth, don't you?"

Angel's mind flashed with an image of Joel Stamford, and he turned away from the beautiful face at his side. The demon laughed.

"Oh well done, Angel!" It clapped its hands and the assembly behind it barked with laughter. *"See, you got there in the end, you worked it out at last. Joel, Joel Stamford. He will be the unwitting instrument of our purpose. And I will tell you something else, my Angel, we, my true kin and I, will have little to do when it comes to it. Dear Alex and Joel, they will gradually fill with lust, little by little, bit by bit, until eventually they will succumb and rut together like these pieces of meat are prone to do, and when that happens, she will be compromised. She will be separated from the strategies of God, and you, my brother, will have to return home in anguish and humiliation."*

Perhaps it was the grain of truth contained within the poisonous words that made Angel react. Whatever it was, some righteous anger welled up in him:

"You shall not touch her!" He lashed out at his adversary. The demon leant in, knowing that it was a greater force than its oppo-

nent. It slapped Angel's attack away, the clash resonating across the spirit world, and Angel stepped back because now was not the time for this battle, and he knew in his heart that, by himself, he could not win this contest.

"Thank you, Angel," the demon said. *"Such delicious outrage, such passion! I approve."*

But Angel didn't hear the words. The demon's half-truths echoed in his mind, weakening him. Alex might indeed fail because of Joel. And what if it did happen? What if Alex did succumb to temptation? What if he, Angel, somehow failed in his mission? And then he remembered that this was Alex they were talking about, and she was precious to him, and his Lord had sent him to look after her. He refused to let the demon set the agenda for this conversation with its vile talk, and some words that were buried deep in his mind came back to him, words spoken to him just before he'd left to fulfil this purpose.

"Love her, Angel, because I love her. Keep her safe because she has come freely to me, desiring to be my chosen instrument."

And he bowed his head and whispered the words of submission to his Lord: *"Not in my own strength, Lord, but in yours. May your will be done."* He gave himself up totally to the will of God and in doing so tapped into that familiar source of inestimable power. He sensed the irresistible will of the Lord and he knew that he was home.

Across from him a howl of anguish erupted from his enemy and the whole assembly of demons screamed in agony and disarray.

And in the physical world, time moved again, as Alex watched Lench step backwards as if someone had knocked him off balance.

"Who the hell do you think you are?"

It was Daisy; she had stepped forward and pushed him, hard in the chest.

LENCH STARED AT DAISY, and anger, raw and unmanaged rose up inside him.

"Who do you think you are, you whore!" he hissed, and slapped her with the back of his hand, causing her to stagger back.

"How dare you!" shouted Alex.

Lench turned from Daisy to Alex as she marched towards him.

"How DARE you," she repeated and Lench flinched. He was gathering himself together when another voice cut through to them all.

"Excuse me!"

They all turned to see a robust-looking woman in a navy blue uniform, glaring at them.

"Is this your vehicle, sir?"

"What?" said Lench.

"I said, is this your car?" she pointed at his Mercedes, still perched on double yellow lines on the main road.

Lench's mouth worked but there was no sound.

The traffic warden stared at him.

"If this," she indicated the Mercedes, "is your vehicle, sir, then you had better move it, now."

"I will be there in a moment," said Lench.

"Now," said the woman.

He looked back at his car, and then at the traffic warden. She had taken out a small camera and was now photographing the car. Lench was finding it hard to control himself.

"I'm leaving now," he whispered hoarsely. The traffic warden ignored him and took a small machine like a card reader from her belt. Lench turned and walked back to his car. He got in, punched the ignition and drove off.

Once the car was moving, he put the window up and allowed

himself a scream of frustration and anguish. He turned the air con to an icy blast and tried to bring his breathing under control. As he began to calm down, he noticed the faint tingle across the back of his hand where he'd hit the mouthy blonde one. It was a curiously pleasurable sensation, but he was under no illusions that this had been an embarrassing and unnecessary encounter.

Alex was silent as they drove away.

"Who was that guy?" said Daisy.

"I don't know," said Alex, gripping the steering wheel and trying to concentrate on the road ahead of her.

"Creepy piece of work," said Daisy. "He'd better not show up here again."

Alex was silent as they made their way towards Caleb's office.

Travelling in the opposite direction, Lench started to shiver. The more he calmed himself, the more foolish his actions seemed to him. There was a pain in his chest, and it took him several minutes to get his breathing under control, and for a while he seemed incapable of driving in a straight line. This visit had been an indulgence, a stupid mistake. He felt more culpable than the Assassin as he thought about his conduct, and he could feel the frustration of the spirits around him.

He assumed he would get a ticket from the traffic warden. The fine meant nothing to him in financial terms and of course it was nothing compared to the fiercely intimate, probing anger that he might yet have to face from his master. At least he knew the worst of it now. They had not removed the threat, there was still an adversary, and that adversary would have to be dealt with. He had originally wanted to return to his office, but now it was probably best to go home. The madness of the company inside him still beat against his chest and his brain, and he needed to rest.

———

At Caleb Wicks' office, Daisy gave him a dramatic account of their meeting with the strange man. Alex remained silent throughout, giving Daisy the chance to let off steam.

Wicks frowned as he listened and glanced at Alex several times during Daisy's story.

"I don't know who he was," said Alex, when Daisy had finished. "I've never seen him before."

"You didn't get his car registration number," said Caleb.

"No," said Daisy, "but that traffic warden would have, she took a picture of his car and gave him a ticket." She smiled wickedly at the thought.

"Let's leave it now," said Alex, "and concentrate on Daisy's interview."

"Of course," said Caleb. "Okay. Daisy, let's go through it one more time."

"Okay," said Daisy and sighed.

———

Alex was pleased that all of Daisy's careful preparation paid off in the police interview. She was precise and honest, and provided a true and consistent story.

The police confirmed that Daisy's version of events was consistent with what the investigating team already knew, and there were no startling revelations in her account of what had happened. They didn't charge Daisy with possession of a class "A" drug but asked that she be ready to act as a witness if required.

Afterwards, Alex and Daisy went back to Caleb's office. He had other business to attend to with Alex now that Daisy's interview was over. Caleb had checked the lease for the building Alex wanted to use for her café and the contract was ready for her to sign. She was taking over an empty shop at the end of the High Street and she had an army of volunteers from church ready to refurbish the place. She signed the contract and felt a surge of excitement as another element in her vision fell into place.

But when Daisy and she left Caleb's office, it was the encounter in the car park that occupied Alex's mind as they drove back to her flat.

12

CONNER MASTERS WAS A FREE SPIRIT. He would go after something, and then if the mood took him, he would change his plans and pursue a different course without worrying too much about the consequences. He was not selfish – in fact he could be very considerate – but he trusted his impulses and followed them whenever he could.

Just after lunch on Friday, he shelved the idea of working on his music that afternoon and instead he packed his bag, said goodbye to his parents and left for the station, striding out at some speed as the clouds gathered above and threatened a downpour.

Max and Helen were not altogether surprised he had decided to go early. When Alex had mentioned that Cousin Daisy was still staying, Conner had expressed an interest in seeing her as well as Alex.

Then of course there was "King of Kings".

"King of Kings" was the biggest Christian event to happen in the city for years. Artists, musicians, actors, singers and other creatives who were also followers of Jesus would be gathering at the biggest stadium in the city. Conner loved big events and he'd bought a ticket for this one months ago. He was well aware of the fact that the stadium would be much easier to get to from Alex's flat than his parents' home in Cheshire. That, and the opportunity to catch up with Daisy, made Alex's flat the place to be this weekend. He bought his rail ticket and boarded the train under a darkening sky, and by the time he arrived in the city, the rain had started to fall.

ALEX'S DOORBELL rang at around six that evening, and Conner's cheeky grin greeted her when she opened the door. He seemed oblivious to the rain and his hair was crowned with little drips of water.

"Alex!" He flung himself at her and she was reminded of Daisy's hug on the doorstep a few days before, although this one came with extra dampness.

"How are you, darling? And before you say anything, yes, I know I'm early, but I just felt like coming over now." She felt as if an enthusiastic puppy had jumped on her.

"Well, yes, I did think you were coming later. Didn't we say you'd get here at about nine or ten?"

"Yeah," he said.

"But you're here now."

"Yeah," he said, "it's great, isn't it? I get to spend more time with my favourite sister."

She shouldn't have been surprised. This was typical of Conner, sometimes endearing and sometimes infuriating, often both. He had already strolled past her, dropped his guitar and bag on the floor, and was on his way into the kitchen.

"Shall I put the kettle on?"

Alex was about to reply when Daisy emerged from the spare room and Conner and she looked at each other for a moment. It was just a fraction of a second, before Conner spoke:

"Hi, Daisy, I'm just making some tea. Do you want some?"

Alex looked at the pair of them and wondered how all this would work out. She loved these people, but they were both quite demanding and they were both in her space, and if there was any trouble, she would not be able to get away.

"I'm afraid you're on the sofa, Conner," she called through to the kitchen.

"I don't mind sleeping on the sofa!" said Conner cheerfully, and as if to prove the point he came back into the living room, flopped down on the sofa and started to unpack some of the items from his bag: clothes, an iPad, even a couple of CDs.

"You want to come down to youth club with me?" said Alex as his stuff tumbled out onto her lounge carpet.

"Here, Alex, I bought you a present." He took a package from his bag and handed it to her. She opened it and inside was a little teddy bear with overalls bearing the words "World's Best Decorator".

"I thought it might encourage you with all that renovation at the new café." He beamed at her, and she couldn't help but love him.

"It's lovely, Conner, thanks." How could she be angry with him? This was how he was, and she had known it for most of her life. "So, do you want to come to the youth club? I'll be going in a few minutes."

"I might come along later. I'm going to have a drink first and settle in a bit." The kettle was starting to hum in the kitchen.

Daisy had still not said anything but had walked across the room and was looking at the CDs.

"That's a bit quaint, Conner," she said. "Still listening to CDs?"

"Old favourites," he said, "and some of my own stuff with the band. I wanted Alex to hear some good music."

Alex watched the two of them as Daisy sat down to look at the music Conner had brought with him. Alex was about to say something, to encourage some conversation between the two of them, but then she checked herself. She didn't need to run around after them, they could sort themselves out this evening. She put on her coat, said a brief goodbye, and left them to it.

Daisy picked up one of Conner's CDs and frowned at it. Something in Conner's manner reminded her so much of Will that she had to blink a couple of times to compose herself.

"This is your band, isn't it?" she said.

"Yes," said Conner proudly.

"Why don't you put it all online?" she said.

"I have," said Conner, "but I still carry these around. Sometimes I give them away to people, you can have one if you want."

"Let's hear it then," said Daisy, "and turn it up. Alex always has the volume set too low on that thing."

"Sure," Conner got himself up off the sofa, walked across the room, and slid the disc into Alex's sound system.

Alex had just reached the front door of her block when she heard the music coming from her flat. She was sure she would never play music as loud as that.

"Fine, whatever," she said, and walked out into rain, the music floating out of her open lounge window. She thought she could just hear Conner's voice. He was laughing at something and then Daisy joined in. She felt pleased for them, but somehow also alone, as if she would not have been able to join in the laughter if she'd been there. She imagined them sharing music, coffee and conversation in a way that she might not be able to keep up with.

Pushing the thought away, she walked up the road at a brisk

pace, hunched under an umbrella, trying to put some distance between herself and the faint cascade of music coming from the open window of her flat.

At the church she found Laura busy setting up for the youth group.

"I feel responsible for them," said Alex, as she helped get some chairs out. "It's like I've got two children in the flat. But they are both twenty years old."

Laura had met Conner before, so she knew what he was like.

"They'll be okay. You know that deep down Conner is really quite wise and sensitive. Does he know about Daisy and this lad Will?"

"I gave him the summary of it. I thought that was the best thing to do."

"Perhaps he'll do her some good; maybe she needs someone to make her laugh."

Laura and Alex had fifteen minutes to get everything set up before the kids arrived. This was always like the calm before the storm, as they got the activities for the evening ready, ran over the five-minute "God slot" they always did, and unpacked some sweets to sell to the kids at the end.

As they finished their preparations, Aiden arrived. He was there to lend some maleness to the proceedings, and it was only right to have a man on the premises, as most of the kids who came to this club were, in fact, boys. Aiden, with his soft accent and subtle, gentle nature had a calming influence on some of the rowdier ones. Alex was pleased he was there.

The club, as usual, was busy. There was a constant barrage of noise as the young people worked their way through the different games and activities that had been laid on for them that evening. There was all the boisterous liveliness of an ordinary bunch of kids, having a good time at the end of a week at school. The table tennis and pool tables, chipped and scratched from years of youthful attention, were as popular as ever.

Later, Aiden did the five-minute slot and talked about how everyone could both receive help and be a helper. Alex opened her little shop to sell a few sweets, snacks and drinks, and there was the usual scraping around for small change as the kids tried to get enough money together for whatever was on offer.

Even as she was busy serving the kids, Alex noticed that one of the girls was hanging about at the back. At fifteen, Alice was one of the older girls. She was quiet and thoughtful, with an intelligent mind and a cheeky sense of humour when you got to know her. But tonight, she seemed quieter than usual, and when the queue had died down, she wandered over, bought quite a few items, and paid with a twenty-pound note. Alex knew something wasn't right, and she decided to scratch at the surface to see what she could find:

"Hi, Alice, how's it going?"

"All right."

"Have you got yourself a job then?"

"No, why?"

"You turned up with a twenty-pound note, cleared out my change. Perhaps it was for your birthday?"

There was a pause, Alice stared at her, and, it seemed to Alex, past her.

"It's just some money I had," she said finally, and with that she collected her half-eaten sweets and walked towards the exit and out onto the street.

CONNER PUT two mugs down on the table by the sofa and sat himself next to Daisy. Psychedelic tones floated across the room.

"Do you like it?" she said. They were listening to her choice of music from her phone.

"Interesting," said Conner, "a bit of psytrance, isn't it?"

"You could call it that."

"Still," said Conner, "you can't beat a band like Undue Influence for a proper live gig."

"Really? A bit of old skool grunge? I didn't have you down for that stuff."

"They were awesome in their day. I've seen them when the lead guitarist does that thing where he eats a wire coat hanger halfway through the set."

"It's not a real coat hanger, you idiot," said Daisy.

"It used to be, before they got new management and a big record contract."

"I can't believe you fell for that," said Daisy. "It was always some kind of liquorice thing."

"Don't be daft. They totally did the metal coat hanger thing. It was their thing."

"Who you calling daft?" said Daisy poking him in the ribs. "You don't know jack-all about anything!"

"Yes, I do," said Conner. "I know how to make good coffee!" He indicated the mugs in front of them.

"All you did was pour hot water onto some coffee granules!" she said.

"I still had to stir it properly!" he protested.

"Whatever," said Daisy, tossing the CD case onto the table.

They were silent for a moment, letting the music float around them.

"I was really sorry to hear about your mate," said Conner eventually.

"Yeah well, Alex has looked after me," said Daisy.

"She's a star, isn't she?" said Conner. "She's like the wise woman. I'm always asking her opinion about stuff."

Daisy nodded. "So what's this thing you're going to tomorrow then?"

"Oh, 'King of Kings'," said Conner. "It's a big praise and worship event. We get together and worship God and listen to some music and pray for peace in the world. It's going to be massive."

"It's going to be wet," said Daisy looking at the steady rain outside. "Forecast says it's going to be like this all weekend."

"Really?" said Conner.

"Really," said Daisy. "You guys are going to be tramping around in the mud like it's a bad day at Glastonbury."

Conner laughed, and then they and the music fell silent; all they could hear was the noise of the rain and the city coming through the open window.

Conner reached for his guitar, took it out of its case, and started to play some chords. He strung some riffs from the Beatles together with melodies from across the last fifty years.

"I tell you what, Daisy," he said, "why don't you come with me tomorrow? We can get you a ticket on the door."

"I don't think it's quite me, Conner. I mean if you're not religious then there's not much point standing in a muddy field for six hours with a bunch of Jesus freaks."

"Well, suit yourself, but I can tell you it will be good, and it won't rain."

"Sure," she said, pointedly watching the drops pattering against the window outside.

Conner smiled at her and said, almost in a whisper, "It's not going to rain tomorrow."

Daisy looked at him as he started to play again. She smiled slightly.

"So," she said, "isn't your girlfriend going with you on this praise thing then?"

He kept playing but he glanced at her and raised an eyebrow as he did.

"No," he said.

"No?"

"No, because she doesn't exist."

A bit of him wanted to say, "Why, are you offering?" but even Conner had the sense to realize that might be pushing the humour a bit too far at the moment.

So instead, he continued to play, and in the gathering darkness, Conner could feel her presence as well as see her, hear the faint murmur of her breath, and now that he focused on it, he picked up the mix of scents from her: the scent of her, and the smell of cigarettes. He resisted the urge to tell her to stop smoking.

He played a couple more songs and then stopped and put the guitar down. She was looking at him but saying nothing.

"What?" he said.

"Look at me," she said, and there was no smile on her face.

He turned to her and raised an eyebrow.

"Alex says you're a good person. A good man," she said. "Are you?"

"Most of the time," he said. "But I'm not perfect."

"Have you ever hurt a woman? Harmed anyone at all like that?"

He looked at her, and hesitated.

"I don't think so," he said. "I've never hit a woman, if that's what you mean."

She stared at him for a few more seconds, and time seemed to slow right down.

"I want you to give me a hug," she said.

"Okay." He twisted himself towards her, put out his arms and they embraced, awkwardly, where they sat.

"This is no good," said Daisy, and she stood up, pulling him up as well.

"Come here." She reached out towards him and they stood face to face for a few moments, and then embraced. Daisy closed her eyes and held him tightly.

Conner felt compassion as well as the tingle of interest that any pretty girl might engender in him. He held her tightly and remembered who he was.

After a few moments he gently released her, and they sat down again. He picked up his guitar and started to play a soulful tune; a melody that spoke of sadness and yet within it there was a grace and beauty.

DAISY FELT herself slip into the music, to be enfolded by it. She felt as if the very chords he played understood her at the deepest level, as if the music were a language that perfectly described her feelings, her sorrow and her sense of desolation.

She remembered Conner's embrace, the first man to touch her since Will had died. She had been safe in his arms, even if that touch had left her confused.

Who was Conner to her? Family and yet not family, like a brother and yet more than that, a different feeling that wasn't quite what she had felt for Will. Above all, she felt safe with him, or at least she felt safe with his music.

She listened to the notes as they turned from sorrow into a sense of serenity and reassurance.

When the tune was finished there was silence in the room. The rain continued to drum against the window, but more gently now, and Daisy found herself wishing for dry weather tomorrow for his event.

"That was beautiful, Conner. What was it?"

He smiled. "I just made it up, Daisy. You could say that God gave it to me for you."

She smiled. "Honestly, you lot."

"Us lot?"

"You Christians, you really are plugged in to God, aren't you?"

"Maybe you're seeing us at our best," he said. "Lots of people can be compassionate, and caring."

"Yes maybe," she said, "but for me," she pointed to herself, "it's you and Alex that have turned up. That's what matters."

WHEN ALEX ARRIVED HOME, the living room floor was scattered with CDs, and Conner's guitar was resting against one of the chairs. Conner and Daisy were sitting together on the sofa; Daisy was asleep and Conner reading something on his iPad; some gentle music drifted out from the hi-fi.

Daisy woke up. "Oh, hi Alex, did you have a good evening?"

"Yes thanks, and you two?"

"Yeah, we're good," said Daisy.

"Time to tidy some of this stuff up, Conner, yes?" said Alex. She didn't want her living room ending up in the same state as his bedroom at home.

"Oh, yes sure," he replied, gathering his belongings together.

"Anyone want a drink?" said Alex.

"Yes please," said Daisy, following her into the kitchen. She stood next to Alex as the kettle started to hum.

"I think," said Daisy, "I need to go back home, to my flat, tomorrow. I'm really grateful to you for looking after me and sorting me out and everything, but I need to get back into college and back to my own routine."

"Of course, it's been good to have you here," said Alex, which was true, although she was looking forward to having her space back.

They all sat and talked together for a few minutes, and then Alex and Daisy went off to bed.

Later, once she was in bed, Alex let her mind wander over the events of the day. It was good to be able to help Daisy, but now her thoughts turned to Alice, the girl from the youth club. Where had she got that money from? Why had she been so mysterious about it? And why had she left so quickly?

There was something about that whole episode that seemed wrong, and she could not quite say what it was.

As she thought about it, she was surprised to find tears in her eyes. It was often like this, when she thought about the young people in the group. Thinking about one or other of them made her tear up. She looked across her room, out past the curtain to the street light just below the level of her window.

There was no such thing as real darkness here. There was only that grey-yellow tinge that characterized the urban darkness. She did not want to think about the good and evil that might be going on right now across the city. It was more than she could bear.

She knew she needed to resign from SLaM and pursue this vision, and she was surprised at how sorry for Lewis that made her feel. She liked Lewis, a lot, but the direction SLaM had taken made her feel sick, and besides, Alice had unwittingly reminded her of where her destiny lay.

She said a prayer for Alice, and then she remembered the four or five other kids she cared passionately about, and she prayed for them also. As she settled down to sleep, she saw Alice's big mournful eyes and that crumpled twenty-pound note that someone out there had given her.

The next day, Conner went off to "King of Kings". He said goodbye to his sister and to Daisy, hugging her for what seemed to her like a surprisingly long time. Daisy wondered if Alex had noticed.

Daisy left soon afterwards to take the train home. As she stared out of the carriage window, the rain started to fall again. She remembered Conner's confidence about the fact that it wasn't going to rain on his event. She was almost sorry to see the raindrops, but she had much more faith in the hardships and disappointments of life than in a God who may or may not turn up and do what people asked for. It was another reason, maybe the reason why she dared not believe: there was enough disappointment in her life already.

As her train pulled into the station, she noticed that the rain had in fact, been a brief shower, and the clouds now seemed to be breaking up.

AT THAT MOMENT, miles away at the stadium, Conner looked up at the sky. The clouds were thick and heavy, but the rain had held off. He dug around in his pocket and found his ticket for "King of Kings". Borrowing a pencil from one of his friends, he wrote the word "Daisy" on it.

So long as the rain held off, he was going to send her a text, or maybe even a letter (he couldn't remember the last time he'd written a letter) and he was going to remind her of his "no rain" prediction. He didn't know what else he was going to say to her, but it was enough to start with. Then he heard a roar from the crowd go up and one of his favourite bands came onto the stage. Putting the ticket in his pocket he uttered a prayer of thanks to God and let himself go into the music.

That day, plenty of rain fell to the south of the city, but the stadium remained dry.

13

———

IN THE HEART of the city, warmth gave way to heat, and sunlit days gave way to sultry nights. The weather brought people out onto the streets, the pavements became busy, full of chatter and laughter, frustration and bravado. Summer nights were restless nights, and the people of the city felt it.

The SEEKA ethos with its emphasis on experience as the root of truth touched a nerve amongst the young and the affluent. The tee shirts started to appear, the magazine articles too, and a mineral water supplier started to produce a "SEEKA" brand.

At SLaM, the royalties started to roll in, and a mood of arrogant triumph spread across the office. The big project, the one they had worked so hard on, was really taking off. The workers buzzed around the office and there was a sense of energy that matched the city heat. The trauma of Bridget's murder, now some weeks past, was forgotten and SLaM was getting on with the serious business of making money.

Sitting at the centre of it all was Martin Massey. The success of the project, his project, had been like a drug to him, making him feel important and powerful. The project he had fought for, was proving itself. Of course, he couldn't have done it without his backers, the obvious ones like Bridget, and the more silent ones in the background like Lench and the others in the group, but still this was his success.

He almost wished Bridget were here to witness it. Her disapproval of and estrangement from him now looked pathetic. In the weeks after her murder, as the police chased around after any kind of lead, Martin came to think he'd got the best of both worlds: it had been Lench's idea to have her killed, and it was Lench and his shadowy assassin who'd had to take responsibility for the deed. But her departure from the scene had also worked to Martin's advantage, removing someone who had become a liability.

Dave Somerville had been one of the project's fiercest critics, but now he had completely changed his tune and was speaking up for SEEKA whenever he got the chance. The sales of SEEKA gear had smashed even their most optimistic targets, and that meant a bigger bonus for everyone, including Dave. It had been more than enough to bring him into line.

The success of the project, and Dave's newfound enthusiasm for it, had only served to remind Martin of how much he despised his colleague. He could still perceive Dave's real feelings about SEEKA: the jealousy, the bruised ego, plus the frustration at being proved so completely wrong. Dave harboured a grudge that no bonus, however large, would shift, but he pretended enthusiasm now for all things SEEKA.

Another benefit was that Martin could now look Lewis in the eye. The boss had made it clear that Martin succeeded or failed with SEEKA. Lewis had spent the week sulking when his simpering PA, the saintly Alex, resigned, but as far as Martin was concerned, she was better off out of the way. He recalled that this was the woman Lench had made such a fuss about after Bridget's death, as if somehow, they should have gone after her instead of Bridget.

He realized Lench was a bit of an old woman about these

things, worrying too much, fussing over some imagined opposition. If the Bridget thing was a mess, it was a mess of Lench's own making. However, Martin's project was a winner, and they were all getting what they wanted as a result of his vision and determination.

He sat back in his chair and looked at the sales data on his computer screen. It was the end of another successful week and so tonight he was going to go out and celebrate.

ACROSS THE CORRIDOR from Martin's office, Lewis sat studying his copy of the same chart. There was no doubt about it, the project was making the company a fortune, and that meant it was making him a fortune. He should have been happy. In fact, he should have been able to share some of the arrogant pride that Martin so obviously felt. But he was surprised to find that he felt nothing. Not even a little of the warm glow he usually felt when he was making money. At first, he thought his pride had been offended because SEEKA was Martin's project, not his.

But it wasn't that, and anyway, he should still be looking at the bottom line and remembering that whatever bonuses the others got, he took the lion's share.

But even the money wasn't cheering him up. There was an ache inside him, a heaviness, a lethargy dragging him down, and as he sat there and looked at the money but feeling nothing, he realized what his subconscious already knew, he was grieving for Bridget, and he was missing Alex. Two of the most important women in his life, both of whom he'd consistently undervalued, were gone from his life; one of them was utterly gone forever.

The murder enquiry didn't seem to be making much progress. No one really believed this was a botched burglary, certainly no one who knew the facts. The police had talked about "signs of a struggle", but Bridget had been despatched by two bullets, which told Lewis that this was a hit job. The police had tracked down the gas engineer pretty quickly, but so far, they'd failed to trace the mysterious window cleaner who was also working there at the time. A photofit showing a man with sunglasses and a shock of blonde hair had yielded nothing.

He tossed the sales chart onto the desk and looked out through the glass window of his office. Most of his team had gone home now. He liked to think of them as his team but in truth, most of them were just contractors for hire, his team – his real team – had gone. He could see into Bridget's office from where he was sitting. If she were still alive, she would have been sitting there right now, and he could have walked the ten metres to ask for her advice. He stared forlornly at the empty chair, absorbed by his loss, but then blinked when Martin strode past his door with a load of SEEKA tee shirts and flyers.

"Bye, Lewis," said Martin with a cheery wave and a grin as he passed.

"You off out tonight?" said Lewis.

"Yep, going to Abundance. They can't get enough of us, and I thought I'd help Dave out by spreading some of the promotional material. He's got a lot on at the moment, poor old chap."

"See you on Monday," said Lewis, looking back to the papers on his desk. The snide comment about Dave Somerville didn't escape his notice.

But Martin had stopped and was peering in through the door.

"So what are you up to this evening?" said Martin, "Going home to your slippers and cocoa?"

Lewis looked up and he could almost feel the arrogance radiating off Martin. He would normally have shrugged it off, but he was tired, and in no mood for Martin Massey and his gloating. The two men looked at each other, and Lewis let his contempt show. Martin stared at his boss and his own features soured in response.

They held each other's gaze for a moment and then Martin turned away.

Lewis heard Martin walk along the corridor to the exit, and he had a sudden premonition that SEEKA would be the thing that destroyed his company.

THE LARGE WAREHOUSE in the south of the city was filling fast. Eager customers of the famous Abundance club were lining up to transition from excitement to disorientation and possibly to oblivion, immersed in a provocative mix of pulsing EDM, with a little bit of old skool house in a separate room for the more nostalgic patrons. There was plenty of alcohol available of course, but that wasn't everyone's drug of choice, and in quiet corners around the venue, trade was brisk.

Martin surveyed the gathering. The music was mesmerizing; he could feel the power of it even as he stood there at the edge of the club, sipping his soda water. He had already been offered enough gear to knock him into the middle of next week. He wanted none of it, of course, not tonight anyway. In fact, he was concentrating, listening to the words whispered under the cover of some of the tracks:

I'm a SEEKA after the truth,
And I am my sacred space,
I'm a SEEKA after the truth,
And I'll be the god of this place.

He laughed out loud, uproariously and unheard above the noise when he thought of those words. They sounded like pointless drivel to him, but Lench had been happy enough with them.

What he didn't laugh at was the success of it all, the money he was making, the power he was influencing. That was serious. He had argued the case, taken the risks, and won it all. He was the one at the centre, not Lewis, and now he came to think of it, not Lench either.

Through the shadows and the crash of the music, nobody could hear him celebrating.

"This is my work," he said, staring up at the lighting rig above him, "my effort, my success, I made this. Do you hear me? I MADE THIS."

For the rest of the night, Martin bathed in a sea of self-congratulation and moved around as if everything he touched might turn to gold.

———

Some miles away across the city a lone figure sat quietly at his desk and slid open a drawer.

"Well, Ms Larson," he said to himself, "I think it is time." With gloved hands, he reached into the drawer and pulled out a large envelope. From inside the envelope, he took out a bundle of papers, at the top of which were the photocopied versions of the two slim reports that Bridget had taken from Martin's office. One was the research Martin had commissioned, and the other was the sales and marketing plan for SEEKA. Attached to the reports was a copy of the first section of an internal memo detailing how SEEKA could and should feed on and encourage the city's drug culture.

He hesitated for a moment, checking the list of instructions on the desk next to him. He took the copy of the memo and placed it next to another envelope. In front of him stood a reel of tape, some scissors, and a copy of yesterday's paper. Slowly, painstakingly, he cut out a series of letters from the paper and pasted them onto a blank sheet of paper. Finally, he pasted the letters of a name and address to the front of the large brown envelope and put the sheet of paper and the memo inside. Applying the correct value in stamps, he took the package and went for a walk, sliding the envelope into a postbox about a mile from his house.

MONDAY STARTED BADLY FOR LEWIS. He had been distracted by the issues surrounding SEEKA as he drove in and had scratched his car against a wall as he'd parked. But this was nothing compared to what he found on his desk when he got into his office. Amongst the jumble of notes and letters, there was a large brown envelope. Inside he found a single sheet of paper, a series of letters had been neatly glued in a straight line. They said: "STOP SEEKA".

Attached to the note was the one thing he had not wished to see again – a copy of Martin's beloved research with his own introduction extolling the relationship between SEEKA and the drugs culture. There was also a copy of a memo Martin had written talking about the symbiotic relationship between the SEEKA project and the market for illegal drugs. Lewis remembered feeling uncomfortable about how blatant the connection was, especially in a written document; even Bridget had been embarrassed. He had asked all of them to make no copies of the report and to keep it locked away. Clearly that had not happened.

Now someone had a copy of the research and Martin's note, and they were trying to blackmail him, not for money, but to stop the project. He was rather tempted to do just that right now, but there was something else, something deeper going on here. What really made his guts squirm was the idea that somehow this might be connected to Bridget's death. He let out a long sigh, picked up the phone and called Martin.

"Martin, something's come up. We need to talk as soon as possible, in the boardroom."

There was a pause before Martin said, "I'm actually a bit busy, Lewis. Can we make it this afternoon?"

"Now, Martin. This is important." Lewis was in no mood for Martin's cocky arrogance this morning. He put down the phone.

Some minutes later, Martin entered the boardroom to find Lewis already seated at one of the chairs. There were some papers on the table in front of him.

"Come in and sit down," said Lewis.

Martin smiled at his boss and dropped himself into one of the chairs at the other end of the table.

"What's this all about then?" he said.

"Look at this." Lewis pushed the photocopy of Martin's research and his memo across the table. Martin picked it up.

"It's a copy of our note about SEEKA. So what?"

"It's a copy of your memo, Martin; and it's come from outside this office."

MARTIN HESITATED. The questions started forming in his mind. Who sent this? What did they want? How should he react? When he did speak, he was frustrated to hear that his voice sounded faint and scratchy.

"What are you going to do, Lewis? Are you going to close me down?" He got up and started to pace around the room, his old restlessness coming back to him.

"Oh, for goodness' sake, sit down," said Lewis. "I am not going to 'close you down' as you put it, Martin. You are my employee: I can hire you and fire you, but I cannot close you down." He went on before Martin could reply.

"If you mean, will I be discontinuing the SEEKA project, the answer is no. But you need to understand that if things go sour for SEEKA, they have the potential to go sour for SLaM as well, and I won't let that happen. Have you still got any copies of that report?"

"One, in my files."

"I want that copy," said Lewis. "Now. I do not respond to threats, and I am not going to respond to this one, but if this project starts to cost me more than it already has done, I will close it down."

Martin heard the words, but even now he was thinking of the man he really answered to. Lewis thought he was hauling Martin over the coals, but this was nothing compared to a cross-examination from Lench.

"Martin, are you listening to me?" Lewis slapped the table. "Who else has seen this report? Who else has a copy?"

"You had a copy, and so did I, and Dave also had one. Any of those copies could have been seen by someone else. But relax, this won't come to anything."

"How the hell do you know that?" shouted Lewis.

"Calm down," said Martin, his anger starting to rise as well.

"Don't tell me to calm down; someone is trying to blackmail us."

"If you have decided to hold your nerve," said Martin, leaning forward, "then do it, hold your nerve. We'll get on with SEEKA, and if we need to stop, we'll stop. It'll burn itself out in a few weeks anyway."

"I want your copy, Martin," said Lewis. "I already have Dave's one, and I'm going to take them all and destroy them – off-site. Did Bridget have a copy?"

"No, it was just the three of us."

"From now on, as far as SLaM is concerned, the report never existed. We'll sweep all of our computers, all the backups, every trace gets wiped, understand?"

"Of course."

"Go and get your copy now, please."

Without a response, Martin rose and left the room, returning a minute later with his copy of the report. He didn't really care what Lewis thought. Let him have his little rant. He did, however, care about Lench. He wondered whether he should tell his real boss about what had happened. Lench wanted regular reports on SEEKA, and he clearly expected the whole project to last for a while longer. Martin could feel his resentment for both Lench and Lewis growing. But he knew which one he feared the most.

ON HIS WAY home that night, Martin made a decision. Stopping in the lay-by as usual, he lowered the window and reached for his phone. He remembered with clarity the moment he had puked across the upholstery of the car when he had heard that Bridget was going to be murdered – he didn't want a repeat of that episode tonight. He speed-dialled the number and waited.

"Hello." The same precise civilized voice.

"Hello, it's Martin."

"Martin, how are things?"

"Very good. The sales figures continue to rise; things are going extremely well. We have had another two clubs sign up for the posters, the video mix, all of the stuff. It is spreading." There was a pause. Usually, Martin could spend any amount of time talking about the successes of SEEKA but tonight he stopped after about fifteen seconds, and was silent, and that silence continued. He heard Lench breathing on the other end of the line before the man spoke again in a calm, almost caring voice.

"What's happened, Martin? Has something upset you today?"

He always knew, this guy always knew, thought Martin. Lewis was a pussycat compared to Lench.

He told Lench the whole story: the report, the discussion with Lewis, their argument, and the decision to continue.

"What did the blackmailer ask for, Martin?" said Lench.

"That was the thing, the note just said 'STOP SEEKA'; there

was no demand for money. I suppose we should be grateful for that."

"Quite so." Lench sounded supportive, but it was difficult to tell over the phone.

"I suppose," continued Lench, "that we shall have to wait and see what our blackmailer does next. By the way, who do you think it is? Who had access to these reports?"

Lewis hadn't actually asked him who he thought the blackmailer was.

"I don't know, perhaps someone broke into the office, stole the papers maybe?" He cursed his own feebleness. Was this the best answer he could come up with?

"Well, let's see what happens over the next week or so. By the way, we are meeting again next week at the usual place. I trust you will be there."

"Of course I will be there."

"Excellent, well goodbye, Martin."

Martin switched off the phone and sat motionless for a minute. He had an uneasy feeling that he had been tested and failed, but there was nothing he could do now. He started the car and swerved, tyres screeching, into the first lane of traffic. It was only now, as he replayed the conversations with Lench and Lewis in his mind, that he remembered one of Lewis' comments that had seemed strange, but he'd forgotten:

"If this project starts to cost me more than it already has done, I will close it down."

What did he mean by that? The start-up costs for SEEKA had been relatively modest. Did he mean Bridget? Or even his little pet PA, Alex? Everyone knew she was offended by SEEKA, and nobody cared except Lewis. For some reason he'd been soft with her, maybe they'd been lovers? Martin hit the accelerator and longed for the journey home to be over. All he wanted to do now was to get in, lock the door, drink an excessive amount of alcohol, and forget about it all for the night.

LENCH REALIZED he was grinding his teeth, a distasteful habit but perhaps understandable in the circumstances. He was now certain he would need to deal with this fool in his group. He had allowed Martin to join them because he perceived Martin held a strategically important position in a company that could affect many young people. Martin had been the key to manipulating the culture for the master's own ends, and in that objective, they had been at least partially successful, albeit on a tactical rather than strategic level.

But Martin was clearly not worthy to join the group on his own merit. He was, after all, just a common spiv, a small person whose arrogance so outweighed his true importance that Lench was constantly amazed by the spectacle of it.

He reflected on one of Martin's comments:

"That was the thing, the note just said 'STOP SEEKA'; there was no demand for money. I suppose we should be grateful for that."

It was so typical of Martin to think that the worst thing that could happen might be financial loss. Lench would have preferred to hear that there was a demand for money. But no, this person had an altogether different agenda, and what Martin could not know, of course, was that the blackmailer was very likely to be the recipient of the package that the woman Bridget had sent before the Assassin had got to her.

For the first time since the project had started, Lench began to weigh the value of the SEEKA project against all the trouble it had caused. He had compromised himself when he had visited Alex Masters, but he'd explained that to himself as a need to see the potential prey. It was unlikely she was the blackmailer: she would not have left her job and then started this course of action. That would have made her the first suspect. It had to be a legacy of the woman Bridget, and therefore more difficult to deal with. After all, what leverage can you bring against the dead?

So what was he to do? He looked at the phone on the desk, and a number of options ran through his mind. They all led to the same thing: he needed to distance himself from Martin. It would be difficult, but it had been done before, and if the worst came to the worst, there was always the Assassin. He had always considered this option a very blunt and heavy-handed instrument, to be used sparingly. Death always drew a lot of attention, but if there was no SEEKA then there was definitely no need for Martin to be part of the group.

He would start by asking Martin not to report in every day. That could be disguised as satisfaction, and Martin would be too stupid to guess otherwise. Then he would have to decide whether to encourage the demise of SEEKA. He would have Martin's house searched for any connection with the group. After that, he would put distance between himself and this useless fool, and then whatever happened, Martin would have to deal with it himself.

14

ALEX STOOD in her newly rented café and surveyed her work. The walls were gradually transforming from the drab greens and greys she had inherited into the riot of colour she had envisioned.

This space would soon be filled with tables and chairs and life. It really was all coming together.

But for all the achievement and all of the promise, for some reason she could not fathom, her heart still ached. There was sadness deep within her, a sense of disappointment in her bones, and while she delighted in what she was doing here, that sadness would not go away.

Angel stood by and watched. He had sensed the thrill of her achievements, and the sorrow in her heart. He knew why she was sad, and that the unease she felt had not one but two causes, but there was nothing he could do, at least at the moment, to help her.

Angel reflected on the fact that in some ways human beings are very complex and in other ways they are quite simple creatures. Alex's deep sorrow had a very simple cause: she was lonely. She wanted someone to love and be loved by; it was as simple as that. But she had suppressed those feelings, all of that desire, because she was so scared of trusting someone, loving someone and then losing them again.

But that was not Alex's only fear. She also felt afraid for someone. Borne out of her compassion, she feared for Alice, for what might have happened to her, and what might still happen yet.

Alex sighed as joy and sorrow welled up in her. The café needed her attention, but all of these emotions swirled beneath her consciousness, distracting her and blunting her energy. She was just about to dip her paintbrush into the tin once more when the melodic jingle of her mobile interrupted her. It was her friend Laura.

"Hi, Alex, are you still at the café?"

"Yes, I'm going to be here for a little while yet."

"I thought I might send Joel down to help you for a couple of hours. He's only watching the TV here and I've got some mums round and I'd really like him out of the way."

"Oh yes, that would be great," Alex's mouth had become dry, "I can find something for him to do."

She could feel her heart surge, even as her friend finished the call.

"That's great," said Laura cheerfully. "He'll be with you in a few minutes."

She put the phone on the new counter and walked back to her painting.

"He can put in those sockets I need," she said to herself. "That'll be a good thing for him to do, some good work."

She picked up the paintbrush and started to push it back and forth against the wall.

Soon enough, there was a knock on the whitewashed glass of the door. She opened it to see Joel dressed in his overalls. He smiled at her.

"I thought you might need a hand with some of the rewiring," he said, holding up a toolbox.

She stared at him as if he had spoken to her in a foreign language.

"Is that all right, Alex? I mean if someone else is doing it, that's fine. I'm sure there are plenty of other jobs to do." He hovered at the door like a hesitant lover.

"No, of course, that would be great, Joel. Please come in."

He put the toolbox down and walked in, tripping on a strip of wood that had been screwed to the floor where an old shop counter had been.

He approached her and they embraced, and as they held each other she sought to protect herself by making a study of the café windows. The glass frontage had been poorly whitewashed, but she could still see people walking by outside, oblivious to them. The exercise absorbed her for a moment before she gave in and acknowledged that the feel of Joel's arms around her satisfied a hunger she didn't want to acknowledge. Reluctantly, she withdrew from him.

"So what would you like me to do?" he said, smiling.

"A couple of sockets in the back office please. Is that okay?"

"Sure," he said and walked through to the small room that would serve as a store and office space. There were pencil marks on the wall showing where Alex wanted the sockets to go. She watched him as he busied himself with finding the fuse box, getting out his tape measure, making an effort to focus on the job.

Alex continued to paint, and Joel drilled out the channel for the wiring and then started to lay the wiring in the wall. Each of them concentrated on their respective tasks and Alex felt a temporary reprieve. But the work was a postponement, not an escape. Something was coming, something she knew they would both have to face.

At about nine, Alex went into the room where Joel was working. He'd put the cable in and was now wiring up the sockets themselves.

"Looks like you're nearly done," said Alex.

"Nearly there," he said, smiling, "just got to finish with this wiring and then fit the socket panel. Maybe another twenty minutes or so."

"Thanks, Joel. I do appreciate it." They looked at each other for just a moment, but it was too much for her, and she turned back to her work.

As she reached for the paintbrush again, Alex became aware of how tired she was, how much of her ached. She'd been there most of the day, sanding and painting, working hard. Now she wanted nothing more than to relax in a warm bath and wash away all of the grime, and the pain, and the challenges she currently faced. She yawned and stretched before returning to her work, and it was at this moment that Joel chose to turn and look at her.

JOEL SAW her put down the paintbrush and stretch her tired limbs, and as she did so, his eyes ran over her body as she stood side on to him. Her head was tipped back slightly, showing the shape of her chin and neck. The tee shirt showed the gentle sweep of the curves of her body, while the leggings defined the rest of her all the way down to her ankles. He looked away and closed his eyes but still the image was there, playing out in his mind again and again.

He blinked and stared at the almost completed wiring in front of him.

"It will be okay," he whispered to himself, "it will all be okay."

He knew he just needed to do the job and go home. It was that simple. But somehow that one glance had been enough to breach all of his defences. His concentration was waning and he was tired, and phrases from scripture passed through his mind:

"The devil prowls around like a lion, seeking who he may devour.

My power is perfected in weakness."

After a few more minutes, he heard Alex call through to him.

"I think I'm going to pack up, Joel," she said. "I don't want to do any more tonight."

She came into the little office space and looked at his work.

"Are you happy to finish now?"

"Sure," he said, "I can come back and finish this in the next couple of days."

"That would be good," she said, "I really do appreciate it."

Every word she uttered seemed to contain hidden meanings, subtle nuances. He heard the traffic grumbling outside, and he realized that, with the electricity off and the evening drawing in, there was a dusky feel to the place. A sense of dislocation over-whelmed him, he felt as if he was in another place, far away from the rest of his life, with just him and Alex.

He stood up and there was a half-smile on his face. He came over to her and sensed just a hint of perfume she must have put on that morning, as well as that subtle scent that always seemed to characterize her. It occurred to him that even if someone were looking through the imperfect whitewash of the shop windows, they would still not be able to see the two of them in this room together.

Alex bowed her head as if the call to resist were just one battle too many for her. She rested her head on his shoulder and he felt no desire to move it. His only problem was that if she leant any more on him, he would topple over from his rather awkward standing position. He was disinclined to move as if to do so would break a spell that had been cast upon them; the mood had captured him like an insect on the spider's web.

He thought of Laura, and how he would touch her in a way that was open only to him, and she would be in a place some-where between accepting or declining his offer. He felt that now with Alex, that fine balance, that gentle offer of intimacy.

Across the room, Angel stood and watched. He knew there was nothing he could do now; it was too late for that. This was the moment when lives would be saved or destroyed.

When it arrived, as Angel knew it would, the demon did not try to taunt him; in fact, it had not even given much attention to Alex and Joel. In a sense, this moment was theirs; they could do what they wanted and both Angel and demon had to stand by as this played itself out.

And this was the moment of crisis. If they did not back away now, if they succumbed to each other then so much that had been planned for both of them would be lost. Even if they walked away from this encounter physically uncompromised, but wanting more, the next time an opportunity arose, they would find it even harder to resist.

Angel uttered a simple prayer for them in his own language and moved away from the room so he could not see what occurred next. They were in God's hands now, as well as their own. He would know the outcome soon enough.

IN THE OFFICE, Alex and Joel were almost motionless. In her beating heart, Alex felt the hunger rise. In the dim light of the room, everything around her blurred and warmed, and she could feel her own sense of right and wrong blending in with the dusk. She wanted Joel, to touch him, to feel him, to kiss him. The words that described her view of him spun around in her head:

Brother... Friend... Co-worker...

Lover...

Lover...

The idea of Joel as a lover, attractive and forbidden, beguiled her. She was tempted, and in a strange way, she drew some comfort from it, some relief that the temptation was at last out there, clear and obvious. And with it came a revelation – she could no longer deny that she wanted someone to share her life with. She knew she'd been hiding from this truth; she knew she was scared of loving and losing again, but she didn't care.

She put her arms around Joel and buried her face in his chest, feeling the texture of his overalls on her cheek, hearing his heartbeat. This was what she wanted, this was her desire, to love and be loved, to give and receive, body and soul. She let the unthinkable words come into her mind: she wanted to share her life, her love, her desire, with a man.

But not this man.

Slowly she raised her head and stepped away from him. Her eyes fixed on the blank wall to the side of her. She didn't know what stopped her in the end. It wasn't the café project or all of the vision and purpose that God had placed inside her; these things had seemed distant and irrelevant to her at that moment. Rather, it was love, love for the man she knew she wanted to be with, love for the future life she wanted to lead, love for her friend Laura, and for this man who had been kind to her and loved her as a sister as she loved him as a brother, even if they'd forgotten this truth for a moment.

And she knew that the crisis had passed.

"You are right," he whispered, "I have been a fool and I'm sorry." He stepped back from her and she looked at him, her friend's husband, and she felt such a different affection for him that she could only blink and smile.

He turned and started to put his tools away, and she went back to the paintbrush and tin and started to tidy up.

WHEN HE WAS FINISHED, he came through into the main café area.

He walked over to Alex, but they did not touch.

"I'll see you on Sunday, Alex," he said, "and I'll get Aiden to come and help me with this."

She nodded.

"Bye, Joel, and thanks for your help. You are a good man." She smiled and placed her hand on his shoulder. He nodded and turned to the door. He didn't look back as he walked out of the café and into the cool evening air.

Out on the pavement, he whispered a prayer. Nobody would have heard it, swamped by the traffic and the urban noise, but he prayed anyway, petitioning God for both of them:

"Jesus, protect us, and show me who she is to me."

And as he prayed, the Spirit prompted him to look inwards for a moment, into his soul. He searched for Alex there and felt as if he were on a journey to meet the people who were most precious to him. There was Laura and his son Josh right at the centre of that journey, at the heart of everything. Then there were his parents, and a couple of his closest friends from church; his brother and sister, and next to his sister he saw Alex smiling at him. He had looked into himself and there he had found her, a sister in faith, someone like a sibling, to work with and to love with respect and dignity. It was as if he was looking on from the Lord's perspective, and the moistness gathered in his eyes.

As he walked back to his car, he felt like a soldier returning from the battlefront, conscious that he'd narrowly escaped injury or death. He knew deep in himself that neither he nor Alex would succumb now. He believed he was strong enough, and he thought she was even stronger than he was. They would need to be careful, but they would be okay.

BACK IN THE CAFÉ, Angel watched Alex as she slowly tidied up, and he rejoiced in the fact that this age still contained heroes; he was beginning to think she was one of them.

The demon was still on its knees, howling at the frustration of a temptation unfulfilled. It knew the war would go on, but an important battle had been lost. This had been its best chance and it had failed. It knew what was to come.

Alex had just sealed the tin of paint when her mobile rang again. She had left it by the counter and so she ran, still holding the can of paint, over to where the phone was buzzing. On the way, her foot hit the same strip of wood that Joel had tripped on earlier. Unable to steady herself since her hands were full, she fell over on her knees. The paint tin bounced off the floor, knocking its lid off and spinning it over onto its side. Paint spewed out in a ragged arc as the tin spun around.

And the mobile stopped. Alex sat down breathless, shocked and disheartened. It seemed so unjust! She had struggled to keep her life holy, she worked hard for God, she had been really, really brave and good, and she was glad that she had been, and then this happens! Under her breath she whispered a prayer, in hope and anguish:

"When are you going to do something for me?"

LAURA PUT THE PHONE DOWN, concern clouding her face. Why hadn't Alex answered the phone? What was going on? Her first thought was that Alex had hurt herself, but then Joel was there with her so he could have answered. So what could have happened?

Joel was there with her.

In fact, Joel had been gone a bit longer than she had anticipated.

Laura was not a stupid woman; she could see the friendship between Joel and Alex, but she trusted them both. Really, she had to trust them both, but trust only stretched so far, and she had seen a tension in Joel recently that he would not explain.

These last few weeks had been a difficult time for her. She had wrestled with the issue of going back to work, whether it was right or not, and for how long, and what they would do about childcare for their young son Josh. And Joel had been a bit distant, a bit preoccupied with his own work and the church. Was this the reason why? Did he feel something for Alex? But he was her husband, not Alex's.

"Keep your hands off him. He's mine!" she said and was shocked to hear herself utter the words.

She listened, trying to determine whether her voice had woken Josh, but the house was quiet.

Jolted from her thoughts by the sound of the front door opening, she turned and smiled at Joel, and immediately noticed there was something different about him, as if a weight had been lifted from his shoulders.

"Hi," she said, "everything go okay?"

"Yeah, fine," he said and then he kissed her. "Look, I thought I would get us a little something." He had bought a tub of double chocolate ice cream with brownie bits in it. Joel knew that she loved ice cream, especially this flavour, and he had not bought any for quite a while.

"Want some?" he said as he headed into the kitchen.

"Why not," she said.

She closed her eyes and took a deep breath. She felt light, joyful, as if some burden had been lifted from her. Then she thought again about Alex, not now as a competitor for her husband, but as a friend who had not answered her phone.

"Joel," she said, "was Alex okay when you left her?"

He emerged from the kitchen. "Yes, I think so, why do you ask?"

"Because I just tried to phone her, and I got no answer."

"Well, why don't you give her one more call? I'm sure she's okay."

Laura picked up the phone and dialled the number. This time there was an answer.

"Alex, it's Laura, I tried to phone just now. Are you all right?"

She could hear Alex's voice at the other end of the line. "Yes, I'm okay, I had a bit of an accident with the paint when you called so I didn't get to the phone."

"Oh no, what happened?"

"Oh, I just tripped and dropped a can of paint on the floor. I'm okay now, only a few splashes of paint to wash off. I'll be okay."

"Are you sure?" said Laura.

Joel stood in front of his wife with two bowls of ice cream in his hands.

"No, I'll be fine," said Alex. "I give you a call tomorrow."

"Okay, see you soon."

"Well?" said Joel.

"She's fine. Just had a bit of an accident with some paint but she's okay. I'll talk to her tomorrow."

They went into the lounge and relaxed on the sofa with their ice cream.

"How's Josh?" he said.

"Fine. He went down about seven, and I've not heard anything from him since then."

"Good evening with the mums?"

"Oh yes," said Laura, "it was all mother and baby gossip. You did the right thing getting out of the way for a while."

He smiled and nodded, and then they sat back and watched some TV as the sky finally darkened.

"You want some more ice cream?" he said, standing and taking her bowl.

"No, that was enough," she said. "Take me to bed now, please."

Joel stared at her for a moment.

"What did you say?"

"You heard me."

"I, yes, of course, I'll just put these in the kitchen and lock the front door."

———

WHEN JOEL WAS DONE, it was Laura who led him to the stairs, and they walked hand in hand up to their bedroom. Laura disappeared into the bathroom, and as he was waiting for her, it dawned on him that she might have guessed why he'd been so distant these past few weeks. The thought distracted from the mood of the moment, but he knew Laura was happy, and he had enough wisdom to know that things were okay, and sometimes it was best not to complicate matters by worrying.

15

As Alex continued to prepare for the opening of her café, Daisy asked if she could help and became employee number one. Alex wondered if her cousin needed the money. Perhaps she had already burned through the inheritance money she'd received, or maybe she just wanted to belong somewhere, to something, to a community. Whatever the reason, Daisy got stuck in, coming to the café every day in the week before opening, helping to check that all of the equipment worked, looking over the stock, and making some last-minute amendments to the decorations.

With a late burst of assistance from all sorts of people, Alex had her café ready to open with a couple of days to spare, and the day before the grand opening, Laura persuaded her to have an evening off with some of the girls from the church. They headed into the city for dinner and a trip to the cinema. Daisy had insisted that Alex go and so Daisy was left with a few last-minute jobs, making sure the cutlery and crockery were all in place, and setting up some playlists for the sound system.

That evening, Conner arrived at Alex's apartment, ready for the big opening the next day. He'd promised to do a couple of sessions with his acoustic guitar, and he also wanted to be around to support his sister.

With Alex out with her friends and Daisy at the café he had the place to himself for a while, and so he slumped into the sofa and turned on the TV.

After ten minutes spent flicking through the channels, he eventually succumbed to restlessness, grabbed his jacket and his guitar, and headed down to the café. He told himself that he wanted to try out the sound system and now was as good a time as any.

He also told himself that it had nothing to do with the fact that Daisy was there, that if he'd wanted to, he could have made himself stay at Alex's flat and waited for Daisy to return. He kept telling himself this story as he left the flat and headed out of the building.

At the café door, Conner rang the bell for an unreasonably long period of time and peered past the edge of the curtain. From behind the counter, Daisy saw him and waved.

After their last meeting, he'd sent her a letter. It was an odd thing for him to do. Who sent anyone a letter these days? He'd written to say hello, and to inform her that his big Christian event had stayed dry while the rest of the country was drenched. He didn't really know what she'd made of it, she hadn't referred to it in the messages they'd exchanged since then.

She opened the door and let him in.

"All right, Daisy. How are you, mate?"

"All the better for seeing you, cousin." She smiled at him.

"What? Are you really pleased to see me? Oh, say you are, Daisy!" And even while she stood at the entrance he had launched into song:

"Daisy, Daisy, give me your answer do,

I'm half crazy, oh for the love of you!"

"Shut up, Conner!" She laughed and pulled him into the café, shutting the door once he was in. "So what are you doing here anyway?"

"I'm not going to disturb you. I just wanted to check the sound system."

"How can you not be disturbing me when you're going to be standing there making a load of noise?" she asked, hands on hips. "How's that going to work, with you going 'testing one two one two' like some kind of roadie?"

"Keep smiling, Daisy," he said, and walked into the café and up to the stage.

"What?" she said, and when he didn't say any more, she went back to her own work.

He took out his guitar and started to play a few chords, and then he connected the amp to the sound system and tried out the microphone.

After a few minutes, he paused, and Daisy looked up from what she was doing, then he started to play again. He played a tune that she recognized from their evening together. She had to stop and listen as he played the piece. The music was calm at first, but then it seemed to build to an intensity that tingled in her spine; this was no sound check, not now. She felt again the mix of feelings she had experienced in Alex's flat those few weeks before. He looked up at her while he continued playing, and without thinking about it she blew him a kiss.

He smiled and winked back. Daisy felt a pressure in her chest and stomach, and she put down the plates she had been stacking and walked over to the stage where Conner was still playing. She started to dance, just moving gently to the music. He continued with the piece as she moved over to him, and he afforded himself a good look at her.

She was wearing jeans that betrayed every curve she had, and a tee shirt that eased and moved with the curves of her body. There was a picture of a sunflower on the front of it, the emblem for the café. As his eyes explored the design, he almost lost his way, and it took him a moment to refocus on both his musical and moral bearings. As he pulled himself together and carried on with his sound check, Daisy took three steps towards him and, cupping his chin in her fingers she kissed him on the lips. He heard himself play the same chord four times while she kissed him, as if his musical brain was on hold while the rest of him was away on other business.

"You know, Conner," she said, "I could drop off the keys to the café at Alex's place, and then you could come back to my flat. We could text Alex and tell her you'll be back later." She looked at the expression on his face. "Oh, don't worry, I'm not going to seduce you, and I know you wouldn't get involved with me anyway because you're a Christian and I'm not." She smiled at him innocently. "But we can be friends, can't we?"

He didn't feel that he could decline, and he wasn't sure he wanted to anyway. He was staying at Alex's, but he had a key and she'd told him he could come and go as he pleased. Besides, he quite liked the idea of an hour or so with Daisy.

He raised an eyebrow and stared at her, and one thought went through his mind on repeat:

I must behave myself with Daisy, I must behave myself with Daisy, I must behave myself with Daisy...

It was a mixture of self-resolve and prayer.

He started to pack up his guitar while Daisy finished off her tasks and then she set the alarm and locked the place up.

"So how far is it to yours anyway?" said Conner.

"Just a bus ride," said Daisy. "It won't take long to get there."

"I'm in no hurry," he said, smiling, and they walked, arm in arm, back to Alex's flat, and then to the bus stop.

THE NUMBER 62 lumbered along the clogged streets of the metropolis, easing around parked cars and roadworks, with Conner and Daisy tucked into the seats at the back.

"So how is the band going?" said Daisy.

"Oh," he said, and sighed, "we've got recordings of our work out on the web, and a YouTube channel, of course, we're just trying to build up our fan base at the moment."

"But there was a sigh in there wasn't there," she said.

"I'll be honest with you though," he frowned, "I mean really honest, this social media thing can sometimes be a drag. I feel like I always have to be putting stuff out there, content and more content, and sometimes I just want to say, 'Hey guys, nothing new is happening with the band. It's all pretty much the same as yesterday. Maybe we'll have something new next week, or in a couple of weeks' time, but for now go and enjoy your life, and we'll get back to you.'"

"Fans always want more," she said. "That's how they are, that's how social media works, you always have to feed the beast."

"It's just so lame," said Conner. "I mean, I don't want to be posting about what tee shirt I'm wearing or what I had for breakfast or what colour my underwear is, I mean who cares, it doesn't matter."

"Some of your fans might be interested in the colour of your underwear."

"Yeah sure."

The bus slowed, hissed, grumbled and came to a halt, letting a few people off and on.

"Okay," she said, "so maybe the music is the most important thing."

"Of course the music is the most important thing!" He said it so loud someone in front of them actually turned around and looked at them for a moment before they descended again into a mobile phone-induced daze.

Daisy patted his knee. "If the others are as good as you are, I'm sure you'll make it."

"We'll see," said Conner. "You're actually right, what you said earlier, the music is only part of it, there are lots of talented musicians out there."

"Well, you scrub up pretty nicely as well," she said. "Are the rest of your bandmates as nice to look at like you?"

"Well," he said, genuinely embarrassed, "I don't know, I suppose they are, I mean apart from our bass player, he's really mean-looking. Don't tell him I said that if you meet him, please."

"I won't. So are you all religious, I mean are all your songs about Jesus and all that?"

"To answer your first question, yes, we are all Christians. And to answer your second question, no, our songs are not religious, whatever that means."

"You know what I mean."

"Let me ask you a question," he said. "This café thing, you've signed up to help, yes?"

"Yep, as much as I can around my college work."

"You know Alex is doing this in part so she can preach Jesus to the local kids."

"Sure," said Daisy, "but she does want to help them, and I do trust her. And I don't really care what she believes. She stepped up for me when I needed her, that's what counts."

"You're still doing your bit for Jesus," said Conner, winking at her.

"I'm not doing it for Jesus; I'm doing it for Alex." Her tone was almost sharp. The passenger who had turned around to look at them earlier twitched but didn't look up again.

"I'm doing it for Alex," Daisy whispered, "and it's work, Conner, it pays."

"Sure," he said, "nothing wrong with that."

She turned to him. "I need the money, Conner; I don't want to have to go back to my parents' house."

"I know," he said, "it's okay."

They said no more to each other until they reached the stop near to Daisy's flat. As they got off, Daisy took his hand, and he made no attempt to resist her.

He looked around at the cluttered terraces; he'd never ventured into this part of the city before. Daisy's flat turned out to be a small apartment in some purpose-built accommodation. A bedroom, a kitchen diner and a bathroom; living space for one.

There was art, and the trappings of art, everywhere. The walls were covered in designs. A round Dundee table sat in the kitchen, its top covered with pens, pencils and sketchbooks. A dirty plate sat beside a sink that was full of pots and pans.

"You want a drink?" said Daisy. "Coffee?"

"Got any tea?"

"Only some chamomile, that okay?"

"Sure."

"Go and put some music on in there," she indicated the bedroom, "I'll bring these through." She opened a cupboard and pulled out a couple of mugs.

Daisy's bed was covered in pages that looked like they had been ripped from a sketchpad and spread out to cover the duvet.

There was a little bedside table with an ashtray bearing a cigarette-stained kitten, and a packet of pills. Conner resisted the temptation to read the box label. A "No Smoking" sign had been partially scraped off the door, reducing it simply to the word "Smoking".

Conner found the CD player and turned it on. Next to it was a pile of CD cases. He found something by a new band called Snail Mail, pushed the CD player closed and filled the room with sound.

Daisy called out something from the kitchen.

"What?" he called.

"I said, turn it down a bit."

He slipped off his shoes and sat on the duvet. Daisy came in with two mugs.

"They're great, aren't they?" she said, pointing at the CD with a mug in her hand; tea spilt onto the duvet beneath her.

"I love those vocals," said Conner. "It's like she makes you believe her."

"They're all good," said Daisy.

"Yeah." Conner leant back and closed his eyes. "Music…"

"So what are you going to do next?" she said.

He looked over at her. "Well, I'm going to drink this crazy tea you made me and try to behave myself."

"No, I mean with the band." She dug him in his ribs and hot tea slopped onto his jeans. "Oh, I'm sorry! I'll get a cloth."

"Stay here, Daisy, I'm okay." He put a hand on her shoulder. "Just sit and relax." Leaning back again, he closed his eyes before continuing:

"I'm going to give it a year and see how things go, either we need to get a contract or we need to really build up our own presence on the web. But I can't think about not playing music, I don't want to think about what that looks like."

"So you'll either end up a rock star or some bum who is busking for a living," she said.

"Something like that. Still, life is full of adventures; I'll find something to do."

"Of course you will," she said, "you're terminally cheerful, and your homeboy Jesus has got your back. Not like the rest of us, I sometimes wonder whether Will's been lucky to get out of this life when he did."

Conner opened his eyes and stared at her for a moment. "Daisy, there's so much to live for."

She looked at him and then laughed in his face.

"Is there?" she said. "Do you really think that? 'Choose life.' Conner, is that what you're saying? Choose kids and mortgages and consumption and social media and filling the ocean with a load of plastic?" She leant forward as she spoke, as if close proximity might help to reinforce the point she was making.

He could sense her anger, boiling away under the surface.

"That's no life," she continued. "You might as well go out and enjoy yourself and screw the rest of it."

"Is that what you really think?" he said. "No day but today? Go out in a blaze of glory, or misery?" He didn't raise his voice, but she could hear him clearly enough above the music.

"So like I said, Conner, what about you?"

"Well, I'm with you on us not filling the ocean with plastic and the air with carbon dioxide," said Conner, "and I don't believe in consumption or Marxism, or any other dumb ideology that's been found out again and again over the years. You know my choice."

"Jesus?" she said with a mirthless laugh. "What do you know about it all anyway, good little Christian that you are."

"I'm sorry," she said immediately, "that wasn't fair."

"It's okay," he said, "but I have seen the darkness, and I don't blame anyone for wondering what we're here for. Life is brutal sometimes, unforgiving, and Jesus doesn't make all the bad things go away."

"What's the point of Him then?" said Daisy.

"The point of Him is He offers salvation."

"A chance for all the good people to go to heaven when they die?" said Daisy.

"A chance for everyone to live the best life they can, right now," said Conner, "not just a promise of the hereafter. Jesus is for life before death as well as after it, we can have something more now."

"Something more?" she said. "There's nothing more to be had here. I've had enough of life already, I've had it for twenty years, and most of it has been crap. It's one long struggle, and for what?"

He looked at her but stayed silent.

"I'm tired, Conner." She spoke softly now, her voice barely audible above the music. "I'm fed up with the nothingness, the pointlessness, the raging people, each in their own little bubble, everyone shouting and nobody listening, everyone outraged, and no one really cares. I don't want my life to be dictated for me by some religious bigot, but I do want something other than," she waved her arms trying to express how she felt, "something other than all this. If this is life, then maybe the alternative isn't so bad. Maybe getting stoned or wasted is just making the best of it."

"You're right," he said, "there are some people who think that's all there is, and I don't blame them, not really. God knows it's hard, isn't it?"

He looked at her and his eyes glittered with tears.

"Well, isn't it?" he said again.

She nodded.

"So you know that too, do you?" she said, as if she'd just recognized something in him, a similar burden that Daisy thought only she carried.

"Yeah," said Conner, looking away, "I know that too. But there is one thing I do that helps. Sometimes I just go away somewhere, to a place that helps me to find peace."

"So where's that?" she said.

He was silent now, as if to tell her would be to give up something precious.

"Don't worry," she said, "you don't have to tell me, all this is enough."

"All this?" he asked.

"You talking to me now, being honest with me."

"I'll always try to be honest with you, Daisy."

"Look at me," she said, and he glanced up at her.

"Look at me," she said again, and this time he did.

"You make sure you do that, Conner, you make sure you are always honest with me."

He looked into her eyes, right into them, so he could face her fully when he promised her the truth. But the words faltered as he looked into her, and he saw something in her features, something that was her and not her, like a crowded noisy place, full of longing, and hunger and fear. He was looking at Daisy, but he didn't know what was looking back at him.

"Really?" he said, "you want that."

"There's nothing else worth having."

"So can I ask you a really tough question?" he said.

"Sure," she said.

"Do you believe in demons?"

"What?" she said, frowning at him.

"Do you believe that demons exist, I mean really exist?"

She laughed; a short rather derisive sound that suggested this was territory she did not want to cover.

"No, of course, I don't! Why? Are you going to suggest that I'm possessed?" She pulled away from him.

"I don't like the word possession," he said. "I think sometimes demons just hang around people, like uninvited guests."

"Are you saying I have one of these things around me?"

"I don't know."

"What the...who the hell do you think you are, Conner?" She sat back from him, confusion filling her mind, "What do you think you're doing, talking to me about demons?"

"I'm sorry, Daisy, I don't want to offend you, and I'm not trying to hurt you."

Oh God, he thought, *what have I said?*

"It's just that this pain in you, this anger, this restlessness, it feels like it isn't really who you are."

"I can't believe you can say this sort of thing," she said. "I mean, who do you think you are? Who do the lot of you think you are? I suppose you think I'm going to hell, don't you? Well, damn you, Conner!"

"I'm sorry, Daisy," he said, "I've upset you and I'm sorry. I think I'd better go."

He put down the cup he was holding and started to walk to the door. She watched him through the moistness of her eyes, the outline of him blurred with tears.

Not for the first time, Conner wondered whether what he thought was some profound insight from God was in fact just him putting his big foot in it. When he got it right it could really make an impact on the person he was speaking to, but the problem was, when he got it wrong, it also could also make an impact, and for all the wrong reasons. Sometimes he would make a complete fool of himself and often upset the person in the process, and this was turning out to be a classic example of just how wrong he could be.

But this time, he didn't think he was wrong.

He turned and she saw his features through the blur of her tears. "I'm sorry, Daisy," he said one more time, and looked away from her. "You see, I love you, and I want the best for you."

She swore at him under her breath, she didn't know if he'd heard her.

As he left Daisy's flat, Conner was already checking for the change in his pocket and hoping the bus wouldn't be too long. He didn't know what he would say to Alex.

Daisy sat on her bed and tried to summon up the rage and indignation she wanted to feel. But she could not. She could not make her anger fit with the respect and concern he had shown her. In fact, she wanted to call him back, even if it was only to shout at him again.

She heard the front door of the apartment block slam, and

something that seemed beyond her own volition launched her off the bed, into the kitchen, and over to the window that looked out onto the road below. She pushed open the window and watched him, a receding figure heading for the bus stop.

She drew a deep breath of night air and shouted as loudly as she could.

"Conner!" The entire street must have heard her, and she was suddenly aware of how loud her voice could be when she really wanted to get someone's attention.

She saw him turn around and look up to the window.

"Come back," she called.

He didn't move.

"Please," she said.

He looked as if he was about to shout something back, but instead he started walking slowly back towards her.

Within moments he was walking into the kitchen and facing her.

"Listen, Conner," she said, "if you don't talk about demons again tonight, I won't spill tea on you – is that a deal?"

There was a moment of silence between them.

"I do care about you, Daisy," he said finally, "even if I'm talking rubbish, it's only because I care."

She came towards him and put her arms around him, and he put his arms around her, and they stood, together, feeling the pressure of each other, reconciling themselves through it.

"I do have a question for you though," he said.

"Come and sit down again, first." She walked into her room again and sat down on the bed.

He followed her in.

"Go on then, Conner," she said, "ask your question."

"Who do you think moved the stone?"

Daisy traced back their conversation to see if there was something she had missed, some issue or question that had gone unanswered. She could think of nothing.

"What? What stone?"

He sat up in front of her. "The stone in front of Jesus' grave," he said. "Who do you think moved it? The Romans, the Pharisees, the disciples, an angel maybe?"

"Do we have to do this now, Conner?" she said. "I mean, right now I don't care, it could have been the fairies for all I know." She leant back on the headboard and sighed.

He was about to say something else when she interrupted him.

"Okay," she said, "I'll give you an answer. It wasn't any of those people you mentioned. Jesus was actually an alien and after they buried him, the alien Mothership came down and a bunch of other aliens came and moved the stone and took him away. That's what happened." She looked at him.

"Really?" She could see from his expression that he couldn't work out if she was being serious or not.

"Yeah of course," she said. "Now do you want some more of that chamomile tea?"

They sat staring at each other for a full ten seconds before Conner gave in and burst into laughter. Then she laughed, and there was such a sense of release in laughing with him that she nearly started crying again.

"Here," she said. "What do you think of this?" She got up, tapped her sound system and the room swelled with some gentle trance.

"What's that?" he said immediately.

"Tony McGuinness one of his deep sets."

"Yet again, I applaud your taste in music."

She brought more tea, and sat down next to him, closer to him now.

"You know what we were saying earlier, about despair," he said.

"What about it?"

"I don't blame anyone who loses their hope. People who've been through it all, every penny, every relationship, every scrap of self-respect, their dignity, their values. I've seen it, real people real lives – screwed up, wasted."

"Really?" she said. "What have you seen?"

"Imagine yourself," he said, "living in a squalid room, huddled in a blanket, and you don't notice the smell anymore, and the mattress is still there because who the hell would buy something like that? And it's like there's some maggot eating away at who you are, not in great lumps but in tiny little bits so that every morning it doesn't take you so long to justify the next desperate act that you know you're going to commit. Then, when you've sold it all and you've got really good at justification, justifying every last degrading thing you do, what do you say then? You say it's worth it because the alternative is worse, because life is just greed and indifference and hypocrisy, and worthless. And do you know what? The people who say that would have a point, if it was true, if that really was true, then you'd be right, you would, because there's nothing more, nothing."

She opened her mouth to say something, but he raised his hand.

"But here's the thing, Daisy, if you thought that, if I thought that, I'd be wrong, wrong that it's all pointless, wrong that nobody cares. We don't just exist; we are made to live, with all the sorrow and joy that comes with life. I don't have to just exist, you don't have to just exist, you, Daisy, you don't have to just exist. You can choose life, and the thing about life, real life, is that it's better than anything you can swallow or shoot or snort. I choose that life. Do you know why? Because I am loved and I have a purpose, and it's not all pointlessness and despair. That's so scary and wonderful, and so full of potential. It's the most outrageous truth in the world; there is love, and there is purpose, there is more than all this scrambling in the dirt, more than just 'consume and die, and consume and die'."

He stopped, as if all the breath and energy had gone from him. "I know love here inside myself, I am loved, and so are you. You are loved, and you have a purpose, and you have hope. And you matter, you, Daisy, you are beloved."

"No," she said, "please don't do that, Conner, please don't talk about love and hope. I can't do it, I can't hope, it's not the way I live, I don't dare to hope, I don't deserve hope or the disappointment that follows it."

"That's it though, isn't it?" he said. "None of us deserves hope. It's the only way it could all work, if we had to earn God's love none of us would deserve it. But whether we deserve it or not, the love is there."

"I know it's there," she said, surprising herself. "I know it's there, it's just that I can't reach it at the moment, Conner. I wish I could, but I can't. It's too far away, and it's too dangerous, hope is too much to hope for. I want to believe in it all, I want what you lot have got, I want this Jesus, but that's not how my world works. I can't do it, Conner, I'm sorry."

"I know you can't," he said, "and it's okay, really it's fine. This is enough for now."

"Is it?"

"Yes," he said, "more than enough, it's fine."

She suddenly felt exhausted.

"I don't know what you and Alex and all the rest of you have found that gives you so much assurance, so much love. No wonder you spend most of your time behaving yourselves."

He laughed at that.

"We're human like you, Daisy. That's why we take the offer in the end, what else do we have?" he said.

"Okay, it's enough," she said, and she lay back against him and he put his arm around her again, and they were both quiet.

And they stayed silent, and the music played, and the sky grew dark, and they lay still together and for the first time in a long time she was not angry, she was not afraid, and she was not disappointed, either with herself or with others.

And it was enough.

16

ON A BRIGHT SATURDAY morning in July, Alex Masters opened her café.

Outside, there was a very mixed crowd waiting for the doors to open. Some were church people who wanted to show their support, others were kids from the youth club or their friends, and others who had just heard about the café one way or another and wanted to see what the place was like. A rather flustered man with a pencil moustache turned up from the local paper. He demanded that Alex stand in front of the café with a big grin on her face holding a mug. His photographer sidekick, a sallow-faced guy who looked like he wasn't used to being out in daylight very much, took pictures of everyone and everything. As the photographer worked, Conner stood behind him pulling the most ridiculous faces and photographed the photographer with his phone. Alex ended up laughing at him. The reporter seemed happy enough and promised there'd be a small piece in the next edition, around about page thirteen or fourteen.

Daisy and Laura were on for the first shift of the day. Alex would take over later, but for now she wanted to be able to meet her first customers. The place filled up quickly, and very soon there was music and light and talk and laughter.

Alex had spoken to most of the people in the café when Joel's friend Aiden appeared. He was dressed in his suit and obviously on his way to work. A little fish symbol stood out on the material of his lapel. He waved to Alex and went over to the counter to get a coffee.

Alex smiled and made her way over to him.

"You look very smart," she said.

"Seeing a client later," he smiled, "but I thought I'd check in and show my support first. This is a great day for you, Alex."

"Thanks, I just can't believe it's all happening."

Aiden leant forward. "Well, it is happening, and only you could do it, certainly here in this part of town. I really hope it works out for you."

"Thanks, I appreciate that," she said and placed her hand on his arm.

He was about to say something else when a woman whom Alex vaguely recognized interrupted them. She was dressed in a beige jacket, smart skirt, scarf and gloves; there was a rather elaborate brooch on the lapel of her jacket. She was clutching a handbag and staring around the café.

"Excuse me," she said, "are you Alex Masters?"

"Yes, that's me," said Alex.

"I'm sorry to trouble you. My name is Brenda Marsh. My daughter Alice goes to your youth club."

She turned to Aiden.

"I'm sorry to interrupt but I have something urgent to discuss with Alex."

"Of course," said Aiden, "please carry on. I'll see you later, Alex."

Alex watched him join a small group of people they knew, and then she tried to focus back on Alice's mother.

"I'm afraid Alice has disappeared." The woman's voice wavered as if she were about to cry. "She went out on Thursday night, just to the shops she said, and she never came home, and I don't know where she is, and none of her friends know where she is. Have you seen her?"

The café was noisy, and people were still waving at Alex, beckoning them to join her, she gave a brief wave back and then leant in towards Mrs Marsh.

"Come through here to the office and tell me what happened." Alex led Alice's mother through to the little office at the back of the café, she indicated a chair and then pushed the door closed, shutting out most of the noise.

Once seated, Brenda Marsh removed a small handkerchief from her pocket. She looked as if she'd had very little sleep in the last couple of days; dark grey rings circled her eyes.

Alex felt a wave of compassion for this woman. "Let me get you a cup of tea, Mrs Marsh, and we can think about all of the places where Alice might have gone."

Brenda Marsh looked as though she was about to decline the offer and then she seemed to slump in the chair.

"Okay, yes," she said, "that would be good."

Alex went off to get some tea for both of them.

"Have you told the police?" Alex said once she had returned.

"Oh yes, but what can they do? Loads of kids go missing each year, and she only disappeared yesterday. She was only fifteen you know."

Alex tried to mask the shock at hearing this woman refer to her daughter in the past tense as if she assumed that Alice was already gone forever. She remembered Alice's twenty-pound note, and how distant and distracted she'd been the last time she'd seen her at youth group.

"There's more," whispered Brenda. "We'd had an argument on the Thursday, about this. Do you know what it is?" She produced a little packet from her handbag. It contained a tiny pill with a dollar sign imprinted on it. "I found it in her room, and I wouldn't give it back to her." Alex stared at the pill as if it were an exotic and dangerous insect.

"I'm afraid I'm not sure what it is, Mrs Marsh," she said, although she had a pretty good idea what they were looking at here. "I suggest you take it to the police station." Then on impulse, she said, "I could ask one of my friends here, can I borrow it for a moment?"

"Of course."

Alex took the little pill and walked out to the counter where Daisy was serving.

"Daisy, can I borrow you for a second, please?"

"Sure," said Daisy.

Alex showed her the pill. Daisy looked at it and squinted at the design.

"Well, it's probably E, you know, Ecstasy. This brand has been doing the rounds recently. Where did you get it from?"

"I've got the mum of one of the youth group kids in the office, saying her child has disappeared, and she found this on the floor."

Daisy frowned. "The poor kid could be anywhere. She might be hiding, or she might have gone up to the city. Anything could happen to her there."

Alex frowned. This was not the message she wanted to take back to Alice's mother.

"I can't believe it. She was in our youth club a couple of weeks ago."

"Well," said Daisy, "I think you should give this back to her so that you're not done for possession on the day your café opens and tell her to show it to the police."

Alex looked at Daisy and then at the packet in her hand.

"Isn't there anything we can do?"

"Like what? Do you want to go driving around the streets at night on the off chance that you might see this girl?"

Alex stared at the tiny packet in her hand.

"Yes, Daisy," she said, "if that's what it takes, I would drive around the streets and look for her."

Daisy sighed. "Look, just be careful. If you do find her, there might be others with her; these are not nice people, you know what I mean? And besides, perhaps she wanted to get away – it does happen."

"Sure," said Alex. "Thanks, Daisy."

Alex closed her eyes and tried to blot out the noise and chatter for a moment. She clenched the little plastic bag in her hand.

Lord, she prayed, *what do you want here? Should I get involved, can I help?*

She closed her eyes and waited. She could almost feel the second hand of her watch ticking round. That poor woman would be waiting for her, but the café needed her presence.

She continued to keep her eyes tightly shut, trying to will God into answering her. She started to relax again when a voice or a feeling inside her seemed to speak:

"Make a list of places she might be with Alice's mum, and then leave it alone."

That was it, a rather frustrating response, but she knew by now that when she asked for an answer, she should be satisfied with the one she got. She walked back into the office where Alice's mother was sitting and handed back the packet.

"You should take this to the police, Mrs Marsh. I think that's the best thing to do. But we can make a list of places where she might be now."

"Thank you, but I've done that already. However, if you can think of anywhere she might be, anyone at the youth club who might know where she is, please tell me, I'd be grateful. Yes, I'll go to the police with this. They might take it more seriously if I show them." She leant in slightly towards Alex. "I'm sure this is a drug of some kind, that's what upsets me so. God knows what she's been up to, what people she's with." And with that, she started to cry.

Alex watched her put the pill back in her bag and again felt intense compassion for this poor woman, left in agony by the thought of what might have happened to her child.

"I will do what I can," said Alex, and reached over to the desk for a sheet of paper and a pen. She started to list places that she knew the young people liked to visit, other cafés, fast food shops, pubs and some of the clubs. She passed the list to Mrs Marsh.

"If I see or hear anything," she said, "I will let you know."

Brenda Marsh took the piece of paper.

"Thank you," she said, "I'll let you know as well if we get any news."

She stood up, took a deep breath, straightened her back and walked out.

Alex followed a moment later and watched her as she walked out of the café door and disappeared down the street. To her surprise, Aiden was still there in the café.

"How did it go?" he said.

"Not good," said Alex. "You know Alice from the youth club? That's her mother. Alice has gone missing, and her mum found some drugs in her room last week."

"Oh no, were you able to help her? Is there anything we can do?"

"I've given her some suggestions of places Alice might be, but I feel like God's telling me to leave it alone now."

"Maybe you can touch base with her again in a couple of days and see what's happening." He looked at Alex. "I'm sorry this has come out on the day you open your café."

"Well, that's life isn't it, Aiden," she smiled at him, "in all its pain and disappointments."

"That is so true." He nodded and smiled back. "I'll drop by later if I get the chance."

"Sure, and thanks for coming." On impulse she reached out and took his hand.

He drew her to him and hugged her, briefly, whispering, "I will pray for Alice." Then he picked up his case and went out onto the street towards the station.

THAT EVENING, Conner and his band played two half-hour sessions in the café, mixing up some of their own material with some worship songs and a few covers.

The café had been busy all day but by the evening it was packed, and there was a spill of young people out onto the street, mainly smokers hovering near the entrance leaving a litter of cigarette ends at the front of the café. There was music and laughter and chatter and at the end of the evening, when she had finally ushered out all of the customers and shut the door, Alex realized that they had burned through a third of their paper napkins.

There wasn't much to do that evening, so she checked the till takings, while Daisy and a couple of other volunteers helped clean the place up. She had to add the numbers up three times because she couldn't concentrate. Then she went out and swept up the cigarette butts that had collected near the entrance, and with that, she was done.

The first day of opening for Alex's café was a great success. The novelty would wear off, of course, but Alex felt satisfied: lots of people, lots of business, lots of good conversations, and even though there was plenty more to do, the dream was becoming a reality.

Later on, exhausted and in bed, she thought about her day.

The press had been there, the kids had turned up, the staff had turned up, there had been no trouble, and everyone had gone away with a little card telling them what the café was there for, and why Jesus was real and relevant to them today. It had all been everything she could wish for.

But even as she settled down to sleep, she felt nothing but sorrow, and she knew why.

She fidgeted under the duvet, trying to find a comfortable position. Tears trickled down her cheek and onto the pillow as the image that had haunted her mind all day came to her again, more potent than ever in the quiet darkness: Alice.

Where was Alice now? What was she doing? Who was she with? She shut her eyes tight and squeezed out the tears, and her nose began to run as well. At last, she sat up, and reached for a tissue. Then she turned on the light and looked up at the small crucifix hanging on the wall opposite her bed. Opening the café had been such a success; it had all gone perfectly, better in fact then she had hoped for.

And yet, here she was, in tears.

"It has been a terrible day, Lord," she whispered. "Please, please God, look after Alice."

17

Even as Alex drifted into sleep, in one of the city's police stations, Richard "Ricky" Riches was helping the police with their enquiries.

It was going to be a long night. Ricky was a small cog in the machine that was organized drug crime in the city, and he'd had the misfortune of attracting the attention of the forces of law and order. He sat in the interview room, breathing the stale air, perched on the edge of a chair, his dark blue suit clinging tight to his damp body, and he stared with wide bright eyes at the two officers facing him.

The larger of the two was well known to him: Sergeant Hughes. Hughes was a big, cheerful copper who'd served for fifteen years. He'd interviewed Ricky so many times that they were on first name terms. Ricky tended to make the mistake of feeling comfortable with Sergeant Hughes and saying things he later regretted.

The other officer in the room was Inspector Nisi Allen. Allen was an altogether different proposition for Ricky. She sat, silent and expressionless, watching him as he grinned and fidgeted in front of them. He was trying really hard to concentrate on

Sergeant Hughes, but his eyes kept flicking towards Allen. The more she sat there saying nothing, the more nervous he got, as if her silent presence would be enough to make all his grubby little secrets spill out onto the table in front of them.

They had been sitting here for nearly an hour, and Sergeant Hughes was clearly beginning to get bored. He leant forward, and the chair he sat on creaked under his weight. In front of him were his case notes, three empty cups and a search warrant.

"Come on, Ricky," he said, "you know we can't do that much based on the stuff we found you with. But if you don't start talking, me and my colleague here are going to take this warrant, and we are going to get it signed by a friendly judge, and we are going to crawl all over your horrid little flat. Now you think about that, Ricky, think about all the secret little things you've got hidden away, because you know I'll find them all."

Ricky opened his mouth, but Hughes continued before he could speak.

"We can be very thorough if we need to, Ricky, but I think you know that. I'm not just talking about a little look around with a flashlight. We'll be in all the cupboards, under the floorboards, in the loft, in the toilet cistern, everywhere."

Inspector Allen chose this moment to lift a black canvas bag from the floor and rummage around, before producing a box of latex gloves. She lifted one eyebrow and looked back at Ricky.

"I'll be as honest with you as I can," continued Hughes, "my governor here, she wants to nail you for good this time, and who can blame her with your sort of form? She wants me to have a really good rummage around, you know what I mean? All the little knick-knacks you put in the drawer with your Y-fronts, all the little packages behind the sideboard, perhaps a little something in the fish tank? A thorough check-up, you might say."

"Do you keep fish then, Ricky?" said Inspector Allen.

Her voice made Ricky physically jump in his chair. He looked at her as if she'd asked him a trick question.

"Huh?" he said.

Sergeant Hughes shook his head.

"Fish?" repeated Inspector Allen. "Do you keep them? Only, you don't strike me as the type."

"No law against keeping fish, Inspector," said Ricky. "I love my fish; they help to keep me calm."

"Well then," said Hughes, "you won't want anything to disturb them, will you?"

"No." Ricky frowned. "I think I need to go to the toilet."

"Come off it, Ricky," said Hughes, "that's the third time in the last hour."

"Your colleague makes me nervous." Ricky nodded at Allen. "You don't want me to pee right here, do you? It's your floor."

Sergeant Hughes bowed his head and sighed. "Interview terminated at twenty-two fifteen. Mr Riches is visiting the lavatory." The tape clicked to a stop.

"We'll be back in a minute," said Hughes rising from his chair.

Ricky Riches, a veteran of police interviews, rose from his seat and stretched. He shuffled over to the door, feigning a dazed carelessness. But it was all for show; inside his brain, there was feverish activity. All the deals and all the favours, all the contacts he had made over the years, but now for some reason the police wanted to come down hard on him. He hadn't had that much gear on him, not really, but if they searched his house, they'd find all sorts of interesting things.

That was the real fear he had; if they went through the place properly, they would find stuff even Ricky had forgotten he had. He could just imagine ending up in the local news, some top brass copper, standing at the table with the cameras rolling over bags and bags of gear, giving some lecture about a breakthrough in the local fight against drugs.

Along with the fear, there was the confusion. Why were they picking on him? Why didn't they just get their warrant signed and turn his place over? Clearly, they wanted something from him, but he hadn't worked out what it was yet. So, what did they want? That was the real question burning in his mind.

What did the police really want from him?

Ricky hated the idea of telling the police anything. He didn't mind if they charged him based on what they'd found in his pockets, he'd stay quiet and take that hit. But searching his place? That was going to lose his employers a lot of gear, and that was going to make them very unhappy. Some of his associates were already questioning his methods, making noises about how he was getting sloppy and unreliable, and they had a point. He was getting to be so messed up that he had to think for a couple of seconds before he could remember his real name. And now this; a load of their precious stock about to go up in flames. If he didn't end up in jail this time, he would probably soon be dead.

He paused, caught between the indignity of snitching to the police and taking a bit of a rap for what they had found on him, or staying quiet and having them comb through his flat and putting him in serious trouble with his friends.

He wondered if, even now, Allen and Hughes were watching him through the one-way mirror.

"I think," said Allen, "Mr Riches wants to say a few words to us."

"I think you might be right there," said Hughes.

The three of them froze as if trapped in some bizarre tableau – Ricky halfway to the door, Hughes standing, Allen still holding the box of non-powdered latex gloves. The tape was off; this conversation didn't exist. That gave certain advantages to all parties.

Ricky heard the creak of Hughes' boots on the floor; the Sergeant now stood with his lips about six inches away from Ricky's ear.

"Don't disgrace yourself on my floor, Ricky, I'll let you go to the lavatory in a minute, but first you listen very carefully to me because my colleague is getting a bit upset with our lack of progress here. You deal with us, Ricky, because we are ever so much nicer than the people you usually deal with."

"And if I don't?" Ricky stared at the glistening face of the Sergeant.

It was Inspector Allen who replied, making Ricky spin around to face her.

"If you don't, my Sergeant here and I are going to get this warrant signed and while you're still locked up in here, we are going to strip your flat clean."

"You might not get your warrant," said Ricky, "the judge might..."

Sergeant Hughes cut him off.

"You what? Are you serious, Ricky? You think the Judge might say no? What do you think he's going to say, heh? 'Oh no, Sergeant, not Ricky, he's as pure as the driven snow. I'm not signing a warrant for you to search the flat of a fine upstanding citizen like Ricky Riches, heaven forbid.' Do you think that's how it's going to go down, Ricky? Really."

Ricky thought, and nothing but fear came into his throbbing head.

He looked at the two of them and decided he really did need to go to the toilet now.

"Oh, Ricky," said Hughes, "it's all so hard, isn't it? I'll tell you what, we have had four or five dealers in here today and we've heard all sorts of things, we're already acting on some of it. You can tell your friends that you've said nothing to us, it'll be believable."

"What do you want?" said Ricky in a small voice.

"We need some information from you," said the Inspector.

"Just a little bit," said Sergeant Hughes. "Nothing any one of a number of the people we've had in here might have said to us."

"I thought you said your governor wanted to nail me this time," said Ricky.

"Only if you don't cooperate. We've got bigger fish to fry," said Hughes, and then laughed. "No pun intended about the fish."

"What?" said Ricky, genuinely confused.

"Never mind. Look, time's up, Ricky. Are you going to give us something or not?"

Ricky closed his eyes and swallowed. He looked at Hughes and then he looked at Allen. He stared at her for long seconds, and she stared back at him. Finally, he made a squeaking noise and turned and faced Sergeant Hughes.

"What do you want to know?" he whispered.

Inspector Allen asked him a question, and Ricky whispered a few words of an answer and then Sergeant Hughes nodded at his boss, and it was done.

Hughes took him to the bathroom, and they gave him some water, and then they took him back to the cell where he paced around for two hours before falling into a fitful sleep. The records showed that Ricky had said nothing further of interest and he would be released on bail in the morning after they'd charged him with possession with intent to deal.

THERE WOULD BE no early night for the drug squad now; they had work to do. In a room above the cells, Inspector Allen briefed her team. She wasn't really interested in Ricky, although he had been useful in confirming something she had already suspected. She was after a bigger prize, and all of the information they'd collected that day might well give her exactly that.

"So when we go in, we're not only looking for the usual stuff," she said. "We want to pick up anything with this design on it." The Inspector showed her team a range of items, each with the SEEKA emblem on them. "We're starting to see this SEEKA gear all over the place at the moment, and I want to know more about how these people are working with the gangs, if that's what they're doing. We know where it's coming from, but I want to tie them to this event we're crashing this evening. Any questions?"

Everyone was silent; they knew what they were doing.

"Okay," she said, "let's go."

DAVE SOMERVILLE STOOD in front of Martin Massey's desk, rolling up a magazine in his hands.

"This whole SEEKA thing is getting too hot, Martin," he said. "Even you must be able to see that."

"Really?" said Martin, with a dismissive wave of his hand. "You mean it's getting too hot for you to handle."

"You know this is going to go horribly wrong," said Dave. "I can feel it."

"You can feel it," said Martin with contempt. "Go home, Dave, and leave this to the grown-ups."

Dave swore under his breath, turned around but didn't walk away.

Martin smirked and leant back in his chair. In his mind, he indulged in a little fantasy that was keeping him amused during these crazy hot days. He imagined himself as the head of a media empire with everyone around him, including Lewis, acting as lieutenants of various rank and privilege; but the characters in this fantasy weren't people, they were stars and planets. He appeared as the sun, the bright star at the centre of a solar system of other planetary workers. Within that image he called Dave "Mercury", not because of any vigour or energy that the man might show, but because Martin saw Dave as a small rock floating near the centre of things, but actually turning out to be burnt out and irrelevant.

The phone rang and he grabbed it.

"Pat," he said, "are we on? Good." He scribbled something on a piece of scrap paper in front of him. "Yes please, you drive. I'll see you later." He put the phone down, scribbled a note on the paper in front of him, and turned back to Dave who was now facing him again.

"No, things won't go horribly wrong," he said smoothly to Dave, "not unless someone does something stupid, and that's not going to happen, is it?"

"You can't see it, can you?" said Dave, glancing down at Martin's desk.

"There's nothing to see," said Martin. "We're doing what we're good at, riding the culture, making money."

Dave stared at him, and his expression suggested he had made a decision.

"Are we finished?" said Martin. "Because I need to go."

"Yes," said Dave, "we are." He turned and walked out.

"Right," said Martin, "that's that taken care of." He stood up, grabbed his coat and headed out into the night.

He followed a well-worn path to the venue: something to eat, something to drink, then off to meet his contact for a lift. It was a beautiful thing for Martin, to be able to go out and enjoy an event like this, to have Pat, one of his team, drive him there and then to watch as he made money at this place.

The venue was hot, loud and anonymous; the people exchanging their lives as individuals for the life of the gathering. He surveyed them, a sea of bodies, silhouetted in different coloured lights. Water bottles held high above arms covered in bracelets and bangles.

"That's right," he said, unheeded beneath the din, "dance and drink, and buy the merchandise, buy it all, spend your money, spend it on me."

But then he remembered they weren't spending it on him, they were spending it on SLaM, on Lewis. Martin closed his eyes and listened to the music, and he knew that whatever he got out of SEEKA, it wouldn't be enough.

He was just about to curse into the noise around him when he noticed a tall powerful-looking man moving with athletic speed through the room, scattering ravers as he went. He was about fifteen yards from the stage when he held up both arms as if trying to send a signal of some kind.

A man Martin recognized as one of the organizers ran onto the stage behind the DJ, and the music suddenly cut out, as did most of the lights. There was a noise across the whole venue like the wailing of a dying man.

Martin felt someone grip his arm. He turned to see Pat who leant forward and shouted a few words into his ear.

"Police, we are leaving now."

Martin was propelled backwards to a door behind the stage. He saw a team of about four or five people running with the DJ's equipment in front of them. He was bundled through two sets of doors and then out into the open night. Off in the distance, he could see a flicker of blue light.

Pat bundled him into the old BMW, the door slammed, and Pat jumped into the driver's seat. The engine roared as the car lurched and bumped off towards the road.

Martin squinted out into the darkness and tried to push his seat belt into place. He saw a car swing round to intercept them. His first thought was Lewis, and his second was Lench. He closed his eyes and cursed.

He still had his eyes closed when there was an explosion of light just outside the window. It was followed by at least three others in quick succession. His eyes were watering, but now all he could make out was the fading image on his eyelids and the growing bursts of blue light around and behind them.

A couple of police cars flashed by, ignoring them and within a minute they were away. Pat slowed the car, the engine calmed.

"Someone sold us out," said Martin.

"It happens," said Pat, "but there was a lot of our merchandise in there."

"There's nothing illegal about what we're selling," said Martin. "Nothing."

"All the same," said Pat, "that flashing light."

"What about it?"

"That wasn't the police," said Pat, "that was media, a photographer."

Martin cursed through his teeth.

They said nothing more to each other as they drove back.

***

DOWN AT THE STATION, the Inspector surveyed their haul with her team. Packets of drugs, and quite a supply of bottles, tee shirts and hoodies with this SEEKA logo on them.

"Get this lot bagged," she said. "We'll go through it in the morning. You," she turned to Hughes, "come with me, I want to have a word with our friend downstairs."

"I think he told us everything he knew, boss," said Hughes.

"I'm sure he did," said the Inspector, "but what I want to know is, who tipped off the papers? This nearly all went sideways because they turned up."

Five minutes later, the Inspector was down in the cells right in the face of a sleepy and disorientated Ricky Riches. The strip lights in his cell were all on.

"What?" said Ricky. "What do you want from me now?"

"Was it you, Ricky? Did you invite the media to our little party? Did you tip off any of your old mates and neglect to mention the fact to us?"

"I don't know what you're talking about?" squeaked Ricky. The Inspector stared into Ricky's red-rimmed eyes and was surprised to find she believed him.

They left Ricky to it and walked back upstairs.

"He didn't do it," said Hughes. "He's too stupid to be a good liar. I think it was someone else."

"I think you're right," said the Inspector. "And really, it doesn't matter. We've got a few more characters to talk to, and I can tie these SEEKA people to the scene. I'll be having a word with them next week as well; it's time we rattled their cage."

As a bunch of weary coppers made their way home, in the heart of the city a busy journalist put the finishing touches to a late bit of copy, a perfect complement to the pictures his colleague had sent in. Some of the images had been rubbish of course, but there had been this one, a beautiful image of one of the guys fleeing the scene, a real "rabbit in the headlights" shot. The expression on his face suggested that the photo had been taken just as he had heard some terrible piece of news. His mouth was half-open in preparation for a howl of anguish, and the right hand was shielding one eye, while the other was wide open, perhaps in terror. Taken as a whole, this picture suggested a nice mixture of fear, shock and confusion. It was perfect.

Getting the tip-off about the rave had been useful, finding the police had turned up made it even better, and getting this picture, that just topped it all. And the best of it was, he knew this guy, he recognized him.

It was one thing to print the picture, it would be quite another to name him in the article.

He sent the finished piece across to his boss, and then called him.

"Have you seen it?" he said.

"I like it," said his editor, "but being able to name the guy from just this photo? Are you sure about that?"

"It's him, my source has seen it and confirmed it."

"Sean, you know if we're wrong about this, legal are not going to be happy."

"It's him."

"Okay," said the editor, "go with it, but if you're wrong, when they've finished roasting me, I'm going to do the same to you."

"It's safe," said Sean, and forwarded the copy with APPROVED in capitals in the subject line.

Later, as the presses started to roll at the network of printers across the country, Sean found a solitary cab outside the office and went home.

On the way, he made a call.

"Dave, it's Sean, yes I know what time it is, I thought I'd check in. No, no problem, it all went well, really well, better than we hoped for actually. Just buy a copy tomorrow, you'll love it. Yes, goodnight."

Sean sat back and relaxed as the cab rumbled across town towards his apartment. It had been a good day for the free press, especially his little bit of it.

18

ALICE MARSH WAS LYING on a hard surface. She knew she was on her back, outside somewhere, but she wasn't really sure where.

The air smelt cold, and raw. She moved her head and felt pain, she took a breath and then she felt more pain.

In the last couple of days, she had learnt the value of all the things she had taken for granted, and she had learnt how fragile her body was, and how little the world cared for her.

She had run away from home.

It had seemed like such a bold, defiant thing to do. She had been angry, so angry, although she couldn't fully remember why now. By Sunday night, she was cold, tired, itching and aching – and scared, that was the worst of it, she was very scared. She had just bought some food and some drink and walked around the city. On Friday night, she had slept at a railway station near where she lived. Amazingly, nobody had seen her, and she had caught an early train in on Saturday morning. When she arrived, she had nearly turned back and gone home. But instead, for the next two days, she walked and slept in the city. She'd met a girl called Crystal who'd found Alice sleeping in her favourite doorway. Crystal, who was a veteran of the streets, decided it would be good to help Alice spend her money.

They'd eaten a lot of food, especially Crystal, and they'd spent a lot of money in a chemist's shop where Crystal was obviously a regular customer. Alice had paid for all of it, but by Sunday night she'd run out of cash. It was probably this friendship that had saved Alice from anything worse than the aches and pains she now felt, but once she was penniless, Crystal made it clear that Alice needed to move on.

She tried to open her eyes. There was a bright light out there, the sun pressing down on her mind.

There were more aches now, in her neck, and her stomach.

And she was cold, down to the bone, cold.

She lay still, concentrating on the noises around her. It seemed that even in the last few minutes the amount of noise had increased; cars came into and out of her range of hearing, people were walking past her on the street, some of them sped up as they passed her, their distaste and embarrassment pushing them on to get past another rough sleeper.

And the memories started to come back.

All this because of one stupid pill.

And the row with her mum that had got out of control so quickly.

Alice had been bored. Bored with school, bored with the youth group, bored with her dull friends and their predictable chatter. Bored with the fact that no one seemed to understand what she wanted. Depressed about the reality that she was never going to tell anyone how she felt because no one would understand.

So she'd done something that was not boring. Crazy, out of character, bizarre, yes, all of those things, but not boring. She'd taken out some of her savings and found a guy who could sell her a couple of pills. They hadn't even been as expensive as she thought they would be, and she'd wandered around with a bunch of twenty-pound notes like an idiot for a week.

She had waited until she was on her own in the house and had tried one of the pills.

She'd felt the euphoria, like everyone said she would, but then her throat got really sore and her whole body got itchy, and she got a rash right across her back, and she was all for throwing the other pill away, and that would have been the end of it, but instead her mother found it while she was snooping around in her room, Alice's room; her mother going where it was none of her business. Then the row, and now Alice was here, shivering, aching, angry and sorry, resentful and homesick.

"Hello, my dear, are you all right?"

Alice cracked one eye open and found herself looking at an old, creased face, with sharp features and blue eyes.

"Hi," she croaked back. This felt very weird, a bit like her granny had found her and joined her on the street, keeping her company.

"Oh, my dear, I don't think I've seen you here before. Have you been sleeping rough for long?"

Alice opened her eyes further to get a better look at this face. Her vision was hazy in the morning sun, but she noticed that the old lady had a symbol on her lapel, a golden "S" shape on dark red. Alice frowned.

Was this some kind of super granny? she thought. She closed her eyes again and then with rather more effort reopened them.

The face was still there, and the "S" on her lapel. She wanted to see who this old lady was, so she tried to sit up.

That was a mistake, a big mistake. Her head pounded and her guts clenched.

"Okay," said Granny, "it's okay, I've got you."

"I'm going to..." She got no further before she leant over and started to retch onto the pavement beside her. Trickles of liquid seeped from her mouth, spattering onto the ground.

"Oh dear," said Granny, "there you go." Someone handed her a tissue.

Granny spoke again, more quietly, and not to her. Now there were two voices. They seemed to be talking about her.

"No, I think she's under sixteen, probably a runaway." This was Granny.

"Well, we should take her in and see what we can do for her," said the other one.

Alice looked at the faces. A younger man had joined Granny, and she could see that he also had the "S" symbol, like they were both wearing uniforms.

"Who are you?" Her voice sounded like she was speaking from the grave. She wasn't sure why she'd asked this.

"I'm Marie and this is John. Can you tell me what your name is?"

"Alice, my name's Alice."

"Well, Alice, let's see if we can help you out here, shall we?"

"I don't need any help," she said weakly.

But she knew she wanted their help. The defiance and frustration were now mostly dissipated and hearing a voice that reminded her of her grandmother made her think of herself as a little girl again.

They got her to her feet, and as they did so she whispered, "I just need to go somewhere and get some sleep."

"Of course, Alice," said Granny, "we'll find you somewhere to sleep then, dear."

Some minutes later she was in a minibus, heading north across the city. The traffic was getting busy now and she needed to have a pee. They'd given her a bag in case she was going to throw up again.

The journey ended at a house on a suburban street. A sign on the door declared this to be somewhere called "Faith House". It made her think of Alex and Aiden and some of the others at church and then she felt a kind of sad longing sensation that made her want to cry.

They let her have a shower, and never in her life had she felt so clean. They gave her some clothes, which weren't what she would normally wear, and didn't fit perfectly, but they were warm and dry.

She still didn't want to tell anyone who she was apart from her name, so they left her in a room with a bed and she felt the tiredness overcome her. She lay down and pulled a blanket over herself and was about to drift off when some spark of curiosity made her open her eyes. There was lettering on the blanket, she could see some of it from where she was.

"...L V A T I O N A R M..."

Of course. She was in the hands of the "do-gooders". And they were indeed doing her good, and that felt okay.

When she had been a little girl, she had sometimes put money in a Salvation Army tin for the "poor children", as her mum called them. Now she was getting the benefit; she had become the poor child. With that thought in her mind, she closed her eyes and went to sleep.

As she drifted off, she thought about her mother, and the stupid argument, and the things she had come to value so much these past few days: warmth, food, safety, and of course, love.

19

———

Lewis Ashbury looked at the newspaper photo once more. He supposed there was a chance, albeit a slim chance, that the picture he was staring at was not Martin Massey.

If this had happened even a couple of months ago, he would probably have laughed about it and thrown it in the bin, citing the adage that any publicity is good publicity.

But this was not two months ago, this was now, and there had been murder and blackmail since then. Someone was trying to force him into halting the SEEKA project, using as leverage the fact that SEEKA and the drug culture fitted hand in glove. Last week, there had been an article in one of the tabloids, comparing SLaM and other organizations like it to parasites, feeding off the lives of young people. In his heart, Lewis was beginning to think that what they were saying was true.

Lewis was sitting in his house, alone. And tonight, he really did feel alone. Bridget was dead, Alex had left the firm, and he was reminded again of how much he missed both of them. He sat back and removed his glasses. With his eyes shut, he could see images of newspaper headlines: "SLaM – The drug connection", "SLaMMED – media business SLaM cashes in on drugs misery", and so on. These articles could now include a picture of Martin being driven away from some rave, and not just any rave but one that the police had raided.

With a mixture of regret and relief, he made his decision. It was the end of SEEKA; the best thing, the only thing he could do. And Martin could hardly complain; he'd been instrumental in the downfall of his own creation. He scribbled some notes in his diary; there were a lot of arrangements he would now have to make to unwind that part of the business.

He put the diary down and cursed under his breath. There had always been a nagging doubt in the back of his mind, something telling him that a lot of what he did, a lot of what SLaM did, was harming other people, and was wrong.

He tried not to care, but it was there, it had always been there. He realized now that he'd used Alex as a kind of fig leaf to cover for SLaM's actions. At least he'd always had a nice decent PA, who he respected and who hadn't slept with him. At least he could always say the firm had her on the payroll. Thinking about it like this now, it all seemed so pathetic.

He suddenly felt very tired, weary after all of the worries and concerns that had crowded in on him. As he closed his eyes, he imagined thousands of parents raged against him, people of his generation, people with children whom they loved. Children who were not only being poisoned by drugs, but were also being actively encouraged, by his company, to take those drugs. Of course, he had no children who could be harmed by the very things he was producing. He could almost hear the mothers and fathers now, anger in their voices at the ruined lives of the children they loved.

Love. What did he know about love?

"I know something," he said to himself. "I do know something."

Yanking out one of his desk drawers and tipping the contents onto the floor, he spread out the papers and photos, and just as his search was turning to frustration, he found what he was looking for.

He picked up the brown hard-backed envelope, slid the contents onto the desk and looked down at the two pictures.

The first showed him holding a champagne glass while standing next to a huge card. The caption "Good Luck SLaM" could be seen through the grainy medium of an old snapshot. On the other side of the card, stood a young-looking Bridget, also holding a champagne glass. This was how he would remember her: glamorous, determined, sensual. The photo didn't really do her justice although he could remember the day well; the very start of SLaM when it had been just him and her.

He looked at the other photograph. This was a larger print, and the quality was much better – a publicity shot taken in a studio. This one also showed Bridget, but quite a bit younger, probably not even out of her teens, striking an alluring pose over the bonnet of an Aston Martin. Lewis shook his head at the irony of the vehicle name. The photo showed all the elements that had attracted him in the first place: those lips, a mixture of desire and strength of will, the form of her body, the intelligence and deter-mination in her eyes. As a rule, he had never been attracted to redheads, but that was Bridget: she broke all his rules.

He was surprised to find himself crying, and even more surprised to find that he wanted to cry, wanted to grieve for her loss, and felt no shame in it. Wave upon wave of relief passed through him as the teardrops hit the surface of the desk. This could only have happened when he was completely alone, and in the luxury of his solitude he cried as he had never cried before, astounded as he was by the potency of his feelings and the poverty of his situation. He felt like a man who had gained the whole world but had paid for it many times over with his soul.

SOME FIFTEEN MILES away across the city, Lench sat back, lit a cigar, and reflected on the fact that for once, circumstances had conspired to make things simpler for him. The photo in the paper was all the indication he needed. It was time to finish with Martin Massey, to exclude him from proceedings very quickly, and with the minimum of fuss.

At least this was familiar ground; people joined and left the group, some by their own choice and some by other means. It was unlikely that Martin would even need to be removed completely in the way the Larson woman was; he just needed to be reminded that it was in his best interests to remain silent from now on. The mobile number would soon be untraceable, and he would get the Assassin to make his usual sweep of Massey's apartment.

The cigar smoke spiralled gently into the air, and Lench tried to relax. This project was over, and, phoenix-like, a new one would rise from the ashes. Strategies changed, but the core objectives – the promotion of the glory of his master, and the defeat and humiliation of the opposition – remained unchanged.

But something stuck in the back of his mind, like a piece of grit in a clam, a barb of unfinished business that was nothing to do with the halfwit Massey and his grubby project.

He knew the problem, this loose end, was likely to be the woman, Alex Masters, who Martin had been so dismissive about. He'd found out that, rather than disappear from view like a good girl, she was now making a nuisance of herself by opening some sort of religious tea shop on the High Street where she lived. It really was very, very tedious. He couldn't go and check this place out himself, not after the encounter in the car park. So he would have to get someone else to go, and only one person could do that job. He just hoped the Assassin could stick to the brief; the last thing he wanted was his attack dog going freelance and causing carnage.

He continued to reflect on the best course of action, but then he was distracted by a piece of ash as it fell from his cigar on to the floor. Lench cursed, and before he realised what he was doing he stamped down hard, crushing the ash into the carpet.

20

It was a quiet evening in the café. Alex looked at the clock and saw it was twenty minutes until closing time. She was thinking about sweeping the floor when the café door opened, making her jump. She didn't normally react to the door opening, but there was something about the force that had been applied to open it, something about the way the door swung in, hit the doorstop and then bounced back, the blind on the inside clattering against the glass pane.

A man stood in the doorway. He didn't come in immediately, rather he stood and scanned the room in front of him, as if he were appraising every single person he could see.

Even through his clothing, he looked compact, and tense like a coiled spring. He wore a very long black coat, and he had close-cropped hair and dark frowning eyes. His presence, as well as his entrance, seemed to change the atmosphere of the place. He was not especially large, but somehow, he was imposing, and there was something else about him that made Alex immediately feel uneasy. He stared at the other customers, the layout of the chairs and tables, and finally at Alex. Then he moved with unnatural grace over to the counter.

"Tea," he said, without even looking at the girl who was serving.

"Would you like milk with that?" she said.

"Yes."

He took his tea and walked over to one of the empty tables near the door. Some upbeat worship music continued in the background, jarring with the new mood in the café. The visitor sat with his collar turned up on his coat, but Alex could clearly see a scar snaking across his face as if he had been slashed quite recently with a sharp knife.

Some of the young people in the corner started to fidget, one said something, and another responded with some foul language. It was the first time Alex had heard that since the café had opened.

The man ignored them, staring at his tea. Then the young people all got up and shuffled towards the door, clattering against the tables and chairs as they went, the crude banter carrying on as they spilled out into the street.

THE ASSASSIN CONTINUED to stare at his mug, but he was quietly satisfied with his influence on the place. This might turn out to be quite an amusing assignment.

At least he was relieved to be out and about again at last after a short period of confinement. During his time at the safe house, he'd been doing a bit of "freelance thinking". That was what Lench called it – he wasn't sure what it meant exactly but Lench tended to use the phrase when he was reprimanding him for doing something outside of his express orders.

He'd had his briefing from Lench about this woman and her Jesus café. Lench made it clear that he didn't want any violence; this was reconnaissance only. That was fine with the Assassin, for this visit, but now he'd seen her, he was reasonably sure he'd have to point a gun at her one day.

He'd recognized her instantly of course; the description Lench had given him was thorough as usual, and he'd been able to look at a series of photos taken a few weeks ago.

She had a nice figure and quite a pretty face. As a rule, he didn't like killing pretty women, he gained no perverse satisfaction from it, but business was business. The Assassin stretched out in his chair, smiled and cracked his knuckles just to put some other noise in the air over all this Jesus music they were playing.

Standing in the space next to Alex, but in his own dimension, Angel was able to see both the man and those who accompanied him. Lench's entourage had been fearfully potent, and this lot were spectacular in their own way, like a collection of exotic animals at the zoo. One was clearly in charge of the rest and it reared up and approached Angel on their own plane, standing face to face with him and screaming at his face, completely unbidden, its whole torso and head shaking with the absolute rage and anger that consumed it.

"WE ARE LEGION, AND WE BRING LUST FOR VIOLENCE, AND FOR MURDER," it screamed with a piercing, aching cry. Angel stood motionless, unafraid and unmoved by the desperation in this creature before him. He almost felt a kind of pity for them, the Lord would deal with them all as He saw fit when time came.

The most powerful of the demons stared at Angel, spiritual energy steaming off it. Then, again it arched back and threw itself forward with all the malevolent strength it could muster, screaming obscenities and blasphemies at its angelic opposition while its comrades crowded round, goading Angel into some reaction.

But Angel was at peace. He felt none of the apprehension about this encounter that he had felt when Alex had met Lench, or when Alex and Joel had been alone in the café. He stood his ground as the demon threw itself at him. The thing grew even angrier and started to utter every dark thing it could think of in every language that it knew. And still, Angel watched and waited.

IN THE CAFÉ, Alex stared, mesmerized by this man. Her spine tingled and itched. She felt as if she were engaged in battle with him even though she had done nothing but watch him walk in. She continued to watch him now, sprawled out at one of the central tables, picking the sugar sachets out of their pot, tearing them open one by one, and spilling the contents onto the table. She started to pray.

In the spirit world, the foremost of the legion of demons raised itself up again and faced Angel, head on, staring with fierce red eyes into his face. This time it spoke rather than shouted.

"Angel, look how our man sours the place. That is the power we give him, the power we have in him. WHAT HAVE YOU GOT?"

It gibbered to itself for a moment before continuing.

But now Angel was not listening. His attention had been caught by a thin shaft of light that seemed to appear from a ceiling tile, and flow gently downwards until it landed on Alex. Of course the people who were present in the room would not have seen it, but Angel had, and he knew two things.

First, such divine grace did not always come, whoever was praying and whatever they said. Second, he knew that something spiritual, and possibly something physical was going to happen.

The demon paused and its eyes flicked to the beam of light falling on the human at Angel's side. It sniffed the air; some of its subordinates started to fidget. Now it was Angel's turn to respond.

"You know who that is, don't you?"

"Lies," whispered the demon, it too started to jump and twitch.

"He must leave," whispered Angel, *"and so must you."*

"No," it screeched, *"no. We will not be subdued."*

The demon raised itself up to its full height. It towered above Angel, manifesting as an enraged dragon, scales of bronze and crimson shining in the light of the spirit world in which it existed. It screamed out its ancient rage once more, and its subordinates collected round their champion like frightened children around their mother.

In the café, Alex felt drawn towards the table where the man now seemed to be shaking. He stared at the crumpled packets of sugar, discarded, broken in front of him, and Alex stared at him, and the compulsion to approach the table where this man was sitting grew stronger.

Alex kept moving towards him, part of her mind convinced that what she was doing was absolutely right; the other part convinced that what she was doing was complete madness.

"You must," she said, "have made her really angry."

SOMEHOW, over the noise of the music, everyone in the café heard every word she said. The Assassin stared up at her, dropping a sugar sachet. He took in her face, storing this closer look to memory, registering what he had not noticed before. She must have some Asian parentage, perhaps Indian, certainly one grandparent, maybe even a parent.

"Yes," said Alex, coming to stand at the other side of the table from him, facing him as he faced the door. "She really must have been angry with you."

He was suddenly very aware of his scar. Almost by habit, he scanned the room again. There were three other customers, an older male, perhaps in his seventies, keeping his head down in the corner and trying to ignore what was happening here, and two girls at a table at the back of the café. The Assassin could see they were scared, very scared.

He liked that.

Just as he was about to focus on Alex again, the café door opened and a male of about twenty walked in. He had stopped in the doorway, perhaps sensing the atmosphere, and was now standing between the Assassin and his escape route, a complication he did not welcome. Any environment where something or someone was blocking an exit made him nervous.

At Alex's side, Angel watched as the beings that infested this man clustered around their host, while a form, translucent, white coalesced around Alex.

It was almost shapeless, but not quite, looking to Angel rather like a pair of cupped hands, in which Alex now stood.

"Are you speaking to me, woman?" The Assassin spat the last word out like a blasphemy.

"Yes," said Alex, "and I'm talking about that scar. It could not have been accidental, and it must have been administered by a woman."

The Assassin stared at her in confusion.

"What?"

Even as his mind processed what she'd said, he started to plan his escape.

Five people in the room, one blocking the exit, but with no sign of intending to stop him. The exit about ten metres away, no other obstacles.

His mind resolved into action almost before he realized himself, and he sprang with astonishing athleticism, judging his moment to perfection. He shut down his confusion at what this woman had said, and his body responded, performing as required.

One step took him past Alex's left-hand side. Two more loping strides took him to the door and the astonished-looking youth. With his momentum carrying him, the Assassin tapped the centre of the youth's chest just hard enough to make him step back a pace. At that moment his third stride took him through the open door. A fourth stride took him out to the pavement where he turned right and started to run down the street. As he had expected, everyone in the café simply stood and watched the spectacle. He lengthened his stride and eased into a jog, putting distance between himself and the café.

What happened? he thought as he kept running. *Something happened, I could not answer her; I could not deal with the threat. I was barred from dealing with her.*

The clean getaway could not alter the fact that this felt like a defeat, even though he couldn't really understand why this was. There was no clean resolution; there was no spilling of blood. There was no death, not even his own. At some level, it had all been very frustrating.

The Assassin concluded that this must have been some sort of spiritual thing. Even as he continued to jog, now at a steady pace, he reflected on the question of how much he should tell Lench about his little visit. He was just considering a very edited version of the encounter when his head felt as if something had exploded inside it.

He stopped running and, panting, leant against a wall as his companions screamed in a chorus of frustration and madness. Now he was sure, there must have been something spiritual going on for the whole lot of them to go crazy like this. He continued to walk, muttering to himself, his own anger growing now as the host within him howled and jabbered at him.

He reached his car, quickly checked he had not been followed, yanked open the door and flopped into the driver's seat.

When the door was shut again, he hissed at the voices inside his head.

"Shut up, damn you."

The clamour continued and he held his head, shaking it from

side to side. For a moment he wondered whether he would have to open the car door so he could vomit into the gutter.

"I said silence." He spat the words and gradually, begrudgingly, the howls died away.

He waited, panting and exhausted for two minutes before he started the car and drove back to the safe house.

CONNER FELT the shock of the hard tap on his chest and stepped back. As he did so the stocky-looking man moved past him, jogged out onto the street, turned right and disappeared.

He turned to Alex.

"Who was that?"

"I don't know," said Alex. "He just came in, sat down there, and the whole place went...sour."

They gave each other a hug, and Conner looked at the table.

"Well, he managed to trash a load of sugar for you."

Behind him, the two girls who had sat perfectly still through the whole thing got up and headed out of the door.

Their movement roused the old guy in the corner who eased himself up and walked up to the counter with his mug.

"Thanks," he said cheerily, "see you soon." And with that, he was gone.

"I think I need to have two people on all the time really," said Alex. "I can't have this happen if anyone was on their own here."

"You handled it," said Conner.

"Yes, this time, but what if it had been Daisy?"

"I reckon she would have given as good as she got," said Conner.

"Seriously?" said Alex, and Conner raised his eyebrows.

"She would," said Conner, "but you're right, maybe you need to be open a bit less, have more staff, and well, keep the place safe."

"Well, I'm closing up now." She moved over to the door and flipped the "Open" sign over.

Even as she did this, the door opened again with almost as much force as it had when the menacing man had opened it. A woman stood in the doorway.

"Mrs Marsh," said Alex stepping back.

"She's home!" said Mrs Marsh. "Oh, dear God, she's home. I wanted to tell you and to thank you. Not just for your help but because you cared, I know you cared."

Mrs Marsh drew a deep breath and looked around herself.

"You're obviously closing up, so I won't disturb you anymore, but I wanted you to know."

The relief flooded through Alex. She felt as if she might float up off the ground.

"Oh, I, oh thank God," she said.

"Well," said Mrs Marsh, "like I said, I won't keep you. She'll be back to youth club soon and if you want to come around before then and see her just give us a call."

And with that she was gone, shutting the café door behind her.

"Well," said Conner, "that's a relief, I know you were worried about–"

Before he got any further, Alex had put her arms around him and burst into tears.

Conner held her and kept silent.

"Oh Jesus," whispered Alex, "Jesus, Jesus, Jesus."

21

———

Lewis knew the game was up when two of his contract staff didn't turn up on Monday morning. They had both come into the office over the weekend and had cleared out all of their personal effects, and now they were gone. On his desk were notes from each of them expressing their regret at having to leave and promising they'd send him an invoice in due course. It was unfortunate to lose one contractor but losing two at the same time sent him a clear message.

He shut his office door and spent an hour on the phone, first to his legal adviser and then to the bank.

Then he asked Martin to join him.

A few minutes later, Martin shuffled in. He had none of the bravado of a few days ago, now he looked as though someone had sucked the life out of him. He reminded Lewis of a Labrador looking up at his master from the vet's table just before the last injection.

"It's about SEEKA, isn't it? Have you had enough then, Lewis?" There was no trace of sarcasm in Martin's tone.

"I have had enough, Martin, yes."

"Do you want my resignation?"

Lewis paused. "No, I don't think so. I have lost enough people today already. If you feel you want to go then that's up to you, but I'd prefer you to stay and help me sort out the work we need to do to close SEEKA down."

There were footsteps outside Lewis' door, and they both looked up to see Dave Somerville shuffle past; he seemed to be caught up in the sombre mood as well. Martin frowned as the old anger flared up inside him again, but he didn't have the will for it, not now.

Martin knew that even he was pleased to see the end of SEEKA now. He had worked hard on the project, and for a while, it had been everything, but now it was over.

"Okay," he said, "I'll stay for now, at least to help you tidy things up."

They talked through the calls they'd need to make, the contracts they needed to terminate. Then they divided the tasks between them, and Martin went back to his office and made a start. It was not a simple process, in some instances, there were contracts with suppliers that would need to run for a period of time. The result was that SEEKA would wither away rather than disappear rapidly. There would soon be no more merchandise, no more club mix releases, no more video content, no more anything. The whole process would take a few weeks but by the end of the summer, SEEKA would be gone.

Even as he worked through the tasks Lewis had given him, Martin knew he had one more job to do, in private. He needed to tell Lench that SEEKA was finished.

It didn't take Martin long to make the necessary calls to contacts and suppliers, and he soon had one last unwritten task on his list.

He made sure his office door was firmly shut then he took out his mobile and laid it on his desk. He was surprised to find that, for once, he was not afraid, not scared of phoning this man. He didn't really have anything to prove to Lench anymore, and maybe he was too tired to care. The whole thing with Lench was probably over now anyway.

"You should never have killed Bridget," he said to himself. He had no idea where that idea had come from, but now that he said it, he knew it was true. It had been Lench's fault, all of it. Learning that he was going to have Bridget killed had been the beginning of the end for Martin, he realized that now.

He picked up his phone and made the call.

"This is Lench." That same clipped English accent.

"Hello, it's me, Martin."

"Ah, Martin, how are you?"

He never ceased to be amazed at Lench's observance of manners on the phone.

"I'm well, thank you. Look, I have some bad news. Lewis has decided to pull SEEKA; the pressure has got too much for him. There's been some comment in the press, and a photo."

"I have seen it as well, Martin."

"He thinks it's me."

"It is you, Martin, in what one might call an unguarded moment."

"Well, yes."

There was silence. He almost dared Lench to be angry with him.

"Martin, I am disappointed to hear this, but I can't say I am surprised. Are you at work at the moment?"

"Yes, I'm helping Lewis to shut down the SEEKA project."

"I'm glad you phoned anyway, Martin, because I wanted to give you a little warning. A friend of mine tells me that the police want to have a very thorough look at SLaM, and the SEEKA project in particular. My advice is this: go through all of the files and other material that you have and remove anything to do with SEEKA. All of it, physical and electronic, get rid of it all. Oh, and one more thing: we won't be meeting in the same place next week. I'll be in touch with you, but don't call me. Goodbye."

The phone went dead, and Martin felt slightly queasy. This was still the man who had arranged for the death of his colleague and lover, the man who might deploy a weapon that could kill him as well – he had no illusions about that.

The word "lover" hovered in his mind. He pictured Bridget as he had often seen her, standing at the window of the SLaM conference room, looking out onto the city, hungry to embrace all of the potential out there, to join the battle and claim the rewards. He had often watched her, observing the tension in her shoulders, a hallmark of her restlessness. He imagined her now, imagined himself looking at the way her clothing stretched across her. Sometimes, if they were alone in the room, he would go close to her and they would exchange a token of the passion they felt for each other, made all the more intense by the need for brevity and discretion.

He took in a deep breath and closed his eyes, indulging himself for a moment.

He pictured her there, in the boardroom, the familiar lines of her body silhouetted against the backdrop of the city view. She was wearing that Yves Saint Laurent cream and navy outfit that she loved. In his fantasy, he crept up behind her, and even though he was silent, she knew he was there, she always knew he was there. He felt again the old eagerness for her. He saw himself put his hand on her shoulder and move closer to her, feeling her with his fingers, even as she turned to him.

"No!"

He jerked back in his chair. The fantasy had turned to nightmare as he found himself staring not at Bridget but at the face of the Assassin, wearing her clothes, with her hair, but devoid of life. The head inclined slightly, the completely lifeless eyes holding his gaze, gripping him like a vice. A scar snaked like an adventure across his cheek. Looking at his eyes was like staring into the moment of death.

It must have been the last thing Bridget had seen.

"Good afternoon," said Lench. "I have a little employment for you."

"A wet job, is it?" said the Assassin.

Lench frowned at the crass phrasing the Assassin always seemed to use about his work.

"So quick to jump to conclusions," he said. "Please, have some patience."

And yet, thought Lench, *there's something refreshing about the Assassin, about his approach to things, the focus, the determination and the desire simply to kill.*

"No blood this time, my friend," he said. "I want you to visit Massey's flat, and I want you to remove everything that incriminates us. Specifically, there's a book I lent him, and I would like that back now. And..."

"It's done."

"I'm sure it will be. Try not make a mess. I do not want the place ransacked. This needs to be executed with the minimum of fuss. Is that clear?"

"Very clear." The line went dead.

The Assassin would do a good job. Lench knew that. He was a man of many talents, of which death was just one, and he would want to make amends for the fiasco with Bridget Larson. It was time to erase all trace of Martin's connection with both the group and Lench himself.

AT THE SAFE HOUSE, the Assassin donned his coat and went out into the heat of the day. He didn't like Martin, and he would have been quite happy to kill him, but he was under orders and just at the moment he needed to behave himself. Things needed to settle down again, he knew that. It wasn't only the blunders involved in killing the woman; it was also his ill-advised trip to the café. Sometimes Lench thought of the Assassin as a brute, a blunt instrument, but he was still aware of the realities of the spiritual battle. He was a man under authority like all the others, even Lench.

He parked the car and approached the flats where Martin lived. He pressed the buzzer for Martin's apartment, and there was no answer. He returned to the car and got out the old disguise he'd used for the Bridget Larson job. Nobody questioned him as he went about his work, and in a rare moment of levity, he decided that if he ever had to give up killing people, he would make a passable window cleaner.

At the right moment, he placed the bucket and sponge behind a bush and put on the surgical gloves. The lock on the door to Martin's flat was a simple affair, and he was soon in. There was an alarm, but Martin hadn't even set it. The Assassin knew he wouldn't have long, but he did not rush. He spent thirty seconds examining the layout of the flat, and then another two minutes looking at the contents and design of each room.

He operated with clinical efficiency, checking all the books, looking through piles of correspondence, checking under the furniture, in the drawers, in the cupboards. It took him over an hour to cover every inch of the flat and in the course of that search, he had found the book that Lench had been so keen to get back, and an address book with Lench's phone number in it. He removed a thin metal blade from a small box in his pocket and cut out the page with the number on it.

Nothing was broken, nothing else was damaged, nothing was stolen beyond the items that were required for the purpose of the job. It was clean and efficient, and the Assassin left with a sense of a job well done. It wasn't a kill, but there was still some satisfaction in it. He left the flat with the alarm off and the door locked, exactly as he found it, and then placed the gloves back in his pocket.

IT WOULD, in fact, be several hours before Martin returned to his flat. He'd spent the day unpicking SEEKA and then clearing out every trace of the project from the SLaM office. Paper reports, computer files and emails, all of it. He didn't know if it was enough, or whether the authorities could still track down the evidence, but he'd done what he could.

He returned home just after eight, exhausted, scared, and completely oblivious to the fact that a killer had been in his home.

22

At eight in the morning, the police arrived.

For over an hour, Martin stayed in his office, watching them come and go, boxes of files disappearing out of the door. He made a few calls, tied up a few more loose ends, and then when he was finished, he walked out into the main office area where he could see his contractor colleagues chatting to each other, huddled around the coffee machine. None of them looked surprised at what was happening, and a few of them were organizing their next assignment. No one would want to stay here after this.

He walked past Lewis' office, where two officers were finishing up and taking the last of what they needed. Lewis looked pale, and Martin was tempted to feel sorry for him; it was a fleeting emotion, and it passed.

Out in the main office space, Dave Somerville was leaning against a wall, coffee in hand, watching the police take the last of their evidence away. There was a smug look on his face as if he wanted to tell all of them that this was exactly what he had predicted; Martin's precious SEEKA project would fall apart, and it looked like it might drag SLaM down with it.

Martin looked at him and felt the old anger, the old intensity rising up inside him again.

Arrogant, cocky, smug...

The words fired in Martin's imagination. Dave didn't care about SEEKA of course; he probably didn't care about SLaM either. The feelings of contempt surged up, making Martin's head throb.

He went over to where Dave was standing.

"Happy now?" he hissed.

Dave turned slowly to him and looked him up and down.

"What are you talking about?" he whispered. "If you think I wanted this, then you're even more of an idiot than I thought you were. Things have gone south here because of you," Dave pointed at Martin's chest with his finger, "and your stupid, stupid scheme."

Another police officer brushed past them on the way to the door. The fact that they kept their voices down injected even more venom into their words.

"You hypocrite," said Martin, "I didn't see you complaining when the first bonus got paid. You had your snout in the trough with everyone else then, didn't you?"

Dave was about to respond when another officer eased between them.

"Gentlemen," he said, and paused, "we have a few questions for you. Is now a convenient time to come down to the station?" He looked from Dave to Martin, and then turned to Lewis who was following him. "With your boss."

"Are you arresting us?" said Martin.

"No, sir, it's just a few questions, but it would be better if we could ask them at the station now rather than later."

There was an uneasy pause.

"Come on," said Dave, "let's get it done."

Lewis came out of his office and had a hurried conversation with the remaining contractors, and they all grabbed their coats and left, then everyone else filed out and Lewis started to shut the office down. Just a few days ago this business, his business, had been humming and busy and alive. He had been working hard and making money, good money. Now it was like a mausoleum.

With a click, he turned off the coffee machine. Then he switched off the lights, set the alarm, and shut the main door with a finality that convinced him he was shutting up shop on SLaM for the last time. Now he needed to focus on damage control.

A long time ago, the directors of SLaM had discussed what they would do in a situation like this; they had contingency plan and they put it into action now. Lewis had his solicitor on speed dial and asked him to meet them at the station.

Lewis' solicitor, Mr de Witt, was a small, slight man, cheerful and nervous in equal measure. He carried a large, bulging briefcase that he held close to himself as if it might defend him from an unexpected attack. He sat in an interview room with Lewis, Dave and Martin, and a nervous smile crept across his face.

"Gentlemen," he said, fiddling with the lock on his case, "gentlemen, I don't think you have any need to be alarmed."

"Really?" said Dave.

"For all their bravado," said de Witt, "the police have nothing to go on except a photocopy of the document the blackmailer sent to them and some conjecture linking that to Ms Larson's murder."

"And it is just conjecture," he added, "There's no evidence to connect Ms Larson's murder to her work, and no original copy of the research document at SLaM's offices. There is nothing I am aware of that connects any of you to Ms Larson on the day of her death. Really, they have nothing."

As if to prove his point, within a couple of hours, they were released and back out on the street.

"We need to have a chat," said Lewis, "all of us." He looked at Martin and Dave and the solicitor.

"You want to go back to the office?" said Dave.

"No," said Lewis, "there's that private room at the Kings Arms on Lacey Street. We've used that in the past. Let's go there." He turned to his solicitor. "You able to spare us another hour or so?"

"Certainly," said de Witt and smiled his cheerful smile.

They all knew the Kings Arms; it had been the venue for a few celebrations in the past, and they'd organized a couple of fairly outrageous parties in that private room during the good times. When they got to the pub, the room was free. Lewis bought a round of drinks and they went up there and closed the door.

"Okay," said Lewis turning to the solicitor, "what's our next move?"

Mr de Witt smiled at them. "I believe that the police want to try and find some connection between the death of your colleague and this new venture of yours – SUKKER, SECKER?"

"SEEKA," said Lewis.

"Yes, of course, but I don't think they've got much else. In fact, I don't think they've got anything else. They can't really tie SEEKA to drug dealing, so legally I don't think you have much to worry about. There will be public relations implications I'm sure, but unless they find something really damning on those computer files or amongst all the papers they've taken within the next few days, I don't think you'll have anything to worry about."

"So we should be able to get back to work soon?" said Dave.

"I think you can reasonably expect the police to return all your files and computer equipment," said Mr de Witt, sipping his gin and tonic, "and then you can get back to business as usual, all will be well." He smiled at each of them.

"Good, I still have a magazine to produce," said Dave. "At least we still have some reason to be in business."

"What do you mean by that?" said Martin.

"I mean that if we had just relied on your SEEKA thing we'd all be out of a job now, wouldn't we?"

"Well," said de Witt, fidgeting a little, "as I was saying, I think in a few days–"

"Yes, and we know why it's all gone wrong, don't we?" said Martin, butting in over de Witt. He stared at Dave.

"It's because you sold us out. You were the one who had the police run their eye over us, you were the one who sent the blackmail threats, and you tipped off the cops. IT'S YOUR FAULT!" Martin was shouting now, and de Witt looked as if he wanted to slide under the table and hide until this was all over.

Dave, though, was unmoved.

"You're a sad case, Martin, you know that?" he said, sipping his beer. "You are so wrong. Okay, so I never much liked SEEKA – a view that I think is well justified now – but I would never have sent our stuff to the police. You need to look somewhere else for your blackmailer's identity because I'm going to tell you one last and final time, it was not me. And if you come at me again with your accusations, I'll–"

"That's enough," said Lewis, "the pair of you, you're upsetting Mr de Witt here, and I'm paying for his time so let's settle down and finish this."

"Yes, well thank you," said de Witt.

"It doesn't matter who did what now anyway," said Lewis, "because SLaM is finished."

Martin and Dave looked like two boxers caught in mid-blow. Their mouths dropped open and they turned to their boss.

"I'm giving you three months' notice, full pay," said Lewis. "I would be grateful if you could collect your personal effects from the office in the next week because after that SLaM will be shutting up shop. We may meet again if the legal circumstances require it, and the company will pay all costs relating to any defence you have to make in this matter."

"You're what?" said Dave. "You're shutting SLaM? Really?"

"Yes, really," said Lewis. "It's over."

He stood up and looked at Martin and Dave.

"Gentlemen, as far as you are concerned, this is the end of SLaM. Goodbye and good luck to both of you. Try not to hit each other on the way out."

With that, he beckoned de Witt to come with him and left the room.

Martin and Dave looked at each other.

"Well, that's that then," said Dave, getting up and following Lewis out as quickly as he could.

MARTIN SAT ALONE with his beer; he took a little satisfaction from seeing Dave leave first, running like a frightened rabbit. But he had more to worry about than his former colleague. He picked up his mobile and dialled Lench's number. It was better to get this over and done with quickly.

He waited for it to ring but there was nothing. Then a sanitized voice told him that the number was not available.

He drank some more of his beer and sat back. Another part of his life had been closed down, and Lench had cut him loose.

But what did that mean? How much of a liability did Lench think Martin was now?

Fear started to creep up his spine, up to the back of his neck as he thought about the Assassin, and what he was capable of. Dave Somerville really was the least of his worries. He would need to be careful now, very careful.

He drained his drink and left.

THAT EVENING, Dave related the events of the morning to his friend Sean. They sat in a quiet corner of a little pub, out in the country away from the bustle and the business of the city. No one could see them or hear them.

Sean was clearly delighted with what he heard. He told Dave it would all make a great follow-up story to the "rural rave" piece that Dave had helped him with, and they might even reuse the picture of Martin looking stunned in the back of the car; it was such a great shot.

"So who was this blackmailer then?" said Sean.

"Don't know," Dave confessed quite truthfully. "Maybe it was Bridget, or one of her friends; she was probably getting her own back from the grave."

"Well, there's no anger like that of a spurned lover," said Sean. "She must have arranged it."

"It certainly wasn't me. I'd have asked for money," said Dave, and they both laughed. Dave drained his glass and counted his blessings. The cheque he had received from Lewis included bonus payments and would cover him till he found something else, and that wouldn't take long. All in all, things had turned out quite well.

MARTIN RETURNED HOME from the meeting at the pub and spent twenty minutes trying to reassure himself that there was no one waiting in his apartment.

Finally, he sat down and tried to decide what to do next. He looked at the address book he kept by the phone. He wanted to check the number he had for Lench, but strangely, it was missing. When he examined the book carefully, he saw that the page had, in fact, been carefully sliced out of the book.

He swore and looked around again. The flat was silent, and his front door was locked.

He immediately started to search the place, looking for anything that might suggest someone had been there. After about ten minutes, he found the clue that confirmed it. The book Lench had lent him, hidden away under some other papers and novels, was gone.

"Oh my God," he said out loud. He went to the curtains and looked out; there was nothing to see, no one watching his place, as far as he could tell.

Martin felt himself slide into panic.

"I must be calm." He was talking to himself now. He got up and wiped his hands on a towel. "I need to get away," he said. "A holiday, that's what I need."

He almost ran into the lounge and started to pull up the corner of the carpet. When the floor was bare, he removed one of the floorboards and reached down to a metal cash box.

With some excitement, now he opened the box and took out some Euro notes, some American dollars, and his passport. It was time for him to get away from it all, take to the air and enjoy the sun.

He grabbed his wallet and his phone and sat down again in the kitchen. It was all he could do to resist looking out of the window again.

He tipped the contents of his wallet onto the table and rummaged around amongst the cards and receipts. Eventually, he found a crumpled bit of paper and spread it out on the table.

His hands were shaking as he picked up the phone and dialled the number. It rang about fifteen times before a distant voice answered.

"George, it's Martin!" he bellowed down the line. "Look, I'm taking you up on your offer; I'm coming over to see you for a few days."

There was a pause. "Marvellous, Martin, be great to see you. I think you have the address, don't you?"

Martin reassured his brother that he did have the address, and then he had to listen as George told him about how much fun they would have out here by the sunny Aegean. Then they were into the final act, which was, as ever the appeal for funds.

"Look, old chap, don't think me funny or anything..."

Martin knew what his brother was going to say and for the first time ever he really didn't mind. George would be earning his money by keeping him far away and safe.

"Hello? Are you still there, Martin?"

"Yes, George. What were you going to say?"

"Oh yes, look don't think me funny or anything but make sure you bring a bit of pocket money with you. To tell you the truth, old boy, I could do with a bit of liquidity, you know, after all the capital outlay here."

Martin smiled and pretended complete incomprehension.

"Hello, George?" he shouted. "I didn't catch that last bit. What did you say?" Then, without waiting for a response, he finished the call and smiled to himself.

The amusement evaporated quickly as he got up and went to find his suitcase.

Lewis sat down at his desk at home and stared at a patch of wall not covered in some SLaM-related merchandise. He had had enough of it all: the contempt, the lies, the ambition, even the money. Somehow, he wasn't in the mood for any of it anymore.

He felt as if some part of him had died, and he'd only just discovered its passing. He tried to examine his feelings, and it all came back, again and again to Bridget.

The police involvement didn't worry him; the law related to encouragement of drug use by corporations was opaque and complex, and SEEKA, for all its brief success, hadn't really made that much of an impact.

No, this was about Bridget. He was able to acknowledge that truth now. Bridget's death had hurt him, and he wasn't surprised at the ache inside him; he still grieved for her.

And he was missing Alex, and those feelings didn't surprise him at all now. She was the only one he had really trusted, the only one who was honest with him. He couldn't say that about anyone in his life now.

He sighed and looked at his desk.

"I can't just sit here and mope," he said at last.

He went and got a Scotch and ice. He downed it and then went and got another one. As he drank it, an idea occurred to him. It was such a ridiculous idea that he laughed out loud.

"No," he said, "that's not going to fly."

"Why not?" he asked himself.

"Come on, really?"

"And why not? Give me one reason, I mean a good reason."

He shook his head, got up, and went to get another drink. But this time he didn't refill his glass. Instead, he came and sat back down, and took out his phone.

He'd had an idea. It was a crazy idea, but he was always having crazy ideas, and he prided himself on backing the most outrageous ones, and this one was right up there with the best of them. The call went to voicemail. He took a deep breath and left a message.

23

Daisy returned to college with a new sense of purpose.

She had had a good summer. Part-time work in Alex's café had enabled her to keep up the rent on her little flat, and she still had some of the inheritance money she'd received left in her account.

Then there was Conner. She didn't know how she felt about Conner, except that he was making her review all of the things she believed and didn't believe. The curious thing was that with other boys she had known, as the relationship developed, it always moved towards the point where she wanted to sleep with them – it was like a mark of the intimacy they had achieved – but with Conner it was different. She had shared with him such personal things, and she felt so close to him, and yet again her thoughts brought her back to the same point: she still wasn't sure how she felt about him.

At college she attacked the early assignments of the term with a purpose and vigour that surprised both her peers and her tutors. Many of the people around her saw the change in her work and speculated that she'd had some kind of transformative experience over the summer. They looked at her designs: the bold contours, the confident use of colour and line, the passion and energy. Her latest assignments stood in stark contrast to the more bewildering material she had generated in the previous year. Now her work showed courage, and a conviction that had been absent before.

A couple of her friends and one of the academic staff took an even closer look at her work and thought hard about what they saw. They agreed that she had indeed improved – there was no doubt about it. But these people looked beyond that improvement because that was only part of the whole story. For those who could discern it, a close examination of Daisy's new designs was an uneasy, disturbing experience.

The style of every line she drew, bold and hard, the stark use of colour and contrast; all these things pointed to a fury deep in her heart, a fierce, quiet battle. She was a better designer, maybe even a better person, but she was still as angry as ever. She started to spend more time on her own, working on her designs, literally wrestling with the demons within her. Conner continued to stay in touch with her, and she chatted with him on social media, but she didn't want to see him. Instead, she wanted to work, and the passion inside her fuelling that work now shone brightly.

Daisy loved the energy she felt, and the purpose and drive within her, but it was also burning her up. Although she tried to ignore what was happening, Daisy was all too aware of how the destructive energy that drove her work had its source in her own personal pain. She was familiar with that pain, of course, she knew it was born out of the old feelings of fear and rejection that were now challenged by a new sense of self-worth. These different versions of who she was and her own intrinsic value were now at war within her, fighting for mastery of her mind.

She felt like a powder keg that was ready to explode.

She resolved to try and dull the pain in the only way she knew how, by going into the heart of the city, to the bars and the clubs, to reach for the drink.

After a month of this, she received an invitation from Conner.

He was having an evening out with the others in the band and some of their mates, and he asked her to come along. One voice in her head wanted to say yes, but the other told her to ignore him. She didn't want to be surrounded by religious people again. Instead, she wanted to go somewhere where she could forget who she was and lose herself.

She wanted to forget about her experiences over the summer. The love of the people she had met, the morality of their faith, all that being nice to each other. Although she was impressed by the idea of a moral code, she wanted to form one for herself, not borrow anyone else's. She wanted to pick and mix her own way of living, not commit herself to a resurrected Saviour who might start to make demands on her.

It would please her to be able to answer Conner's question: who moved the stone? But she didn't want that answer to have consequences she could not control.

Daisy put on her club gear and went out into the city. Her aim was to spend some money, get drunk and have a good time, but even as she left the house and made her way up to the bus stop, she could feel the battle still going on inside her. She pushed it aside and walked on.

Standing at the bus stop, she tried not to feel too self-conscious. Her dress was short, very short, and she wore it with defiance. As she pulled the hem down for the third time, a small part of her wanted to just go home and put her jogging bottoms on and relax in front of the TV...and call Conner.

"Damn Conner!" she whispered under her breath.

She got on the bus and headed into town, glaring at a couple of boys who stared at her as she sat down.

Without her quite realizing what was going on, the old enemies inside Daisy had been busy. In recent weeks, they'd seen a lot of the hard-won gains with their host evaporate as she came into more contact with the Christians in her family. It had been painful for them, to see all their work begin to unravel like this, but now they had started to rebuild, patiently inflaming the old fears, the self-pity, and a deep indefinable sense of being unloved. If they'd had any names at all, they would have been "fear", "self-pity" and "unloved" – a mark of their work.

As the bus rumbled into the centre of the city, Daisy started to feel the old anger again, the old sense of injustice, rising in her. She hadn't felt it for a long time, and she enjoyed the experience now. Everyone had a claim on her, it seemed: the Christians, the boys leering at her, the landlord, the college. Everyone wanted a piece of her, wanted to mould her, own her. But Daisy wasn't for sale; she wasn't anyone's property. She wanted to be herself, and she was going to be herself, tonight.

It was about ten as she got off the bus, and the city was given over to its nightlife. The streets were busy with chatter and lights, the smell of cooked food on street corners, people in pairs or little groups, already drunk, weaving their way to a bar or a club. Nobody here knew her, and nobody cared. It was what she wanted, and somehow exactly what she didn't want as well. She had been up to town plenty of times in the past, but always with others; it didn't seem so good when you were on your own.

She headed for a nightclub and paid her fee. One of the staff tried to chat her up and in an act of defiance against her feelings, she kissed him, hard. His breath stank and she recoiled at the taste of him.

As she went into the club, she could hear the man she had kissed laughing at something one of them had said about her.

Inside, there was the familiar disorientating noise and heat. It was all here, the things she wanted, the opportunity to fall in with a mindless mass of people, none of whom would judge her. She felt her senses slip from their moorings and move with the ebb and flow of the atmosphere. She headed for the bar and bought a very expensive and colourful drink, then surveying the room, with all its heat and music and light, she remembered a conversation she'd had with Conner about a lifestyle that rejected all of the things she thought her parents stood for: climbing up the career ladder, living the consumable life and playing the corporate game. Right now, she wanted to choose another way of living, a way of life that lives for today. She'd once watched a film where one of the characters had talked about consciously deciding on this sort of lifestyle, of rejecting the consumerist rat race and as they put it, "choosing life". Was it that bad? More to the point, was the alternative any better?

She finished her drink and went into the ladies' room where she adjusted her dress and touched up her makeup. At the door of the toilets, she looked out again into the heaving mass of life. She felt as if she were about to dive into a very deep pool and maybe even lose herself in it. So be it, that was what she was here for, that was what she wanted.

She went back out into the heat and joined the crowd.

CALEB WICKS SAT up in bed. He would have sat bolt upright but advancing age and aching joints prevented any sudden movement these days.

"What are you up to now, Daisy?" he whispered. He confessed to himself that he was getting quite irritated with being woken up at all hours to pray for this girl. Next to him, his wife turned over and settled again. Caleb eased his way out of bed and got his dressing gown and wished that the people God laid on his heart would keep sensible hours.

He wandered through to his study and sat down in his chair. He avoided the sofa on these occasions because he'd just fall asleep again.

He settled down and started an elaborate prayer about Daisy, when God cut him off.

"Conner will call you."

"Oh Lord," he continued, "I want to lift up to your care young Daisy."

"Conner will call you. Be ready."

"Okay, okay I get it," he said to himself. It was going to be a long night. He got up slowly and went to put the kettle on.

DAISY HAD BEEN at the club for about an hour: she had bought three drinks, been chatted up very inexpertly by someone who looked like they were about thirteen years old, and now she realized she was both slightly drunk and slightly bored. She was about to go to the bar to see if they had something else imaginative, she could try, when she heard two clear words spoken through all of the chaos.

"Hey, Daisy!"

For a moment she thought she'd heard Will calling her, and she turned quickly to see who had called out her name.

She scanned the crowd, telling herself it could not have been Will, and indeed it might not have been anyone at all; she might have simply misheard. Then, in the half-light, she saw Conner.

Her brain registered it was him but because she was seeing him completely out of context, she couldn't bring herself to believe it.

He waved and came over to her.

"Fancy meeting you here," he said. "You should have come with us after all. Are you here with anyone?"

"No." She felt ridiculously pleased to see him. "Do you want to buy me a drink?"

She followed him to the bar and as he ordered something, he said, "Come and meet some of the guys from the band."

"Well, I don't know, I mean I'm sure you're busy."

"Daisy," he said, and he looked at her.

She grabbed her drink and he led her over to a corner of the club where a group of about ten people, guys and girls, were clustered around a table. Conner introduced her to them all and sat her next to one of the girls in the group who was also studying fashion and design. They managed to exchange a few words over the noise of the music.

Later, they all danced together, and Daisy felt the hard corners of her heart begin to soften. One of them came out to the beer garden with her for a smoke, none of them commented on what she wore, or what she drank or what she said. She felt like she belonged, and she enjoyed it, she really enjoyed it.

Later, the music mellowed out and if anything, she had an even stronger desire to stay with these people, to be with them – especially with Conner. And without thinking twice about it, she asked him to come back with her to her flat.

"I'm not sure that would be such a good idea, do you?" he said.

"Please, Conner, I need to talk to you, and I need someone to make sure I get home safely."

He looked at her and smiled. He knew he would say yes to almost anything she asked, and he said yes now.

The taxi took them through the darkness of the early hours. They both sat at the back and she put a hand out, and took his. This should have felt good; it should have been a moment of enjoyment, excitement, even passion. Instead, the restlessness she'd felt before, the conflict in her, was right there in her again, and worse than before, like a ball of acid turning over and over in her gut.

She held Conner's hand and watched the street lights pass by as they headed back to her flat.

Why do I feel like this? What is happening to me? She asked herself these questions, and the answers came whispering back to her: *I'm afraid. I'm full of self-pity. I'm unloved.* She didn't even know where the words came from; except that they had always existed, deep in her heart, woven into her being, part of the fabric of Daisy Masters.

The taxi pulled up outside her flat and they got out. Maybe being in her own flat would put her more at ease, but it didn't work. She wanted Conner there and she wanted him gone, she wanted his help and she wanted to push him away.

She thought about the things he'd once said, about her being possessed by demons, not that he'd used that language but that's what he'd meant. She didn't want to believe he was anything close to right. She didn't want to believe that the reason for her torment was more than just something in her mind.

Still, there was that small voice in her head, asking her questions. *What if it was true? What if it was even slightly true?*

And now they were together again, and she knew she wanted to deal with this. She wanted to face this spiritual stuff, and resolve it one way or another, simply so she could be done with it and get on with her life.

She let him come in and then she shut the door.

"Conner." Her voice sounded light and reedy to her.

"Yes?"

"I want to find out whether I'm possessed or not. I want you to do an exorcism on me."

"I don't think the term 'possession' is very helpful," he said. "It's not something I'd say."

"Look, whatever," she said. "I don't care about the semantics, Conner, I want this sorted out."

"Why do you think you're...like this?"

"I've spent evenings thinking about what you said, whatever you called it, and I keep trying to tell myself it's a load of rubbish and maybe it is, but it won't go away, Conner – the pain, in my head, the battle, it won't go away. Maybe I just need some counselling or psychotherapy, but I might need this as well."

"I think a good counsellor or psychotherapist would be really helpful for you, whatever else is troubling you," said Conner.

"Yeah, maybe," she said, "but let's try this first."

She coughed and turned from him, going into the kitchen.

CONNER DIDN'T KNOW what to think. This had taken him completely by surprise. One minute he'd been thinking about how he was going to resist the temptation to get cosy with Daisy, and now here she was talking about demons and exorcisms. In his mind, he whispered the best prayer in the world.

"Lord, help!"

Then in his imagination, he saw an image of old Mr Wicks, a regular visitor to their house after Alex had arrived. The whole family had become close to him, and Alex and he had often talked about him. He just hoped he had the number on his phone.

And there it was.

"Thank you, God!"

He walked into the kitchen where Daisy was putting the kettle on.

"Okay," he said, "we'll do this thing. But I'm going to get a bit of help. You know Caleb Wicks? I'm going to get him."

He looked at Daisy. She stood pale and withdrawn, the little dress she was wearing seemed garish and out of place under the strip light in her kitchen.

"Just do what you need to do, Conner." Her voice was a whisper.

He looked at the clock; it was twenty to one in the morning.

"Maybe," he said, "we could perhaps deal with this tomorrow? You know, like when it's not after midnight."

She looked at him, wide-eyed and pale, and he could see that she was shivering.

"We'll do it now," he said.

The phone rang and rang, and he cringed as he heard it, knowing he was calling at a hideous time for these old guys.

"Hello." It was Mr Wicks, and he almost sounded as if he was expecting the call.

"Hello, Caleb, it's Conner here. Look, I'm really, really sorry to call you at this time, and there's no emergency or anything, but," he looked at Daisy, "well, it's a bit of an emergency actually. It's about Daisy. You remember Daisy?"

"Of course I remember Daisy," said Caleb, "and to tell you the truth, I have been expecting your call."

"You have?"

"Yes, now why don't you tell me what the problem is."

Conner gave a quick outline of what had happened.

"I see," said Caleb, "so tell me where you are."

Conner gave him the address.

"Okay, now stay there with her. Olive and I–"

"Is that Mrs Wicks?" said Conner. "Is she coming too?"

"Of course she is. We're dealing with a young lady here, so Olive will be in charge for this session. Now stay there and relax. We will be with you in about forty minutes." The phone clicked off.

***

DAISY WATCHED IT ALL, feeling the pressure inside her beginning to build. She could feel it deep within herself, and she suspected that "it" was them, and for the first time she was so frightened that while Conner wasn't looking, she whispered a word for the first time in a new way.

"Jesus."

Deep within her, the spirits struggled and writhed. This was a disaster for them, a moment of crisis. They knew much better than Daisy could ever guess what was coming.

While Conner sat at the kitchen table, Daisy went into her room and got changed. She peeled off the dress and put her tee shirt and jogging pants on, and then she sat on the bed and tucked her knees under her chin. Something was inside her; she knew it now. She could feel the damned thing in there. She thought back over the last few months and the circumstances that had brought her to this point. It was as if the whole "Jesus" thing, once so distant and far away had gradually sneaked up on her, and the whole circus – angels and demons, Jesus and the devil, the whole lot of it – was about to come to the surface.

She heard Conner knock on the door of her room.

"Come in," she said.

"You want some tea?"

"Coffee," she said. "Strong, black."

There was something inside Daisy, jabbering at her, she could practically hear it, telling her that Conner was a threat, that he didn't love her, that he felt contempt for her and her crazy lifestyle and messed up head.

She got up off the bed, grabbed her cigarettes and went to the window. Pushing it open, she leant out and lit up one she'd rolled earlier that evening. She sucked furiously on the tobacco and breathed the smoke out into the warm calm air.

Conner came in with a mug and put it on the bedside cabinet.

When she was done, she leant back in and shut the window. She felt sick now, and she started to shiver again. She sat on the bed and called out.

"Conner!"

He appeared at the door.

"Come and hold me." She picked up her mug, slopping some of the coffee onto the edge of her duvet. She sipped at it and put it down.

He came and sat next to her on the bed and put his arms around her, and they sat like that, waiting, shivering, and listening to the quiet sounds of the night and the faint tick, tick of the clock in the kitchen.

As the minutes passed, her grip tightened on him.

Then the doorbell rang.

They both jumped at the sound, and he went to the door and opened it.

Daisy felt her stomach starting to churn; the coffee was sharp and bitter in her throat. She closed her eyes and whispered again the name of a Saviour that she did not believe in.

CALEB and Olive Wicks came into the flat like a calm breeze across the battlefield. They looked as unhurried as they ever did. Olive opened her handbag and took out a small, sealed tub of milk, which she placed on the draining board next to the fridge.

"What's that for?" said Conner, frowning.

"It's milk, dear," said Olive. "We'll have a nice cup of tea when this is all finished."

They had evidently been in bed asleep before Conner had called them. Caleb was still in his pyjama top with an overcoat and trilby hat, and Olive had a coat over her quilted dressing gown. Conner thought they looked like a mad couple from some kind of sitcom, and he almost laughed despite the situation.

"Where is she?" said Caleb. "In the bedroom?"

"Yes," said Conner, "just through there."

When Caleb and Olive walked into Daisy's room, Conner hung back in the doorway.

"Just get on with it, please," said Daisy.

"Come here, Conner," said Caleb, calling him away. He took off his trilby and Olive put down her bag, and they both looked at Daisy. Daisy started to fidget, and looking at her, Olive said:

"In the name of Jesus, be silent!"

There was silence.

"Now Daisy," continued Mrs Wicks, "please listen to me. I am going to try to find out whether there are any demons in you, and then I am going to tell them to go in the power of Jesus. Do you understand that?"

She nodded.

"And are you happy for me to do that?"

Daisy nodded again. "Just get it done," she said.

One might have expected a Hollywood-style deliverance scene, with special effects, lots of growling and the poor clergyman pinned to the wall by some supernatural force, clutching his Bible in an act of self-defence. But in the end, there was very little fuss. One by one, Mrs Wicks told each of them to name themselves, and since she was acting in the power of Jesus, they had to do just that. One by one, she told them to go in the name of Jesus, and so they did; unravelling from Daisy, reluctantly unweaving themselves from her, restoring her to the freedom and dignity she had lived without for so long.

Then came the peace. To Conner it felt as if the room, the whole flat was like a different place, like there was a great ocean of calm and silence that had been waiting to fill this place, and now it could.

"Right, then," said Caleb, "shall I put the kettle on?"

He was humming to himself as he opened cupboards and found some mugs and rinsed them out. Olive suggested that both Daisy and Conner come back and stay with them for the night. Daisy could go in the spare room and Conner could sleep on the sofa. Daisy simply nodded and so Conner said yes as well.

They drank some tea, and Daisy went to her room with Olive to collect some clothes, her toothbrush and her house keys. Conner wandered into the kitchen where Caleb Wicks was drying the cups with a rather tatty old tea towel, he smiled at Conner.

"Well, what an evening, Conner. I expect we shall all sleep soundly after this."

Conner looked at him, wide-eyed. "I want to be able to do that," he said.

Caleb raised an eyebrow. "What, dry cups? Don't they teach you young people anything these days?"

"No!" said Conner. "You know what I'm talking about. The deliverance thing, I want to be able to do that."

"Really?" said Caleb, placing the last mug on the kitchen table. "So am I to understand that God called you to that ministry?" He looked over his glasses at Conner.

"Well, I don't know," said Conner, "but I'd like to be able to do it."

"Tell me, Conner," said Caleb, running his hand through greying wisps of hair, "are you doing all that you can do at the moment to help those in need, to love the poor, the homeless, to show Jesus' compassion to those who are suffering?"

"Err," he said, "well, I've helped Daisy tonight."

"Yes, that was a good job." Caleb nodded. "But what about helping out at church, and seeing what you can do to support others in your community?"

Conner stared at him, uncertain how to respond.

"My dear Conner," Caleb reached out and placed his hand on the boy's shoulder, "do the simple things first," he said. "Do what's in front of you. Love the Lord and those around you. If you're called to this, you'll know, but for now," he put the last of the mugs away, "love your neighbour as yourself; it's really that simple."

And with that, he smiled and closed the cupboard door.

"Yeah, okay," said Conner, again unsure how to respond, and feeling slightly foolish.

"And let's start," said Caleb, "by loving Daisy and looking after her, shall we?"

"Sure," said Conner.

Olive appeared with Daisy at her side.

"Are you ready then?"

"I think so," said Caleb. "Come on then, Conner, let's be going now, shall we?" He picked up his trilby and they went out into the chill of the very early morning.

In the car, Daisy curled up on the back seat next to Conner. She looked exhausted, but more than that, she looked unburdened, free.

24

———————

Martin Massey was in an almost hysterical state as he threw some clothes into a case.

Every five minutes, he had to stop what he was doing to calm himself down and reassure himself that the Assassin was not hiding behind the curtain, or about to burst through the door. When he eventually finished, he sat on the side of his bed and surveyed the room. The answering machine light caught his attention. He had received eight calls, but he did not listen to any of them.

The Assassin had been here. He had thumbed through his belongings. His possessions had all been touched, defiled. That man, who was capable of cold clinical murder, had proved that he could come into Martin's apartment whenever he wanted to.

He let out a long sigh. It was definitely time to leave, time to put this place behind him for a while. But now the time had come, now he was running away from his own flat, he found himself hesitating, dithering. He felt as if something precious was slipping away, like he had sacrificed something important, scurrying away as he was, fearful for his life.

"Rational, I have to be rational," he whispered.

He picked up his bag, went out into the hallway and opened the front door, peering out into the lobby.

"If," he said to himself, "if Lench wanted me dead, that maniac would have done it by now."

He thought this was almost certainly true, and with that crumb of comfort, he set the alarm, picked up his bag, and walked out of the apartment. He shut the door with a final, resounding thud, and locked the place up. The alarm whined for a few seconds and then stopped.

The thought that if he were going to die he would already be dead got him to the car park. He packed the bag in the boot and then he got in the car, fidgeted in the seat, and then, for no firm reason, he got out, and went back to the flat for one final check. Something in his mind told him it was a foolish thing to do. It was time to go, and at this rate, he might even contrive to miss his plane.

He turned off the alarm and looked around the place one last time. He felt as though he was looking into a stranger's home. He checked the kitchen: everything was switched off. He looked in the drawers of his desk: he had left nothing of value. Finally, he pulled back the curtain and looked down onto the road below. It was meant to be the completion of the ritual.

And there he was, an outline, a man standing outside on the pavement, talking on a mobile phone. It didn't look like the Assassin, but he couldn't be sure. Suddenly, fear gave him clammy hands and left him breathless.

He finished locking the flat and then, instead of walking out of the front door, he climbed out of one of the windows in his bedroom, letting slip a muffled curse as he banged his shin on the windowsill and landing in the shrubbery of the communal garden. His shoes sank into the mud from the recent rain. He could see the figure more clearly now. It was a tall, thin young man with long hair, a stranger, nothing like the Assassin at all.

Martin walked around the building to the car park, scampered back to his car, unlocked it and climbed in. He now wished he'd gone to the bathroom before he'd left, but it was too late. He started the car and pulled away, narrowly missing some of the other vehicles around him. The man who had been speaking on the phone completely ignored him.

He took a deep breath, trying to rid himself of the useless energy the adrenaline had created. He glanced at the on-board clock and made a mental calculation; it was eight minutes before eight o'clock. He'd managed to buy a ticket for a flight that was leaving at ten forty; if he wanted to give himself an hour to check in, this was going to have to be a fast journey.

He was just turning on some music when his vision was enveloped in white light. He slammed on the brakes and swerved. The car jolted onto the pavement and stopped. Optic nerves continued to fire and shapes from the car and windscreen started to float in his vision.

"What the...?" he shouted, squinting out of the window into the evening darkness.

He could hear footsteps running away from the car, and his mind went back to the intrusive flash photography that had captured him on the night of the rave. Was this another reporter? Would he see his face in the papers again?

"The hell with it," he muttered, forcing the car back into gear. He told himself he didn't care. He was going away, going abroad, and disappearing for a while. The whole lot of them from Lewis to Lench, from the police to the Assassin, all of them would forget about him soon enough.

He bumped the car down from the pavement and sped off towards the main road.

He parked in the long-stay car park at the airport, having booked himself six weeks there. He'd extend that stay if he needed to, although he thought six weeks with his brother would be more than long enough, whatever was happening back here at home.

He checked his baggage, bought some more euros at the bureau de change and waited in a café with a paper in his hand and his back to the wall.

He had his mouth full of pastry when his mobile went off. He chewed frantically and then swallowed hard, spitting crumbs as he answered the phone.

"Hello?"

"Hello, Martin."

It was Lench.

Lench, as smooth as ever, but sounding somewhat distant. Somewhere near Martin, the PA announced the final call for a departure to Rome.

"Martin, you sound like you're at an airport. Going anywhere nice?"

He had to resist the temptation to just switch the phone off. "I thought I would get away for a few days, you know" he said, swallowing the last of his pastry.

"What an excellent idea. Well, I will come to the point because I don't want you to miss your flight. The end of SEEKA means the end of you as far as the group is concerned, although I think you probably guessed that. I have had to make some arrangements to ensure there is no evidence of any connection between you and either the group or myself. You have been something of a disappointment to me, Martin."

Martin was silent, with the phone pressed to his ear. He felt like a small boy being told off by the headmaster, but some of the old defiance was rising again; he was tired of Lench taking this high-handed tone with him.

"Are you still there?" he said.

"Yes, I'm here," he said.

"Listen to me, Martin, our association is over, finished. The fact that you are running away tells me you know this, and you are afraid. That's good. But don't worry, Martin. I won't be sending our friend after you; I won't even come after you when you come back. In return, of course, I need to be assured of your complete discretion. If I find you have tried to damage either the group or me with some foolish accusation, I shall be forced to take action. Is that clear?"

Martin really wanted to bite back. He really wanted to tell Lench what he thought of him: that he was a damn fool to have had Bridget killed; that his stupid assassin had botched it and caused more harm than Martin ever had; that in the end he had had to do everything himself and all Lench had done had been to make demands on him. He wanted to tell Lench that he was in no position to make threats.

Lench continued: "Martin, it's not like you to be so silent, but perhaps you have a lot on your mind. I think we can safely say that this is the last time we will be speaking. Remember one thing, you belonged to the group once and in a sense, nobody leaves the group. You are one of us now and you always will be, so do be careful. Do you understand? Martin, are you there?"

Martin didn't care now because he'd had enough. Check-in would be opening in eight minutes.

"Just be careful yourself, Lench. You are the one who has made the mistakes – you still might have to pay for them." He switched off his phone before Lench could answer. He was amazed at his own bravado and it was a sweet moment amongst all the bitterness.

The ten forty flight for Athens left on time. Martin tried to look forward to the life he might be able to lead out there. Perhaps it was a good idea to be heading out into the sun as the autumn approached, and he did like Greek food, and perhaps some of the girls would find an Englishman intriguing. He bought a Greek phrasebook in the duty-free and made his way to the gate. Perhaps this wouldn't be such a bad experience after all.

———

Lench sighed and dropped his phone onto the table. This fool, this insolent pup had managed to have the last word. He cursed under his breath. The Assassin sat opposite him, frowning, agitated.

The pair of them had spent the last hour going through all of the implications of what had happened. It was probably more accurate to say that he had led the Assassin by the nose, metaphorically speaking, through the implications. Now he needed to work out the limits of his liabilities before he tried to close off this whole sorry affair.

Of course, the sum of the whole thing was failure, and the consequences of failure were ignominy and punishment. In the last few months, they had both failed and would share in the disgrace. The Assassin had been punished for his mistakes with the murder of Bridget. Lench's turn would come soon, and when that time came, his civility and refined tone would count for nothing, he would have to answer for his folly as everyone did in the end.

The imperative now was to see all of the liabilities dealt with. First, there was the issue of this woman, Alex Masters. Perhaps something could be done with her to compensate for what had happened. Recently, he had started to think very seriously about having her removed. It was a dangerous proposition, and he had the feeling there was something he was overlooking, but she was still a threat. She represented a danger to him and all he stood for because she was a hungry Christian, a Christian with a purpose and some integrity. She had too many qualities to be placed in the little boxes he and others like him had prepared over the years. She was too passionate to be ground down into going through the motions of her faith, too strong to be passed off as a weak and feeble invalid, too full of compassion to be castigated as a hypocrite. She led the normal Christian life and demonstrated that such a life was credible. To Lench, she was poison.

Then he thought about the girl that had been with Alex Masters during their fateful encounter, a feisty young thing she had been. He only wished he had encountered her in different circumstances; he'd have soon brought her into line.

He certainly didn't want to visit this woman Alex Masters at her flat again. An encounter with that officious traffic warden or one of her kind was not on his list of desirable outcomes.

Which reminded him, he still needed to pay the damn ticket she'd slapped on his car when he'd last visited.

He thought about the ticket for a moment, and then something like a lump of cold and bitter fear dropped into the pit of his stomach.

The ticket.

If he tried to remedy this situation, the parking ticket would tie him to the car park, outside that flat where Alex lived. The traffic warden might recognize him again. And he had hit that girl; he had hit her in front of two witnesses. He had not thought through the scenario in this context before, but now that he did, a vast black hole began to open up beneath him. What if they had gone to the police? What if either of these women were killed and the police followed the trail back to him?

Then there was the Assassin. The man who had gone into Alex Masters' café and caused a disturbance, the man who had allowed a variety of people to see his scared face. A man now implicated just as much as Lench.

Whether he liked it or not, whether he desired it or not, he could not risk another direct attack on Alex Masters, or anyone associated with her. It wasn't just the foolish risks they'd already taken, there was also a spiritual dimension to this matter; he could sense that both he and the Assassin were barred, restrained from harming this woman. The Assassin might scoff at that idea but Lench knew all too well the power of spiritual forces, working for and against their purposes. Finally, there was the issue of Martin and SEEKA. In a way, this was the most straightforward aspect of the whole thing. Martin was gone and good riddance to him. So long as he kept his mouth shut, which Lench was confident he would, then that would be the end of it. If there was any flak from SEEKA it would hit SLaM, and possibly Martin as a senior employee, but it would go no further than that.

It was obvious now that the woman Bridget Larson was the most likely source of the blackmail attempts Martin had talked about. She had probably spent the morning before she was killed gathering the material she needed to strike at Martin. If only the Assassin had been able to get to her earlier. It took Lench a moment to remember why the Assassin hadn't finished the job as soon as Bridget had arrived home. Someone from the gas company had been there with her; that one coincidence had derailed the whole plan. Lench cursed under his breath.

"So what are we going to do now?" said the Assassin, twitching with agitation. He reminded Lench of a barely trained animal, straining to revert back to its own base instincts.

"Do? We are not going to do anything. It's done, finished."

"What do you mean there's nothing we can do? I will kill the woman, Alex Masters, and in due time, the other one if you want me to." He spoke the words as if they were an irresistible statement of fact.

"No!" said Lench. "It's too dangerous, for both of us. Haven't you been listening to what I've said? We have both been fools with her and her friend, and we must pay the price for it." Then he added, "They are protected."

The Assassin snorted and removed a long thin-bladed knife from one of his boots. "What protection does she have? None!" Lench watched the figure in front of him straining against the imposition of discipline. There were occasions when the Assassin needed a firm hand.

"Don't parade your weaponry in front of me," he hissed. "I'm telling you, she is protected."

He repeated the words again, more quietly this time, but with no less conviction. There was silence except for the tick of the carriage clock on his desk. Lench leant forward across the desk, fixing the Assassin with his gaze.

"If she is not protected, why did you run from her presence?"

"I did not run, I made a decision to–"

Lench slammed a fist onto the table.

"You ran," he shouted, "you ran. And so you should. This is not just a fight with blood and bones. You know this! You ran because there was nothing else you could do but flee from that place."

"I can go back," said the Assassin.

"No, you can't," said Lench, "because if you do, you will fail, and in the process, you'll attract even more attention to yourself. Think. Think about this situation."

The Assassin was silent. He rocked back and forth on his chair, and then he slid the knife carefully back into its sheath in his boot. Then without further comment, he rose from the chair and left the room.

Alone in his study, Lench surveyed the situation. No doubt SEEKA had been a useful exercise while it lasted. But that had been just consolation in the light of the other things that had happened. It was only now, when it was far too late, he realized that while SEEKA had been a tactical victory, the other side had been playing the game on an altogether different level. They had managed to put people in the right places. This was a strategy, a long-term strategy, not just a tactical move. Was it possible that Alex Masters and the others were going to achieve things that would make SEEKA seem paltry and insignificant by comparison?

For the first time in years, Lench tasted real, nauseating, fear.

25

————

Daisy spent the rest of the night in deep peaceful sleep. For the first time in her life, she felt neither the condemnation of others nor the need to fight against that condemnation. She was free.

When she woke, she began to recall the events of the previous night, as if they had happened to someone else. Maybe she was someone else now, certainly, a burden so profound that it had almost become a part of her was now lifted. Some oppression, weighing her down for years, had been taken away. The Christians around her had done their thing, and by her definition rather than theirs, she was no longer possessed, she was free.

Even waking up felt different. Before today, she had been called awake by a brutal voice, challenging her to do something to justify herself that day, weighing her in the balance and finding her wanting, condemning her because there was nothing she could do to change the situation she was in. It was a revelation to her now that up to this point in her life she had been condemned, even before she had got out of bed.

This morning, there was no voice, no judgement. There was nothing to fear, and the pain from the lack of love was gone, its power shattered by the actions of these two old guys who seemed to have no other motive than a concern for her welfare. Not forgetting Conner, the boy who had treated her with kindness and dignity.

She got out of the bed and thought about Conner. His love had driven him to take all sorts of risks with her. She knew he found her attractive – he was real in that sense – but it was an indication of the strength of his love that he had not taken advantage of her in any way. There had been no bullying, no psychological pressure, no denigration of her.

Grabbing her dressing gown, she left the bedroom and walked down the stairs. In the silence, she could make out the sound of snoring coming from the living room. Daisy pushed open the door and looked in.

Conner was lying on the sofa, sprawled across the cushions, his left leg dangling in mid-air. He seemed to bring his own sense of disorganization to everything he did, even sleeping. She glanced at the clock on the wall. It was just after eight fifteen. Quietly, she shut the door again. In the kitchen, she could hear someone moving around, and the sound of a kettle boiling. Olive emerged and smiled at her.

"Ah Daisy, come and sit in the sun lounge with me, dear, and we'll have some tea."

It seemed to Daisy that these people were in the same league as Miss Goldsworth when it came to making tea, as if a hot drink could solve most of the world's problems.

Daisy nodded and walked through to the little conservatory at the back of the house. She could already feel the warmth of the early morning sun.

This room, even more than the others in the Wicks' house, seemed to radiate a sense of peace. If she believed in holiness, she would say that it dwelt here, a room that looked out onto the back garden of the Wicks' suburban home.

Olive came in with some tea and placed it on a little table near to where Daisy was sitting. Stacked under the table, Daisy could see back copies of a magazine her mother used to read. A brightly coloured jumper lay half knitted in amongst some balls of wool on the floor.

"I call this hour of the day my quiet time" said Olive, as she poured some tea and picked up the bundle of knitting by the side of her chair. "I find it's a good time to think about things. There's no noise, no distractions. I expect we will be able to sit here for a while before the men disturb us." Her language reminded Daisy, of a rather elderly great-aunt she remembered from when she was a very small child.

That old lady had often referred to male company as "the men", and always called her husband by his surname when refer-ring to him in front of others. Olive leant forward in conspiratorial fashion:

"You see, dear, Caleb isn't much of an early riser and an expe-dition across the city at one o'clock in the morning is quite reason enough for him to have a lie-in. And as for young Conner, well I think you have looked in on him already. I don't think we'll be seeing much life there for a while yet." The knitting needles started to click erratically.

The silence descended again, and Daisy tried to describe how she felt – the sense of release, the lightness of a burden lifted – but she couldn't find the words. The sun continued to shine into the conservatory where they were sitting, giving a gentle warmth. In the garden, she could see the carefully tended roses, and a clematis climbing across a fence. Somehow the flowers and shrubs had an air of "aliveness" about them, a quality of texture, colour and vibrancy she had never noticed before; she could not think of a better word to describe it.

"How are you feeling today, anyway?" said Olive.

Daisy thought about the question before answering. "Relaxed and confused." She wondered if they all expected her to suddenly "see the light" and get religion. These people had given her back her life, she could feel it inside her, and they deserved her respect, but she still didn't know what she believed about anything.

The knitting needles continued to click.

"By the way," said Olive, "Caleb and I have no expectations of you now, if that's concerning you."

"You don't?" Daisy's reply betrayed her surprise. *Could this woman read her mind?*

"Oh no, dear! We have done what we were required to do. We have helped to release you from something that should never have had a hold on you, and now we will give you some breakfast and send you on your way. What we don't do is make the choices for you that you need to make for yourself. That would not make us much better than the things that bound you."

The needles continued as if the old lady had decided that whatever else happened she was going to get this jumper finished.

"I think Conner will expect something from you now though," she said, "but you should not worry too much about him. He is still young, isn't he? Bless him."

Daisy nodded, and then she looked out of the window again and studied the flowers. There was something out there, in the garden, some truth represented in the colour and life there. She did believe there had been something in her, she didn't know what, and now she felt in herself that it was gone, in fact, they had gone. She looked out at the garden again and she thought she heard something, a voice, a song.

Daisy frowned. A song? What song was she likely to hear in this garden?

There was a voice, a silent voice, speaking to her:

"Come into the garden and hear my song."

But all she could hear was the click of the knitting needles.

She got up from the chair and looked out of the window.

The knitting stopped for a moment. "Would you like to see the garden? It's looking splendid at the moment."

"Yes please."

Olive unlocked the conservatory door and Daisy walked out into the sunlight. She stepped forward a few paces and stood amongst the flowers and looked at the scene around her. The colours seemed to have such an intensity that her eyes watered. She closed her eyes, and the voice came again.

"This is my song, my song of love to you Daisy, my beloved,
For the winter is past, the rains are over and gone.
Flowers appear on the earth; the season of singing has come."

A sense of love surrounded and enfolded her. She felt the focus of an energy, a person. She couldn't tell whether the tears in her eyes were from the brightness of the sharp colours or from the sense of acceptance she now felt.

And there was more. She knew with a certainty and clarity that she was loved. And she believed this fact with such a deep and profound sense of realization that she could feel it changing her. This was not a development over months; this was instantaneous and absolute. Love was there in that garden with her. Personal and intimate, closer than anything else she had ever experienced, far removed and far more profound than the physical contact she had received from the variety of sexual engagements she'd had. Her experience of sex had been her primary frame of reference for finding the love that had been absent from her life, until now.

Now she was experiencing something else, and the comparison was, in fact, no comparison at all. This was a completely different kind of intimacy. If she had been loved in her own home by her parents, she might have been better equipped to quantify the experience, but all she could do was marvel at the scale and newness of the love and acceptance that she now felt.

Olive continued with her knitting, glancing up occasionally to see Daisy walking in the garden. She whispered prayers of love and encouragement as the knitting needles continued to click.

The door from the house opened and Conner walked in. He was still half asleep as he wandered into the conservatory, rubbing his eyes.

"Hello, Conner." Olive smiled at him; he looked a complete mess.

"Hi, is that Daisy out there?"

"Yes, she's just having a few moments in the garden."

Conner looked out at Daisy who was now standing perfectly still.

"I think you might want to put on some clothes before you go too much further, dear," said Olive.

Conner realized that all he had on was a tee shirt and some boxer shorts.

"Oh yeah, sure." He turned around and wandered back to the lounge where his clothes were scattered across the floor.

He pulled on his trousers, flopped onto the sofa and, out of habit, checked his texts and emails.

He was still surfing the web when there was a knock at the door, and Daisy came in with a cup of tea.

"Mrs W thought you might want some tea," said Daisy.

"These guys survive on tea," said Conner. "I think it makes their world go round."

She smiled at him.

"So how are you today?" he said.

"I'm fine. A bit tired, you know."

"We did have a bit of a night of it."

"Yes, we did," she said.

"Well," said Conner, "hopefully they can give us some break-fast, I'm starving."

"Mrs W is in the kitchen rustling something up."

"Excellent!" Conner stood up and pushed his phone into his pocket.

"Look," said Daisy, "I just wanted to say thank you to you. You've been the anchor through all this for me, you and Alex, so, thanks."

He smiled at her. "You're more than welcome," he said, and she put her arms around him and hugged him, and after a moment he hugged her back; they held each other, tight in the silence for several long seconds.

"That's better," she said finally. "Come on, let's get some breakfast."

LATER THAT MORNING, Daisy and Conner walked down to the station together. Going back on the train had been their choice. Daisy hadn't wanted the Wickses to miss going to church if they wanted to go.

The other thing she wanted was a chance to talk to her friend.

"Conner."

"Yep?"

"We need to talk."

She took his hand. It was the most affectionate thing that had happened between them.

"The thing is, it's true to say that something has happened to me. I don't know what it is, but I know it's real, and it's significant."

"That's good," said Conner.

"But it doesn't mean I know what I believe now."

"Okay," he said.

"What I do know is that I am loved and accepted; it's like a huge weight that was on my shoulders has gone. But in some ways, it's raised more questions than answers."

"I'm not making any assumptions about what you think or believe, or what you want," he said. "It's okay for you to do your thing, you know?"

She carried on, trying to articulate the thing she most wanted to say.

"And I don't know what I think about us."

They released hands and he turned to her. "Look, Daisy, you've been through a traumatic time, having a bunch of demons untangled from you. That's pretty heavy stuff. Take your time and see how things go for you."

"I will," she said, "and please stick around, you know, as a friend."

"Sure," he said, "it really is okay." He took her in his arms, and they embraced again, standing by the side of the road. The intermittent Sunday traffic passed them by, and together they found out a little more about the love they now shared.

26

It DIDN'T TAKE Alex long to work out that the café would not be enough.

She thought it would keep her occupied but soon enough the old restlessness crept in, that hunger to make a bigger difference, to engage with the culture more directly across all of its manifestations: music, art, literature, film, social media, even fashion and food.

Every idea seemed crazy; every thought impractical. She wanted it all, and it was all too much. But Alex wasn't interested in giving up, in hearing that her vision was too much. After all, no one thought she could run a café and yet here it was.

It was on a typical day when typical thoughts like these were running through her head that she came home from a shift and found a message on her answerphone, from Lewis.

She was surprised at how pleased she was to hear from him, they'd had no contact since he'd told her about what had happened to Bridget.

She listened to the message twice to make sure she had the gist of it right.

.   .   .

"ALEX, it's Lewis here. I hope all is going well for you. Listen, I've got an offer to make you. It's going to sound pretty strange but I'm just going to come out and say it. I'm closing SLaM down, shutting up shop. After everything that's happened, I can't carry on. But the thing is there's still some value in the company. It's going to take me six months to work off our notice on the office rent. You might as well have the place during that time, if you want it. We have all these printers and servers, and the studio and mixing equipment, all of the licences and software we got for the social media projects – anyway, you know what we had. I know you've always dreamed of doing a Christian version of this stuff, and frankly, I don't want it anymore, so I want to give it to you. I don't need it, and you might as well put it to good use, if you want to. Give me a call sometime soon and we'll discuss it, yes? Okay, call me soon, thanks, bye."

OF ALL THE crazy ideas Lewis had ever come up with, this was probably the most outrageous.

She sat down and thought about it, and prayed about it, and thought about it again.

And it felt good. It felt right. She knew what kind of equipment SLaM had, and even if she could use some of it, that would help to make the next stage of her vision a reality.

She sent Lewis a text thanking him for his message and telling him she'd get back to him as soon as she could.

Over the next couple of days, she went back over her plans, trying to decide how this offer could help her. She talked to Celeb and Olive Wicks, and to Daisy and Conner to get their opinion as well. Everyone was keen, especially Conner when he heard about the recording rig. Caleb was more considered but equally enthusiastic.

After a few days of reflection, she contacted Lewis and they met for a coffee, and a chat.

LATER THAT YEAR, the deal went through. Alex used some of her own funds to make a token payment for the remains of SLaM, despite Lewis insisting she could have it all for free, and then once it was all agreed, Lewis looked forward to pursuing some of his other interests, to do a bit of travelling and have a break.

When the transfer was completed, she invited Conner over to look at the recording equipment she'd acquired.

It was situated in the basement of SLaM's office, where a soundproofed space had been created for the work they needed to do.

Conner looked at all of the equipment and mumbled phrases like: "This stuff is brilliant," and, "We could really use this, but…"

"But?" said Alex.

"But the real value in an outfit like SLaM is the creative talent, the ideas and the content, you know what I mean?"

And she did. She was working in the creative industry now and turning her equipment into real value was going to be the challenge, and she didn't feel qualified to manage that challenge herself, and so she made an impulsive, crazy decision.

She picked up the phone and dialled. It was answered in two rings.

"Alex, what a pleasure to hear from you. How are things?"

"Hello, Lewis. Things are good, thanks. Listen, have you got a moment to chat?"

"Sure."

"How would you like to come and work for me?"

He actually laughed and made no effort to hide the fact.

"Work for you?" he said.

"Yes."

"You know I'm not religious, don't you?"

"Well, thank goodness for that," said Alex. She had never been a big fan of the term 'religious'.

"Look, Lewis, I know you're not a Christian, but that doesn't matter. I need your business knowledge, your understanding of how creative businesses work. I want you to act as my adviser on contemporary youth culture."

She thought, but didn't say, that she was definitely not hiring him for his management style.

LEWIS SAT BACK in his chair. It was not often that he was genuinely rendered speechless, but he was now. After what seemed like an eternity, he gathered himself together.

"Alex, are you sure about this? Don't you know some other people who might be more suited to your vision?"

"Frankly, no I don't," she said. "You're the person I want for this job, and I want to make you my first hire. So what do you think?"

He promised to call her back once he had considered it and rang off.

After the call, he started laughing.

"She wants me to be her first hire," he said, and then he laughed long and loud for maybe a minute and then he stopped and tried to think about it.

Could he really do it? Work for Alex, be a consultant in what was once his own company?

"No, surely not," he said, "it's too ridiculous. What would Martin say?"

He paused for a moment and then said:

"Who cares what Martin would say!"

Then he picked up the phone and dialled her number.

"Hello, Lewis," said Alex.

"Hi, Alex," he said, "I'm in."

AND SO, to the great surprise of some of her friends and supporters, Alex took Lewis on as an adviser, and she made it clear to all of them that she considered this man to be a valuable member of the team.

It felt more than a little strange for Alex to be travelling in again to the offices of SLaM, or what used to be SLaM.

But now she was in charge, she was the one who could call her team together, and this was exactly what she did on a warm autumn day, a few weeks after taking over what was left of Lewis' old company. Out of habit she ordered in some snacks and fruit for the meeting; it was just like old times!

Caleb Wicks, now a fellow director, joined her at the front door of the office.

"Good morning, Alex."

"Caleb," she said, "how are you?"

"I'm well, thank you. Things are going well."

They walked up to the second floor of the office complex, to the old SLaM boardroom.

The large table was still there, in the middle of the room, and Alex regarded it with a kind of dread fascination; even the familiar dull insistent hum of the air con made her twitch. She had come to associate that noise with the conflict and suppressed hatred that had so often characterized SLaM meetings. She turned to Caleb, and he stopped shuffling his papers for a moment.

"Please can you do something for me?" she said.

"Of course, Alex, what is it?"

"Can you pray over this room? Some things were said and done in this place that were not good. I'm going to get it professionally cleaned but I want it spiritually clean as well."

"Of course I can do that," he said. "And I'll pray for you as well, Alex, because it seems you have been given that most deadly of commodities, power. So God help you." And with that he invited the Holy Spirit to come both into the room and onto Alex.

As he prayed, Caleb was strongly reminded of the moment from scripture when Samuel anointed David to be King over Israel. This too was a time of appointment and anointing, and he was excited to see what the future would hold.

From the corner of the room, Angel watched as a skein of light descended and spread out to fill the whole of the room, flowing over every surface, permeating the air.

He looked at Alex, his charge, his precious duty, and he felt a sort of pride for her. She had reached this point in her destiny, and it was no small achievement. She had had to deal with a whole range of challenges along the way, both spiritual and physical, but now she was poised, ready to take another step for their master. She now had the potential to do things that a billion angels could not do: it was time to reclaim some ground. Alex Masters, an orphan, a student of Jesus, and a precious child of the Father, was about to meet her destiny. The real battle was about to begin.

THE END

The Masters Series will conclude with Book 2: 'Cain's Redemption'

STAY IN TOUCH

You can stay in touch with A. J. Chamberlain by visiting:
www.andrewjchamberlain.com

And on social media at:
Twitter@storycraftpress
Instagram@thestorycraftpress

And on Goodreads at:
https://www.goodreads.com/andychamberlain

READ ON FOR A PREVIEW OF THE FIRST CHAPTER OF BOOK 2 IN THE SERIES: CAIN'S REDEMPTION

CAINS' REDEMPTION: CHAPTER 1

SENATE SQUARE, **Helsinki, January**

DARIUS LENCH LOST his footing again and cursed the ice. He walked on, crunching across the flagstones and glancing at the ground beneath his feet.

The maintenance crews were sprinkling salt onto the greying slush, and Lench's soft, city shoes slithered over the uneven surface. Before him the floodlit cathedral dominated, the ethereal glow on the masonry hinting at things unseen. Elevated above the square, the building spoke of permanence, the saints stationed at each corner, directing the mortals below to a more righteous calling. In the crisp, cold, air he saw the clean points of the golden crosses, and in his heart he despised it all.

He'd needed to get away from everything so that he could regroup and focus, and an old friend had offered him the space to do that. Here he could clear his mind, listen and submit to the master.

He was looking forward to this moment, despite the promise of torment. Now, at last, he would find out how to repair the damage, and face the punishment for what had already happened. No amount of success in the other areas of his life would protect him from the reckoning and when it came, and he would offer no excuses.

He looked at the crisscross patterns of stone receding from him in all directions, and felt the freezing water tease its way into his socks.

"I am coming, my Lord," he whispered. "I will submit."

He removed a slim silver case from his pocket, took out a cigarette and lit it. The smoke hung heavy in the frigid air. He rubbed at an ache in his shoulder as he continued to pick his way across the uneven surface, his footsteps rapping out a brisk, uneven tattoo on the stone.

Lench presented himself to the world as a very successful man. He visited the gym regularly and, drawing on sheer strength of will, maintained the brutal regime he had set for himself. He was fitter than he'd been ten years ago, despite his tobacco habit. His body looked good for his age and his mind had lost none of its precision, and his propensity for caustic wit was as strong as ever.

But none of this would be any use to him when he stood before the master to atone for his failings, but like any good leader, he took responsibility when required, and this was just such an occasion.

A year ago he had been humiliated by the SLaM debacle, but since then he had enjoyed professional success and now Darius Lench was a seriously rich man.

His wealth kept him busy; he owned and rented, bought and sold. He had guessed right in the market and made money as others had lost it; and in all this time he had worked and worked on the art of dominance. Darius Lench could be civil when required, but beneath the refinement he cultivated a ruthless edge.

His personal life reflected the same approach. In the last few months he had refined and purged his group. He had driven out the weak people and cast them aside. The process had started, appropriately enough, with Martin Massey.

He had only ever let Martin join the group because of his position in a company called Sound, Light, and Music, or SLaM, as they liked to call themselves. Martin and his colleagues at SLaM had their fingers on the pulse of youth culture, and Lench's Master had determined that these people were a suitable instrument to work his will into that culture. And so, Lench had tolerated Martin Massey's excitable arrogance as the man developed 'SEEKA', a nihilistic, drug-related project that nudged young people towards one of Lench's favorite creeds: do what you will. That was the basis of Lench's life and philosophy.

But Massey had been nervous and stupid, and Lench had always despised him. He had had to endure the sight of Massey's pathetic little ego bobbing up and down with the ebb and flow of the SEEKA project. When that project failed so did Martin's association with the group, and he had been discarded like the trash that he was.

After that, Lench removed some of the others. One by one they had been pruned. Some fell away from the faith; or were tempted by a less demanding regime. There were a couple of New Age "hangers on" who stumbled across his path on their great search, and some who spoke of the master in terms of a vague metaphysics. He had nicknamed them the "lukewarms". These people weren't even sure that their Lord existed; they talked glibly of "forces" and "nature" as if the reality of spiritual conflict would pass them by. He despised them even more than the followers of the enemy. There was no place for such people in his group and he was pleased to see them weeded out, disposed of, forgotten.

The people around him now were of an altogether different order. They had been selected and hardened, and they shared with him a preoccupation for the master's will. These people understood that life was a contest, and winning was everything.

There would have been no room for the likes of Massey in the current line-up. Poor Martin would have looked like a little boy, lost in a museum, frightened by the towering exhibits. With these new acolytes, Lench felt more able to fulfil his ambition and to serve his master and exercise power in all its forms.

But even as Lench built up his group, so also SLaM had thrived. Time and again he had felt compelled to track the fate of his enemies; to see whether they had disappeared like a cancer succumbing to therapy.

At first he thought SLaM would wither, as the misfits who took it over struggled to make themselves heard in the cacophony of contemporary culture. He smiled when he discovered they had taken on Lewis Ashbury as some kind of consultant. He jeered as he recognized little Conner Adams and his band achieve some notoriety at the fringes the music scene. He actually laughed out loud when he discovered that the woman, Alex Masters, had taken on her whore of a cousin to dream up bits of merchandise for them. They were a pathetic collection of amateurs and he was confident that their little venture would flounder and die.

But SLaM did not die. Indeed, it flourished and gained something of a reputation for what it did. He watched it all from a distance, and uncertainty stirred in his gut. Perhaps he had under-estimated them, this raggedy crowd; perhaps they had more money than he realized; perhaps they would not just disappear into the noise. Over time the derisive laughter stopped, and the smile became a grimace. The success of SLaM was his failure, and so now he felt compelled to present himself to the master, to give an account, receive instruction and endure the appropriate punishment.

He did not immediately notice a man approaching him from the edge of the square, a black outline against the floodlights, coming into his field of vision. When he did see the figure, Lench recognized immediately the bulky silhouette of his old friend

Tarmo Ketola. Tarmo lumbered up and Darius Lench took one last resentful suck on his cigarette before dropping it into the slush.

"You are eight minutes late," he said.

In response Tarmo laughed, his mirth turning into a rattling guttural cough. He spat out phlegm before he spoke.

"Darius, my friend, you need two things: decent shoes and a drink."

Lench smiled despite his mood. "Maybe," he said, "but first I have work to do."

The wind blew across the open square and snagged at Lench's thin jacket. He pulled it around himself as they walked together away from the floodlights of the cathedral and into the darkness.

"Tell me," said Lench, "does it ever get warm in this god forsaken land?"

"Not forsaken by the gods though, eh?" Tarmo turned and inspected his friend, like a doctor examining a sick patient. "You most definitely need a drink."

"You do know why I am here, don't you?" said Lench impatiently.

"Ah Darius, you are so clever, but you are also a fool. I will help you to rescue yourself from this mess."

"Don't flatter yourself," said Lench, stamping into slush as the cold seeped into the bones of his feet. "And why are we meeting outside this dung heap of a place? Is this another example of your warped sense of humour?"

Tarmo laughed again. "It's an easy landmark to find. I didn't want to make things any more difficult for a foreigner like you, Darius, now come!" Tarmo picked up the pace and Lench followed on, taking an extra stride to catch up with his friend.

"At least let me get you some proper boots," said Tarmo. "You are not in the City of London now." The big man launched into another coughing fit, and the pair of them trudged on.

"I should tell you," said Lench, "that things have deteriorated again. SLaM is now a running sore. That woman, Masters, has kept the thing afloat somehow."

"Our friend," said Tarmo softly, "is he not able to remove this woman you spoke of?"

"If only it were that simple," said Lench. "She is…" he searched for the right words, "…she is not open to us. We cannot harm her, although we may yet have opportunities to do a great deal of harm to the people she loves. But she is closed to us, and I have spent several hours trying to explain this to Josef."

"Ah, poor Josef," said Tarmo, smiling. "He could never quite grasp the subtleties, eh? I think that's why I am fond of him. He's always ready to slip the blade in first and ask questions afterwards."

"Yes, well that's not always the answer, is it!" snapped Lench. He continued before Tarmo could respond. "Josef has his uses but it doesn't take much to get him into a rage, just someone spelling his name wrong, 'Joseph' instead of 'Josef', is usually enough."

Tarmo nodded and smiled.

"Yes, that's Josef for you," he said, "I know you have to handle him carefully."

"There are other reasons why Josef has become something of a liability," said Lench, "and you know them well enough."

"The scar," said Tarmo, "and the blood."

"Yes," said Lench, "the scar and the blood. The current restrictions are for his own sake as much as any question of strategy."

The hulking figure betrayed no reaction to this; but Lench could sense the disappointment and anger. Josef was one of Tarmo's favourites.

"I am sorry for him," said Tarmo.

"Yes, yes it's a shame," said Lench, "but there it is. Josef's trade carries a certain amount of risk. His contact with the outside world is our point of weakness and it should be minimal. He should move unseen. But that is all rather difficult now that he has been compromised."

"I think you have not told me the half of it, Darius," said Tarmo. "I know he failed with the Bridget Larson job, as did you for sending him there in the first place; but what else is there, what else has he done?"

Lench sighed; he had not intended to spend time going over the Assassin's indiscretions.

"Alex Masters runs a café," said Lench, "and without my permission, Josef visited the place. I understand that he became 'upset' while he was there. He thought I would be asking him to dispatch one or two of them, and so he decided to go on a little reconnaissance mission."

"And?"

"And," said Lench, impatiently, "rather than slip in and out unobserved, an activity in which he is supposed to be an expert, he made a spectacle of himself, frightened the customers, and got himself noticed."

Tarmo sighed. "I did not realize that he had let himself go." He slowly shook his head. "So you have been quite merciful with him really."

"He has been a good servant in the past," said Lench, "and I respect loyalty despite what others might think. But his usefulness is probably coming to an end."

Tarmo grimaced, the pockmarks showing on his face in the floodlight.

"I understand," he said, "but don't discard him just yet."

"Oh, I won't do that," said Lench. "I still have plenty of work for him to do."

There was silence between them as they continued across the square towards a row of parked vehicles.

"Anyway," said Lench, "let's not get too morose, we still have much to do and the service of the master brings both rewards and penalties. Josef has had his share of rewards in the past, and, like me, now has to face the penalties, which I am sure he will take like the man he is."

"He will," said Tarmo.

"But I am not here to talk about Josef, or to decide what is to be done with him. My business with the master is my real concern. I obey his call."

"And the woman is protected?"

"We cannot harm the woman," said Lench, "or that tart of a cousin she hangs around with. They are protected."

"That is a pity," said Tarmo, "but I presume there are others."

"Of course, and any one of them might warrant further attention – that idiot brother of hers perhaps – but I need to identify where the master wants us to direct our attack."

"It will be revealed to you," said Tarmo. "Come, the car is here."

Tarmo's four-wheel drive was warm after the bitter wind of the square, and Lench was soon cocooned in the comfortable, leather interior as they drove away. He was exhausted and he knew it. He had taken an evening flight to come here directly from work, and he feared that Tarmo would find him asleep and snoring when they got up to his villa. It wasn't a prospect that he relished. He needed to remain alert and strong for this encounter.

He thought again about power, his own power, and pride, both of which had been diminished by this *girl*. He used the anger to keep himself awake.

"I take it everything is prepared," he said as the car picked up speed.

"Of course," said Tarmo, "you may spend yourself as extravagantly as you wish." Then with an abrupt movement, the driver's side window glided down and the warmth that had built up in the car fled in a moan of icy air. Tarmo broke into another coughing fit and hawked a gobbet of phlegm out into the racing darkness.

The window purred back in to place again.

"You will have your answers, Darius," said Tarmo, "and no doubt you will pay dearly for them, but maybe you can have some relaxation after that, eh? I have a little wine, and maybe I can arrange for some company for you?"

Lench felt tiredness creeping on him as again the interior of the car warmed up. "Keep your whores to yourself tonight, Tarmo."

The big man grunted and the car lurched across the highway, sloughing through the snow that banked up on the side of the road.

Twenty minutes later, Tarmo's villa loomed before them, a dark grey mass amid the faint glow of the night. A single light shone from the attic room. The car crunched to a halt on an expanse of gravel and Lench noticed the glitter of settled snow on the ground and in the trees.

"Do you wish me to stay with you?" said Tarmo, switching off the ignition.

This was no small offer and Lench did not answer immediately; the world around him was silent except for the occasional tick of the car engine as it cooled. He rubbed his shoulder as pain stabbed down his left arm, adding to the general tiredness he felt.

"No, thank you," he said, "but I appreciate the offer. I have to do this alone."

At the oaken front door of the villa, Tarmo dug into the pocket of an old leather jacket and fished out a formidable collection of keys.

"Again, I welcome you to my house, Darius, I hope you find what you are looking for here."

They walked through to the lounge. The embers of an earlier fire were still glowing in the grate of a soot-caked fireplace and the air was heavy with stale smoke. A large sofa draped with animal pelts sat before the fire, facing the flames.

Lench noted the familiar wood panelling, darkened with the years of smoke, and the trophies of the old gods on ledges and window shelves around the room, memories of the power of deities long since forgotten by the rest of the world. In one corner, he saw a heavy black oak table laden with spirit bottles.

"Lead the way," said Lench. "I want to engage with our master as soon as possible."

He followed his host through the house and up two flights of well-trodden stairs, to the door of the attic room. At the door he stopped and removed his shoes and soaking socks. Tarmo wheezed over and picked them up without a comment, and then he placed his heavy hand on Lench's shoulder. It was an expression of support and Lench accepted it as such.

"I will come and find you when you are finished," said Tarmo.

Lench nodded, then he entered the room alone, shut the door and quickly set about the preparations. He shivered, and stretched his neck left and right against the persistent shoulder ache, and then he sat down on the bare oaken floor, breathed deeply to centre himself, and closed his eyes.

9 781916 175846